SECOND CHANCES

SECOND CHANCES

SOPHIA IRIOTAKIS

ARCHWAY
PUBLISHING

Archway Publishing books may be ordered through booksellers or by contacting:

Archway Publishing
1663 Liberty Drive
Bloomington, IN 47403
www.archwaypublishing.com
844-669-3957

ISBN: 978-1-6657-3602-2 (sc)
ISBN: 978-1-6657-3601-5 (hc)
ISBN: 978-1-6657-3631-2 (e)

Library of Congress Control Number: 2022924107

Print information available on the last page.

Archway Publishing rev. date: 12/29/2022

DEDICATION

I would like to dedicate this novel to my Dad, who is no longer with us. He supported and encouraged me to follow my dream. I am just saddened that he is not here to see the outcome. He taught me to never give-up, as long as it takes, and it took a while! Thank you for that!

Also, to my sister, Effie Maimonis, whose constant support was unwavering throughout this entire process.

And to my best friend, Diane Obradovic, who was relentless with me finishing the novel, even when I wanted to give up.

Lastly, I would like to thank my wonderful husband, Dimitri, who supported and encouraged me throughout this entire journey. I would not have come this far had it not been for him.

I thank you all from the bottom of my heart.

1

As Nicole stood in the doctor's office and awaited his return, she couldn't help but feel anxiety setting in. She hadn't been feeling well recently. She was extremely tired all the time. She didn't feel sick or anything, but she didn't feel right either. Waves of nausea hit her again, which was what initially brought her to see Dr. Hamel. He had been her doctor since she was a young adolescent. When she had missed her period last month, she suspected that she might be pregnant.

The secretary, an older woman, called her in. She told Nicole, in her politest manner, to make herself comfortable and that the doctor would be in shortly. Nicole was in for the results of the blood work she'd had done two days before. As the secretary left the office, Nicole stood there for a moment before deciding to sit down on one of the two chairs in front of the large oak desk. She looked around, observing the warmth that the office provided with its soft shades of white and cream. It was quite appropriate for a doctor of his status. She felt immediate comfort being there. After only a couple of minutes of sitting, she walked over to the window, which overlooked the main street.

Could it be possible? Could she really be pregnant? In the last year, she could count on one hand how many times she and her husband had made love. Nicole Newman was thirty-two years old, tall, and slim, with brown shoulder-length hair and crystal blue eyes. She was a beautiful girl, but at this precise moment, all she was starting to feel was pure anxiety. She continued to look outside, for it was a beautiful, sunny June day. The sky was blue with not a single cloud in it.

As she waited, Nicole couldn't help but think of the last time she had been to see the doctor for this reason. Absentmindedly, she touched her abdomen in wonder. Could there be a child growing inside of her? Her eyes started to well up with tears as she thought of the last year. It was just over one year ago that she had lost her son, Jonathan. He had barely been over two years of age when her little angel had drowned in their pool. She had been in the basement, doing a client's hair, when her little boy had gotten bored with playing there and managed to go into the backyard, unlock the gate that separated the yard from the pool, and step onto the other side.

She instantly shook her head to rid herself of that awful, fateful day. She crossed her arms and continued to look up at the sky as her tears now threatened to escape. How could she have been so careless? How could she have not noticed that Jonathan was no longer in the basement, playing quietly with his toy truck, which he had received as an Easter gift from her parents two months prior to the accident? Questions. Unanswered questions that continued to haunt her, and still no definite answers.

She had been married to Jack Newman for the past twelve years. As she thought about him, she felt instant sadness. They had been high school sweethearts, having met when she was in ninth grade and Jack in twelfth. She fell in love with him the moment she laid eyes on him. He was only eighteen at the time, but he was tall with a muscular build, green eyes, and dark-brown wavy hair. She'd thought he was the next best thing to a Greek god. They'd dated throughout her high school years, while he had continued with his education and gone to university. They'd spent every possible waking moment together. Everyone that knew them had said that they were made for each other.

When Nicole had finished high school and gone to beauty school, they had gotten married, despite their parents' wishes. Their parents had persuaded them to wait a couple more years, because they were so young, but they had gone ahead and married anyways. They were young and very much in love. Waiting to be together hadn't been an option for them, and nothing was going to stand in their way. Their parents had eventually given up and gave them a small, but quaint, wedding ceremony. It had been the most wonderful day of Nicole's life, or so she thought.

Close to a decade later, they had been blessed with a beautiful baby boy. Although her wedding day had been very special, it didn't hold a candle to how she had felt when the doctor had put her baby boy on her chest. It was an absolute miracle to see this small, helpless baby that she and Jack had created. It didn't compare to anything else in the world. She then understood what other mothers felt at the time of their children's births. It had been at that precise moment that she had felt complete and a love so great she didn't even know existed.

Nicole smiled as she thought of that day, over two years ago. She remembered it vividly. Jack had been by her side the whole time and after. He had bent down, stroked her hair, and kissed her on the lips, and then he had done the same to his new son. It was the most magical feeling in the whole world. She had never felt more love than she had on that day. And while becoming a new mother had been challenging at times—with the night feedings, the temper tantrums, and the terrible twos—she had never regretted a moment of it.

What's taking the doctor so long? Nicole asked herself, glancing down at her watch. Her appointment was for two o'clock, but it was now close to three. She would never understand why doctors always seemed to fall behind or why they even bothered to make appointments. It was a Friday, and she'd had to leave the salon early to make it to the doctor. Yet here she was, still waiting. She glanced around the office, noticing the photographs on the desk. There was one picture of the doctor and, she guessed, his wife. It looked to be taken while vacationing. There were another two photos, one on each side of the picture of the doctor and his wife, presumably of their adult children with their spouses and children.

Nicole again thought of her little boy and how much she missed him. The emptiness she felt was overwhelming. Even though it had been over a year since he'd died, nothing had changed. She remembered that awful day when she had noticed that Jonathan wasn't there. She remembered calling his name, thinking he was just hiding. He had always loved to play hide-and-seek. She remembered running upstairs, hoping to find him in the family room, watching his favorite show, *Barney*, and discovering he wasn't there either. She had frantically searched the entire house, hoping and praying he was there, safe and sound. As Nicole turned back time, the visions were always the same. Her client had heard her shouting his name and gone upstairs, hoping to find the little boy. It was when Nicole had seen the open sliding door in the kitchen that panic set in.

Tears slid down her face as she thought of the next image. She had discovered the gate open. When she flew to the pool and saw her little boy facedown, floating at the top of the pool, she had lost it. The rest was a blur. However, she did remember diving in, retrieving him, and ferociously swimming to the edge of the pool while dragging his lifeless little body, blue and cold to the touch. Nicole closed her eyes tightly at the memory of realizing he was dead. She had screamed so loudly—she was told—that the whole street must've heard her.

"Hello, Nicole. Sorry to have kept you waiting," Dr. Hamel said as he walked into the office, closing the door behind him. He stopped short of leaning his back on his desk, realizing that he had jolted her back to reality. He watched as she quickly composed herself, wiping a tear that had escaped down her cheek. "Nicole is everything all right?" he asked softly.

"Yes, Dr. Hamel, everything is fine. I'm sorry. I guess I was just nervous, that's all," she replied, sounding very unconvincing. "So do you have any good news for me today?" She cleared her throat and managed a smile.

She had always respected her doctor. He knew what she and Jack had gone through to get pregnant the first time. They had decided to wait to have children for the first five years after getting married. Jack's business in construction had just taken off, and they had wanted to work hard for a few years, save some money, and buy a house before having a baby. However, it hadn't worked out quite the way they'd wanted. Nicole had assumed that once she got off the pill, she would just magically get pregnant, and they would live happily ever after. It had taken another five years before she conceived. Five years of waiting and crying every month when she got her period. It had been like she was in mourning every month. Even after they had both tested and been told that nothing was wrong, she just couldn't understand why they couldn't conceive. Now her fate was in her doctor's hands as she waited for some news.

"I do, Nicole." He nodded, looking directly in her eyes, and smiled. She knew instantly that she was pregnant.

"Really? Are you serious? Oh my God. I can't believe it!" she exclaimed, thrilled. She stood up quickly and lunged toward him. She hugged him and planted a kiss on his cheek.

"Wow, that was some response!" he said, obviously taken by surprise. "And this is why I love my job. Congratulations, Nicole, I'm very happy for you and Jack. You both deserve all the happiness," he said with genuine sincerity. "You are two months pregnant, and you know what that means, right?" he asked, gently touching her shoulder.

"Yes, I know," she nodded, embarrassed by her sudden affection toward him. "It means I should be eating right, getting plenty of rest, and start on my prenatal vitamins, right?" she said, sounding more like a doctor than a patient.

"That's right," he said, laughing. "I wish that all of my patients were as bright and cooperative as you. It certainly would make my job a lot easier. Anyway, as you probably already have guessed by now, you're due to have the baby by the middle of January."

"Oh my goodness! Thank you, Dr. Hamel, thank you so much!" she said, feeling exhilarated. She was practically jumping out of her skin with excitement.

"Don't thank me, thank that wonderful husband of yours! I just deliver the news. Anyway, my dear, take care of yourself. And I should start to see you monthly. Just make sure to make an appointment with my secretary, OK?" he said, giving her a warm friendly hug.

"I will, and thank you again," she replied, smiling for what felt like the first time in ages. She left his office and booked herself an appointment for the following month. As Nicole left the medical building, she couldn't help but feel somehow lighter, happier. The sky suddenly seemed bluer, and the sound of birds chirping sent tingles up her spine. As she walked to her car, she decided that she would go to the grocery store and pick up some things. This called for a celebration, and she was going to make a special dinner for Jack before giving him the news about the baby.

She pulled out of the parking lot and drove to Metro, a local grocery store. She practically flew in and picked up some asparagus, some baby potatoes, and a leg of lamb. She also picked up some fresh spinach and a French baguette. She paid for the food, the whole time feeling like the world had been lifted from her chest. Her heart was pounding so loudly, she thought the whole supermarket could hear her. She then made a quick stop at the liquor store, picking out a bottle of white wine, non-alcoholic of course. She absolutely couldn't drink now that she was pregnant. She paid for the wine and drove home.

As she pulled up to their driveway, she quickly retrieved her grocery bags from the trunk of her Honda and entered her house. It was a simple house—a detached three bedrooms with a two-car garage. She checked for messages, realized she had none, and proceeded to start her dinner. She hadn't felt so excited about cooking in such a long time. She had always loved cooking and baking, but after the death of her little boy, everything changed. She hardly cooked anything anymore, and as she proceeded to spice up the leg of lamb and the potatoes, she concluded that cooking was like driving—once you'd mastered something, it didn't matter how much time passed, it always came back to you. She put the food in the oven, and started preparing her spinach salad, making sure to wash all the spinach leaves well. She drained them in the colander and then tossed the baby spinach in her salad bowl. She segmented some mandarin in it and tossed in some cherry tomatoes, then made her famous raspberry vinaigrette. *Oh, what the heck*, she thought, *might as well toss in some walnuts.* She wanted to make this dinner something that Jack would never forget. She then started with the asparagus, washing them well, draining them, and then sautéing them with fresh garlic, butter, and fresh herbs. She wanted a little crunch to them because she hated mushy vegetables.

Glancing over to the kitchen table, she decided that they would have their dinner in the dining room. After all, this was a special occasion. She carefully selected a simple white tablecloth, making sure it wasn't wrinkled. She took out her better flatware and set the table. Then, she went to her buffet and retrieved two crystal wine glasses that had been given to them as a wedding gift from her parents, along with the dining set. She lovingly placed them to the right of each setting and then decided there was something missing. "That's it!" she said aloud, "I need some fresh flowers." She went into their backyard and carefully picked off three white geraniums. They were beautiful this time of year. She picked out one of her favorite vases, also a gift from her bridal shower, and put just enough water in it. She thought it looked beautiful as she placed the geraniums in the vase and placed the vase in the center of the table.

She walked back into her kitchen and put the wine in the refrigerator to chill. She carefully cut the French baguette and placed the bread in the breadbasket covering it with a matching white dinner napkin. The aroma of dinner in the oven was already filling her nostrils, making her even hungrier. She then decided to whip up a quick dessert. It was one of Jack's favorites, crème caramel. It didn't take long for her to prepare. When the lamb and potatoes were done, she would then put her dessert in the oven to bake. It was perfect timing, she figured, since the dessert would be the topping to a very romantic dinner. *He'll be floored*, she thought. She envisioned the two of them sitting at the table, holding hands, and looking into each other's eyes while she broke the news to him. He would give a toast to their new beginning and then take her in his arms and carry her up to their room, where he would gently make love to her. Nicole couldn't help but smile as she thought of what the perfect evening would be. She felt so giddy. *Today*, she thought, *will be the turning point for us.*

The past year had been a shaky one for them. Jack and Nicole had both had a very hard time dealing with their loss. Nicole had noticed that Jack came home later and later every night, smelling like beer, but she never questioned his whereabouts. She just thought that, with time, he'd come around, and things would be like before.

She ran upstairs into their en-suite bathroom and took a quick shower. She shaved her legs, put moisturizer all over her body, and sprayed Jack's favorite perfume behind her ears and on her décolleté. He had initially bought her that perfume while honeymooning in Mexico, and she had never changed it. He had always told her that it turned him on, and with tonight's plan, she was hoping it would again. Nicole walked into their large walk-in closet and decided on a white linen skirt, and a sleeveless turquoise blouse. Glancing over at her makeup bag, she carefully applied a light shimmer of blush and two coats of mascara. For her lips, she decided on a light-pink, natural-colored gloss to accentuate her full, plump lips. She put some mousse in her hair and blow-dried it upside down, getting most of the moisture out. It didn't hurt that Nicole was a hairstylist, and whatever she did with her hair, it always looked good. It also helped that she had a slight wave to her hair. She took one last glance at herself in the mirror and was content with what she saw. She looked pretty and fresh and was so happy she was practically glowing.

Nicole lifted her blouse and looked down at her abdomen, placing her hand over it. She wasn't quite showing yet, but in time, she would, and she couldn't wait. She still couldn't believe she was pregnant, since their sex life was almost nonexistent. Jack had distanced himself considerably, and his workload didn't help matters. The little time he did spend at home, he watched television, drank beer, and fell asleep in front of the television. Oh, she had tried many times to talk to him, to reach him, but to no avail. He always seemed so distracted and not interested in anything that, at one time, had meant so much to him. He had stopped exercising, which was something he used to be a fanatic about. They used to go out occasionally for wings or just for a walk, and that had stopped as well. Those things were just a faint memory to her.

She glanced at the clock on her nightstand and noted it was five thirty. Nicole thought she should call him, see if he'd be home soon. She went downstairs and into their family room. The aroma of the lamb and the potatoes cooking was now enveloping the whole house. Her stomach was starting to growl, and she realized that she hadn't eaten since her coffee and oatmeal in the early morning. She picked up her phone and dialed his work number.

"Good afternoon, Newman Construction. Can I help you?" replied the secretary. She was an older woman that Jack had hired a few years ago. She had a pleasant, good-natured voice.

"Hi, Karen, it's me, Nicole. Is it possible I could speak to my husband?" she asked, hoping that he wouldn't be there and would already be on his way home.

"No, I'm sorry, Mrs. Newman. Mr. Newman has left already. Could I take a message?" she asked politely.

"No, no message, thank you. Do you know if he's at a jobsite or if he's done for the day?" she asked as she glanced at the framed photographs on her mantle just across from her.

"I'm not sure, Mrs. Newman. He didn't really say. How are you doing? I haven't seen you in a while," she asked. Knowing what had happened to them the year before, she felt genuinely sorry for them both.

"I'm fine Karen, thank you for asking. I was just hoping to catch him before he left. I'll try his cell," she said.

"Alright, well, you take care now," Karen answered, her usual sunny self.

Nicole hung up the telephone and decided, without hesitation, that she would call Jack's cell. It rang a few times, and finally, she heard a click on the other end. Her heart skipped a beat, and she was just about to say something when she got his voicemail. Her heart sank as she heard the usual speech and then, "If you want to leave a message, I'll get back to you as soon as I can." She was just about to hang up, but then she left him a message, asking him to call her back as soon as possible. She put the receiver down slowly and hung her head in disappointment. Maybe he was at a jobsite, and his cell was in his truck. *That's probably it*, she thought. Where else could he be?

Nicole sank herself in her oversized, espresso-colored leather sofa. She didn't know what to do with herself, and the photograph of her little boy in the silver frame caught her eye. She got up from the couch, and walked over to the picture, taking it in her hands and seating herself again. She looked long and hard at the little boy staring back at her. The picture was taken about two months before he died. It was a close-up shot of him wearing jean overalls, a red T-shirt, and a blue baseball cap. He was holding a chocolate ice-cream cone in his hand, and his little face, apart from his big blue eyes that he had inherited from his mother, was covered with chocolate. Nicole couldn't help but smile as she stared at her baby boy. *He was such a good boy*, she thought. Oh, how she missed him! Her heart ached so much for him that some days she thought she would die of a broken heart.

She took one long, last look at her precious little boy, stood up, and put the photo back on the mantle next to a photograph of her and Jack. It was a picture taken about four years ago while vacationing in Cuba. She gazed at the photograph, and her heart sank, as it only confirmed the emptiness she'd felt for some time, especially because that photo of the two of them revealed how very happy they had been at one time. They were on the beach, both in their swimsuits, Jack behind her with his arms around her small waist, both suntanned and smiling from ear to ear. They had been so happy then and on top of the world. They had found out that they were finally expecting just days before their trip. Jack's construction business had taken off, and they were very much in love. How things could change so much on a dime; it seemed hardly possible that they were the same two people. When their little boy died, their marriage crumpled as well. Tears started forming again, and she fought them. *No!* she thought. Her pregnancy would change everything around for them. She loved him, and she was sure that he still loved her. With time, they'd get back to how things were before. She was sure of it.

CHAPTER

2

*J*ack Newman contemplated whether he should answer the phone or not. He had noticed on his call display that Nicole was trying to reach him, and he had listened to her message on his voicemail, but he couldn't bring himself to talk to her. In the meantime, he just sat in his truck and put his hands through his thick dark hair. He was finished with work, and he was tired. He wanted to go home, take a shower, and relax, but he simply couldn't face Nicole anymore. It was too painful for him to even look at her since she was a constant reminder of what he'd lost. His son had looked like him for the most part, but Jonathan had had his mother's crystal-blue eyes. He rested his head on the steering wheel, his hard, working hands tightly gripping the wheel, feeling anger and frustration rise within him. After some thought, he concluded he needed a couple of drinks, deciding he would go to the bar down the road.

As Jack drove, he couldn't help thinking of his wife. He knew that he should probably be home with her, knowing it wasn't fair to her either, but he couldn't take the deafening silence in the house that was once filled with happiness—with his happy wife and tenacious little boy. Before the death of his son, he couldn't wait to get home to them, and now, he couldn't get far enough away. They had grown apart in the past year, and it bothered him to some extent, but he simply couldn't help himself. He couldn't deal with his own pain and her depression. He didn't know how to comfort her when he himself felt empty inside. He loved his wife very much, but he still couldn't understand why their precious little boy died and how senseless and preventable his death had been. She blamed herself for Jonathan's accident, but he always assured her that it wasn't her fault, and that it was just that—an accident—and she was by no means an irresponsible mother. But subconsciously, he did blame her and wanted her to pay. He stayed out later and later and avoided making love to her, disconnecting from his wife in the process.

Jack parked his truck and walked into The Blue Lagoon. He went straight over to the bar and took a seat at the far end.

"Hey, Jack, how's it going?" asked the bartender. Jack frequented the bar had become one of their regulars.

"Hey, buddy. Same shit, man. You know how it is. Get me a beer, will ya," he asked, noticing the little blonde from across the bar, obviously a new waitress since he hadn't seen her before.

"Sure, man. Draft, right?" he asked, already reaching for a beer glass.

"Yeah, give me two. It's bloody hot out there!" he said, watching the little blonde take some drinks over to the table across the room.

"You got it, buddy!" the bartender answered, serving him one and already pouring the second. It was busy, but that was normal for a Friday. They had karaoke every Friday night, and it was bound to be packed by seven o'clock.

"Hey, Phil, who's the little blonde?" asked Jack, taking a long sip from his beer and eyeing the young woman. She looked hot in her short, black skirt and tight, black T-shirt, which accentuated her full breasts.

Phil glanced in the direction Jack was inquiring about and then turned back to Jack. "Oh, that's Ashley. She's a new girl that just started a couple of months ago. She's cute, isn't she?" he said, smiling. "And she's pretty good at what she does, let me tell you. She's got the guys here eating out of the palm of her hand."

Jack finished of his beer and started on his second. He glanced down at his watch, noting it was just before six. "So, Jack, how's business, man?" Phil asked.

"Alright. Busy as usual. We got a couple of new contracts that we're working on," he responded.

The little blonde brought some empty beer glasses to the bar. She looked over at him and smiled, which warranted a smile back at her. She tilted her head to one side and then leaned in toward the bar, crossing her free hand over her waist, making sure he got a full view of her swelling, ample breasts. The V-neck of her black T-shirt was quite low, which only worked to her advantage. He looked her over, liking what he saw—her medium-length, wavy, blonde hair, cut in a cute, layered bob, her full red lips that were teasingly parted ever so slightly, and her sensual hazel-colored eyes tented with extra-long eyelashes that were abundantly coated with layers of mascara. She eyed him back with obvious interest. Her short black skirt barely covered her thighs, which only accentuated her shapely, long legs, and as he shifted himself uncomfortably in his bar stool, he noticed how high her heels were. He always wondered how women could stand in heels like that, let alone walk or work in them. Nevertheless, he was certainly enjoying the view as well as the attention. She bent even closer toward him, just inches away, filling his nostrils with a scent that made his head spin. He was attracted to her, and he was certain that she knew it. That's how women operated—they toyed with you and then let you take the lead.

"Hey, handsome, I don't believe I've seen you here before," she drawled. She thought he was hot, in a rough and rugged sort of way.

"Oh yeah, well, I haven't seen you around either," he responded in his deep voice.

She pulled herself away from him, liking what she saw. His green eyes never left her, and she was enjoying the attention she received, noticing that he wasn't wearing a wedding ring. She was tired of the same old geeks that she waited on, or the guys that thought that the world revolved around them. She leaned over and poured herself a glass of water. She brought the glass up to her shiny red lips, and her eyes locked into his as she drank the ice-cold water. Then she licked her lips teasingly, relishing the effect she was having on him. He shifted himself once again in his chair. She stared long and hard at him, intending to keep his attention further.

"If you hang around a little longer, my shift ends in an hour or so. Maybe you and I could get a drink somewhere else?" she asked. "Think about it, big guy," she added, winking at him. And with that, she turned around and wiggled her way to a table that was waving at her for their bill.

As she gave the group of men their bill, Jack watched them laugh—they were obviously equally enticed by their server. He drank the rest of his beer and set his glass down. He glanced at his watch and knew that he should be heading home to his wife, who was most likely pissed off with him by now for not returning her call. She always complained to him that there was no use in having a cell phone if she couldn't even get hold of him. As Ashley made her way to another table, to yet another group of young men and women, he couldn't help but notice that she would periodically smile in his direction, with a knowing look that said she would make his wait well worth it. Jack signaled the bartender, who was talking to a group of men, for another beer, which he immediately got. He took a long swig from his glass, enjoying the buzz that it gave him. It went down nice and smooth, which helped him to relax and unwind. There was a little voice inside of him, telling him to get the hell out of there before he did anything stupid, so he finished off the remainder of his beer and set his glass down. As he turned to leave, he felt a gentle hand on his arm, and he turned around, coming face-to-face with the young blonde. She was considerably shorter than he was, and as he looked down at her, she smiled up at him while gently stroking his arm.

"And where do *you* think you're going?" she asked him playfully, moving even closer to him, her body touching his, an electricity between them.

"I just thought that it's time I went home," he answered, his eyes boring into hers. She leaned up against him even closer, and he could feel her heart thumping a million miles a minute as she wrapped one arm around his neck and placed her other hand on his chest. This girl obviously wanted him, and he was certainly attracted to her, which made him feel like a million bucks. She was obviously challenging him, and for a moment, it made him feel uncomfortable. Could he really do this with a woman he just met? Could he cheat on his wife after everything they'd been through? His heart tugged at the thought of Nicole, his sweet wife that didn't deserve to be treated like this, and suddenly, he was acutely aware of the situation he was in with this girl. She didn't look to be more than twenty-five, so what in hell was he doing with her? He took a step back from the girl, breaking free from her arm that was wrapped around his neck. "Look, you seem like a really nice girl, but I need to leave, and now," he said in a serious tone. The electricity between them was so intense that it terrified him. She, in turn, laughed at him to his face.

"Go on, go home!" she scoffed, taking him by surprise. "You clearly don't have what it takes." She laughed, turning her back to him to leave, which angered him to the core.

How dare she toy with him like this, he thought as he grabbed her by her arm, which startled her. He turned her around roughly, bent his head down to her awaiting lips, and kissed her long and hard. She responded to him, kissing him back with such desire that she instantly wrapped her arms around his neck, letting her body be enveloped by his as he kissed her hungrily. He felt an overwhelming surge of desire for her, and he wanted her, right there and then. They finally broke free, breathless from the kiss they just shared. He gazed longingly into her hazel eyes and wondered what had just transpired between them, completely unaware of the people and the music around them.

"Wow!" she said, trying to catch her breath. "You really surprised me there," she added, feeling slightly faint. "That was some kiss." It was obvious to how much chemistry they had between them.

"When did you say you finished your shift?" he asked, his voice so low that only she could hear him. He was turned on, and he wanted more. The scent of her perfume was driving him crazy with desire.

"Hang on, let me see what I can do," she said, looking up at him, knowing this was going to go further than she'd anticipated. "Laurie owes me a favor," she added, leaving him standing there while she walked over to another waitress and whispered something in her ear. In response, Laurie nodded with approval and smiled in his direction.

Jack felt a little embarrassed from the way the other girl seized him up, and he couldn't help but feel a little cheap, but an unexpected opportunity had presented itself, and he could use a little affection just about now. He had a hard-on at the prospect of what was going to transpire between them, and he turned around and casually rubbed his hand over his trousers in hopes of taking it down a notch before leaving the establishment that, by now, was in full swing. Ashley noticed him looking uncomfortably awkward, and she smiled as she took her little black apron off her, folding it and putting it in her purse, which was in the back of the bar. She then gave a quick wink and wave to Laurie, who was giving her the thumbs up, and walked straight over to Jack, who was eagerly and hungrily waiting for her. He put his arm protectively around her small waist and led her to the door and out of the bar.

CHAPTER

3

Nicole was starting to get worried now. Quite some time had passed, and she still hadn't heard from Jack. She glanced over to the dining room, where it was so elegantly set, and she noticed that she had forgotten the candles. She quickly made her way to the buffet and retrieved her crystal candlesticks, and she put one on each side of the flowers that were in the center of the table. She had already turned the oven off a couple of hours ago, and the food was still in the oven, covered with tin foil to keep warm. The only sound in the whole house was the ticking of the clock, which displayed that it was now close to eight o'clock. *Where could he be*, she thought. Not even a phone call from him to let her know that he'd be late. Anger was starting to set in, although she would've gladly replaced her anger for joy if he would just come home. It was always the same song and dance. He'd come home, give her some lame excuse as to why he was late, and apologize to her, at which point her anger would subside and things would resume. Thinking about it now just made her feel inadequate because she knew she would never do anything about it. She just accepted him the way he was, never questioned his whereabouts, and he knew it.

One night when he had come home later than usual, she had questioned him as to where he had been, and he had gotten so angry with her, telling her that he worked his ass off to pay the bills, and that he didn't need her nagging him. He had left her feeling guilty and more upset because she hated when they fought, and when she had tried to apologize to him, he just slept on the couch downstairs, never bothering to go up to their room. Since then, she had never questioned him again. He was a hard worker, and she just had to live with his occasional outbursts, which were happening more and more often.

She started to pace the room, getting more and more anxious by the minute. "I don't need this, not now," she said out loud to herself as she placed her hand gently on her abdomen. She walked over to the front of the house and looked outside, hoping for his truck to pull up in their driveway. How many nights had she waited for him, as if her standing at the window would bring him home sooner. Love and desperation make you do stupid things, and this was definitely one of them.

She couldn't stand it anymore, and she decided she would call him on his cell again. She picked up her cell phone and pressed his number. "Please," she said aloud. "Please pick up, Jack! Don't do this to me, please!" she cried. It rang once, twice, three times. Her heart was beating so fast and so hard that she felt an anxiety attack coming on. After the third ring, her heart sank as she waited for his voicemail. Then suddenly, there was a click and some muffled sounds.

"Jack? Jack? Are you there?" Nicole asked, almost breathless, relieved it wasn't his voicemail on the other end.

"Yeah! What's up?" he asked, sounding annoyed, all the while struggling to break free from Ashley's hands, which had already unbuttoned his shirt and were in the middle of unbuckling his belt. They had been making out in his truck just two miles down the road from the bar. He took her hand with his free hand and held it in his own while he tried to sound as normal as he possibly could to his wife. *Shit!* he thought. *This isn't happening to me!*

"Where are you, Jack? I've been trying to reach you for hours now!" she wailed. "And why didn't you call me?" she added, sounding breathless on the other line.

Jack shifted himself in the truck, breaking free from Ashley's grip. "I—I had to go give a couple of quotes," he answered, feeling like a complete shit. He had never, in all the years being married to Nicole, done anything like this, and now, here he was, in his truck, getting it on with a girl he'd just met. "I'm sorry Nikki. I'll be home shortly, OK?" he said finally, thinking it was a very good thing she had called when she did. He turned to Ashley, who was brimming with anger and confusion, and he shot her a look, warning her to keep quiet while he covered the mouthpiece on his cell.

"Alright, Jack! Please don't be long! I'll be waiting," she answered with a sound of relief.

"OK, I'll be home soon," he concluded, and flipped down his cell.

"Was that your wife?" she asked him in disbelief. "Are you *married*?" she shouted at him, fuming with anger.

"I've got to go, Ashley is it? I'm sorry about all of this—let me get you a cab, OK? I need to go home, and I think it's safe to say that what happened right here will stay here, right?" he said, more of a command than a question, sounding more like her father than the man who, just a few moments ago, was all over her.

"Are you seriously going to leave?" she asked, flabbergasted, her hazel eyes becoming larger and rounder. "What was all *this*?" she shouted at him, referring to her bare breasts. He had been hungrily kissing them and sucking on her nipples, which were still throbbing from him squeezing and sucking so hard that it'd hurt. He had hastily removed her bra, and it was lying in the back seat of the truck along with her T-shirt.

"Yes, I'm going to leave, OK? I must leave, and thank God before things got out of hand," he said, trying to reason with her, buttoning up his shirt, and adjusting himself. He didn't need a hysterical female right now because he was quite certain he had one at home that he needed to tend to. "Listen," he said more gently, turning toward her. "Just go home, or wherever else you go at this time, and forget about me. You don't even know me—hell, aside from your name, I don't know anything about you," he said, which just angered her even more.

"You're a piece of *shit*, you know that?" she cried, feeling hurt and humiliated, her eyes blazing, and he nodded in agreement. "It's guys like you that think you're so superior! You think you could just come in, do whatever you want, and then toss me aside?" she yelled in his face. "If your wife hadn't called when she did, you'd be fucking me right now, and you know it!" she screamed in his face.

"Yeah, you're probably right, but she did call, and I'm not fucking you, and you should be relieved! I know I am!" he yelled back at her. And with that, he retrieved his cell phone and proceeded to call a cab for her while she angrily reached into the back seat and reclaimed her bra and T-shirt, hastily putting them on. He just wanted to get her out of his truck as fast as possible, and he needed to get his ass home to his wife.

"You son of a bitch!" she shrieked. "Who needs you anyways? And don't bother getting me a cab, I can make it home on my own, you piece of shit! Go fuck yourself!" she screamed, as she climbed out of his truck and slammed the door so hard his whole truck shook.

"Ashley, come on, don't be like that. I'm sorry. I didn't mean to hurt you, honest," he said as he got out of the truck feeling like the biggest piece of shit. "Come on, get back in the truck, and we'll wait for the cab together, alright?" He felt genuinely sorry for her. *Shit! This can't be happening!* He was trying to catch up to her while she stomped away from him.

"Fuck you! Go home to your wife, asshole!" she spat, turning to face him. "I don't need you to babysit me!" she hollered, turning her back to him again, already walking quickly away.

"Come back here, Ashley, seriously!" He tried to reason with her. "This park is secluded, and it's getting dark. I just want you to get in the cab, and then you can curse me all you want!" He looked down at his watch and wondered where that stupid cab was and why it was taking so long. He hoped it would get here and soon, because he didn't have time for this. He quickly caught up to her. She had already started walking toward the darkness that was setting in, and they were in a small open area close to the children's swings. He grabbed her by her elbow and turned her roughly around to face him.

"Let go of me, I mean it!" she yelled as she struggled to free herself.

CHAPTER

4

Jorge Cartagena was driving along when he received a call that his cab service was needed at Marie Curtis Park. He pulled into the park and drove down a long winding road toward the parking lot, looking for his customer. He pulled into an empty spot and noticed that the parking lot was empty except for a black pickup truck parked a couple of spots away. He sat in his car for a few minutes and looked around. It seemed to be deserted, all except the black pickup.

Jorge got out of the car and stood there, scratching his shiny bald head. *Damn! There must be some mistake!* He took a few steps toward the path and noticed from a distance that there were two individuals further down. He watched them for a couple of seconds, and from what he observed, it was a man and a woman, and they looked to be arguing. He couldn't hear what they were saying, but it was obvious to him that they were amid an argument. Oh well, just a lover's spat. He chuckled, turned around, and headed toward his car. When he reached his car, he turned around once more, and at that exact moment, caught the young woman slap the man in the face. *Wow!* he thought. *This is some argument!*

He instantly thought of his wife, Maria. She was a feisty one, like this one apparently was. As he entered his car, he recalled the many altercations he'd had with his wife over the course of their marriage—where he'd do something to piss her off, and she'd slap him, but he never hit her back. He was raised by a single mother and two sisters, and he had learned from an early age to respect women and to never ever raise a hand to them. He smiled at the prospect of going home to his Maria. Dinner was probably on the table, and his little ones running around.

Jorge put on his seat belt and backed out of the parking lot, and as he did, he couldn't help but notice the license plate on the rear of the black pickup truck, only because it was personalized, and it read "NEWMAN" in capital letters. He proceeded to drive out of the park, on his way home for some home cooking.

—

"What's wrong with you!" Jack yelled after receiving a hard slap in the face from Ashley. *She's crazy!* he thought to himself. "Just come back to my truck and let me take you home for God's sake!" he pleaded, feeling very agitated and frustrated with her.

"I'm not going anywhere with you, so fuck off and leave me alone!" she yelled, almost hysterical.

"You know what? Fine!" he yelled back, realizing that she wasn't going to budge. "Stay here if you want, see if I care!" he said, and threw both his arms up in the air. "You're bat shit crazy you know that?" And with that, Jack turned away from her and stomped angrily down the path toward the empty parking lot. *Jesus! What a crazy bitch*, he thought as he approached his truck. *Where is that cab anyway?* he thought. "Stupid bunch of assholes!" he said out loud to himself as he opened the driver's side of the truck and got inside. He looked at himself in the rearview mirror looking for any marks on his face. "Stupid bitch!" he said out loud. Who the hell did she think she was, slapping him like that! He put his hands through his dark, wavy hair and made a fist as he checked himself out again in the mirror.

He started his truck and proceeded to pull out of the parking lot. He was angry. He was angry with Ashley for flirting with him back at the bar, and he was angrier with himself for not showing any self-control. He stopped his truck before pulling out of the park and looked around for any sign of the cab that he had ordered. There was not one person or car to be seen. His heart was pounding, and he felt he needed a little something before heading home. He opened his glove compartment, searching for his small liquor bottle that he kept there for times like this, although, in all fairness, there were never ever times like these before. He had never cheated on his wife, and he couldn't believe that he almost did. He located the small bottle of scotch, opened it up, and drank the last bit of what was left in it. There was a garbage can just a few feet away, and he got out of his truck and threw out the empty bottle. He looked past his truck, looking for any sign of Ashley. He wondered where she was, for it had gotten dark at this point. He wondered if he should go back and look for her. The thought of her now just made him angry. Who the hell did she think she was to slap him like she did! No woman had ever laid a hand on him. He took a few steps past his truck and stopped, making a mental note to never visit that bar ever again. Out of sight, out of mind.

—

It was almost ten o'clock in the evening, and Nicole was anxiously waiting for her husband to walk through the front door. What was taking him so long? It was well over an hour ago when they'd spoken, reassuring her that he was on his way home. Suddenly, a wave of panic hit her. What if he wasn't where he'd said he was, and he was with someone else? That would explain him coming home later and later and avoiding making love to her. Many nights, he wouldn't even make it upstairs to their room. She would wake up early in the morning, and he'd be sleeping on the couch in the family room with the television still on. What was happening to them? So much for the special evening she had planned. Everything was stone cold, and she had lost her appetite.

The sound of the key to the front door jolted Nicole back to reality, and she leaped from the couch and down the hall, only to see Jack removing his shoes. He looked startled when he saw her. She stood there, just a few feet away from him.

"You finally came home" she said in a low voice.

"Yeah, it's been a long day," he answered as he walked past her, not bothering to look at her. He made his way into the kitchen, making Nicole's heart sink. He didn't even bother to kiss her hello or apologize for being late. She followed him into the kitchen while he opened the refrigerator and helped himself to a beer.

"Is that all you have to say to me, Jack? I've been going crazy out of my mind worrying about you, wondering where you were, and all you have to say is that you've had a long day. Do you even care about what kind of a day I've had or are you so self-involved you just don't care?" she asked incredulously as she followed him once again into the family room, where he sat and made himself comfortable in the La-Z-Boy chair. He had the remote control in one hand, and a beer in the other. She waited for a response, but there wasn't one. He simply turned on the television, ignoring her once again.

She walked over to him, grabbed the remote control out of his hand, and turned off the television. She stood directly in front of him, blocking his view to the television, fuming with anger and frustration.

"Hey! What are you doing?" he yelled. "Can't you see that I'm tired?" When Nicole didn't respond, he looked up at her, and saw how deeply upset and angry she was with him, her blue eyes brimming with tears. "Listen, baby, I'm sorry, really I am. I love you," he added, hoping to pacify her and feeling like shit.

"Really, Jack? You say you love me; you say you're sorry, but tell me something," she said, her voice breaking. "Do you even care about what's happening to us?" Tears fell down her cheeks. Her heart was breaking all over again. First, she'd lost her little boy, and now, she was losing her husband.

"Of course I love you. Come on, Nikki! What's happening to us? What are you talking about?" he asked. *Shit!* he thought. *What is it with these women. They're all so fucking emotional!*

"If you have to ask, then I'm afraid you're in more denial than I thought," she said lowering her voice. He looked at her with obvious confusion. "Are you angry with me? Is that why you're punishing me?" she asked him evenly.

"What in hell are you talking about? Punishing you for *what*?" he answered, angrily, wondering where she was going with this.

"Are you blaming me for Jonathan? You think it was my fault, don't you?" she asked, crying openly now. "That's why you've distanced yourself from me, and why you don't even make love to me anymore!" she cried.

"Why are you bringing him up?" he shouted at her. "I've never blamed you! It was an accident! Isn't that what you told the police? Isn't that what it was? Why the fuck are you bringing all this shit up again?" He was angry now. She'd opened a wound, a dark place that he didn't like to visit, and he felt cornered. He turned away from her, tears stinging his eyes.

Nicole knelt in front of him, gently taking his hand in her own. "Don't you see Jack? Are you so blind? I miss him so much, my heart aches for him! Why can't you let yourself feel the pain instead of drinking and distancing yourself from me?" She waited for some response from him and continued. "Tell me the truth, once and for all. Do you blame me for our son's death? Is that why you're treating me like I've got leprosy?" she asked him quietly, hoping to break through the invisible wall that he had put up between them.

"Nicole, stop it!" he shouted at her abruptly, taking her by surprise. "Seriously, stop this shit right now! This is ludicrous! What, you think because you've read a couple of psychology books, you're my shrink now? Jesus!" he shouted, getting up suddenly, pushing past her, and heading toward the kitchen, grabbing himself another cold beer from the fridge. As he walked back toward the family room, he turned toward the dining room, noticing the table setting and the flowers. "What's all this?" he asked, more calmly, puzzled.

Nicole wiped her tears from her face and looked at him. "I made us a special dinner that we were supposed to eat hours ago," she said quietly as she stood motionless.

"Did I miss something, Nikki?" he asked calmly as he approached her, standing only inches away from her.

She put her head down, fresh tears threatening to escape again.

Jack thought for a moment. It wasn't his birthday, and it wasn't their anniversary, so what had he missed? He looked down at her, and as he did, he placed his right hand under her chin, gently tilting her head up to look at him. Her blue eyes were glistening with tears, and it broke his heart. He didn't like to see her so upset, and strangely enough, this was one of the reasons why he didn't want to be home. She and his deceased son had the same eyes, the same damn crystal-blue, penetrating eyes! "Nicole, why the dinner? What is this?" he asked in a low voice.

She looked deep into his green eyes and wondered if this was the right time to tell him about the baby. This was not the way she had planned to share something so wonderful.

She hesitated for a moment, not taking her eyes off him. Her heart was beating so hard and so fast, she was starting to feel dizzy. She wanted to tell him, only now she was scared. She paused, her eyes searching his. "We're going to have a baby," she said softly, looking deep into his eyes and waiting for his reaction as she held her breath.

Jack raised his eyebrows. It was obviously not something he had been prepared to hear. He released her chin and took a step back, not taking his eyes from her. He looked at her quizzically, like he was seeing her for the first time. He couldn't believe what she'd just told him—another baby! "You're pregnant?" he asked incredulously, and Nicole nodded slowly, confirming what he had just asked. He glanced down at her midsection and then back to her face. "Are you serious?" he asked, taking both her hands in his own, looking directly in her eyes and feeling elated.

"Yes, Jack, I'm very serious. I just found out this afternoon," she said, wondering if he was happy about it, because now, she wasn't so sure. "Are you happy about it?" she asked nervously. Her legs were barely holding her up, she was trembling so much.

"Oh my God, we're going to have a baby," Jack said, more to himself than to her. "Hang on, I've got to sit down," he said, releasing her hands and moving over to the couch. He sat down, and Nicole followed, sitting down beside him. He looked at her closely once again and took her hands into his own. "We're going to have a baby," he repeated, liking the way it sounded.

"Jack, are you alright? Are you happy?" she asked again. It seemed to her that things were moving in slow motion.

"How do you feel about it?" he asked.

Nicole couldn't believe he'd switched the question over to her. "Well, of course I'm thrilled, how do you think I feel?" she asked. She was starting to feel a little confused by his reaction to her news. "That's why I cooked this meal, so I could tell you the news over dinner. I felt it called for a celebration," she said, trying to choose her words carefully. He still hadn't mentioned if he was happy about her news.

Suddenly, Jack felt like he was going to be sick. His wife had just been given the most amazing news and had obviously gone to a lot of trouble for him by preparing a nice meal, and he had been out there, making out with a psycho. Not too long ago, he was called a piece of shit by Ashley, and now, it wasn't far from the truth. He looked over to his wife who just stood there, and he raised her hands to his lips and kissed them gently. "Of course I'm happy, Nikki!" he told her. "I'm very happy. My God, we're going to have a baby!" he exclaimed as he pulled her close to him and kissed her gently on the lips.

"Really, Jack? You're not upset, I mean—"

"Of course not! How could you even think that I would be?" he said, interrupting her, planting another kiss on her lips. "How far along are you?" he asked, although he didn't think that she was too far along.

"I'm a couple of months," she answered, smiling from ear to ear. "The baby is due somewhere in the middle of January. "Oh, Jack, are you very sure you're OK with this? Do you think it's too soon after Jon—"

"Of course I'm OK with it!" Jack interrupted happily. "This is the best news ever!" He scooped her up in his arms, like he had on their wedding night. She yelped happily at the sudden gesture and snuggled herself in his large-framed body. He smiled down at her, and as he bent his head down to her lips, she kissed him back with all the love and devotion she had for him. When the kiss was over, they gazed into each other's eyes for a moment. Then he carried her upstairs to their bedroom, where he lay her gently on their king-size bed and kissed her once again. "I love you, Nicole," he whispered to her, and she smiled back at him.

"I love you too," she responded softly with tears in her eyes. At this very moment, all the worry and concerns she'd had melted away as she looked up at the love of her life.

"You know what?" he asked, kissing her on the forehead and stroking her hair.

"What?" she asked, noticing the twinkle in his eyes and almost reading his mind.

"I need to take a shower," he laughed. "Care to join me?"

"You go ahead. I took one a few hours ago," she replied, sitting up. "But don't worry, I'm not going anywhere," she said cautiously. "I'll make myself a little more comfortable in the meantime."

"You do that. I won't be long, trust me," he said. He kissed the tip of her nose and was already on his way to their en suite.

Nicole sat there for a moment and smiled. God how she loved him! How could she have even though such things about him? She quickly stood up and removed her blouse and her skirt, folding them neatly and placing them on a chair in the corner of their room. She stood there for a moment in her light pink, laced, matching bra and panties, feeling like she was on top of the world. She scurried over to the bathroom and bent down to pick up the clothes Jack had just dropped in a heap. *Men!* she thought with a smile. *He can't even put them in the hamper.* But she was only mildly annoyed, because right now, she didn't care. She was just elated too finally be alone with him. She smiled, anticipating what was to come, and as she picked up his clothes, she thought she got a faint aroma from his shirt. It was a nice musky scent, and she brought his shirt to her nose, inhaling it once again, trying to make out the scent, thinking it must be a blend of his sweat and her own perfume. Suddenly, Jack opened the shower curtain, grabbed her by the waist, and pulled her in the warm shower.

"What are you doing?" she laughed, as he hungrily and expertly slid down her panties to her ankles. She brought one foot up and then the other, freeing her legs. She was soaking wet by now, but the warm water that came down her hair and face felt incredibly good. He held her really close to his body as he bent his head down, supporting the back of her head with one hand and cupping her breast with the other. He placed his hungry lips to her neck, kissing her, and then moved to her parting lips, where she received him, just as hungry and wanting. They kissed passionately and with such desire that she thought she was going to explode. He bent his head to her breast, where he expertly sucked on her nipple, first the one and then the other, arousing her beyond anything she had ever experienced with him. She was so hungry for him as she held his head to her breasts, her back arching, her head tilting back and wanting more. He stood up and placed his hand on her head, guiding her downwards, and she complied, kneeling in front of him, and took him in her mouth. It was his turn to throw his head back, and he moaned with pleasure as she pleased him, taking him all in, sucking him with such desire. When he was about to climax, he lifted her up to him so her back was against the shower stall, and she straddled him. Her long, shapely legs wrapped around his muscular thighs while he moved her in an up-and-down motion, with little effort. They moved together in unison, moaning and groaning, and making love like they never had before. It had been a couple of months since they had been intimate, and their climax was long and satisfying.

They were both breathless by the time they were finished. He set her down, and they embraced. Wordlessly, he soaped her down, washing every inch of her body gently and deliberately, sponging her breasts, her abdomen, and the inside of her thighs. He proceeded to wash her hair, slowly and gently, while she stood under the shower head, allowing him to take over her body. It was then her turn to soap down his body, making sure she got every crease and curve. She shampooed his hair, losing her fingers in its thickness. They both rinsed and came out of the shower, drying one another. After drying his wife, he wrapped the white terry-cloth towel around her, covering her body. He stood behind her with his arms around her waist and turned her around to face the mirror that stood before them.

"Do you still have to ask me how I feel about the baby?" he asked, admiring her in the mirror and liking what he saw. They always did make beautiful love together, but tonight was something else. So many emotions were released tonight, and he felt good to be with her once again.

"No, I guess I don't," she said smiling back at him. She had never felt more complete as she did at this moment. "I love you," she added, more seriously.

"I love you," he answered, swinging her around to face him. He kissed her on her nose again, and the nape of her neck. "You know what, I'm starving!"

"So am I!" she exclaimed. "I just realized, I haven't eaten anything all day, and there's all this food downstairs. I could warm it up if you like?" she offered.

"No need to warm it, let's go. And by the way, missy, no starving yourself like that anymore. You're eating for two now, you hear me?" he said sternly.

"Yes sir!" she said, saluting him.

"Come on, let's eat! You took everything out of me tonight. I feel like I can eat a horse!" He gave her a swat on her behind, and like two children, they went downstairs and devoured the food she had prepared so many hours before. They ate like they hadn't eaten in months, and when they finished, Nicole ordered her husband to go to bed while she quickly washed and tidied up.

She shut off the lights to the downstairs, armed the house alarm, and went upstairs to their room, where she found Jack already asleep and snoring lightly. She smiled as she climbed into bed beside him. She turned off the night lamp and just lay there for a few minutes while she listened to his breathing, thinking about the eventful day she'd had. The next day was Saturday, and she had a very busy day at the salon. She was more tired than usual, so she got into her favorite sleeping position and fell into a deep sleep almost immediately.

Nicole had the most beautiful dream. She dreamed that Jonathan was telling her that he couldn't wait to meet his new sister, and that he would always watch over her. In the dream, they were at a park filled with bright-colored flowers, and it was Jonathan, a dark-haired little girl, and herself. But Jack was not there in the dream. It was just the three of them. She slept soundly until the morning hours with her arm wrapped around her husband, who hadn't moved all night.

CHAPTER

5

Morning had come, and Nicole was sound asleep when she felt something on her right leg.

She was sleeping on her side, and she felt a feather-light stroking on her bare leg. With her eyes still closed, she smiled and moved slightly, feeling a tingle of sensation. Jack's fingers moved their way up slowly to her thighs, touching her belly. She stirred at the realization that Jack was wanting something a little more than his usual morning coffee. She felt his warm lips on her shoulder giving her light feathery kisses, while his hands continued to travel up and down her naked body. She shivered with delight, remembering she hadn't bothered to wear any pajamas the night before because it had been a warm night.

"Didn't you get enough last night?" she asked him sleepily, happy to be woken up in this manner. She couldn't remember the last time he had been so amorous with her.

"This is what you get for being a bad girl and sleeping naked," he said, his voice deep and muffled as he continued to explore her body, awakening every inch of her. "Don't you know that it's a crime to sleep next to me all exposed like that?" he said in a low and sexy tone.

Nicole turned to face him, feeling his arousal instantly, and she smiled while she investigated his deep, green eyes. "Well, good morning!" she responded, putting emphasize on the morning. He too had slept in the nude, and she wrapped her arms around him while he continued to kiss her. He shifted his position and got on top of her, kissing her neck and then her breast, tantalizing her nipple, and then moving to the other one. She started to moan, all the while wondering how she managed to go without for so long. She was immediately brought to some sense when she remembered that she had to go to work and didn't know what time it was. She abruptly sat up to see the time and noticed that it was seven o'clock. "Jack, we must get up. I need to get ready for work!" she said in a panic, but Jack had other plans as he moved lower to her abdomen, continuing to give her soft kisses on her stomach.

"Relax, baby! Just sit back and enjoy," he said with total conviction. She laid back in bed and watched him as he playfully kissed and stroked her belly. "There's our little baby in there," he said to her, still moved by the prospect of a new baby—*his* baby—growing inside of her, and it turned him on immensely. He knew he had avoided making love to his wife for a while now for reasons he still didn't fully understand, but he was intending to make up for all of it. He loved her, and he wanted to show her just how much. He shifted his weight lower, being careful not to crush her, and started kissing the inside of her thighs, spreading her legs ever so slightly. He looked up at his wife and watched as she closed her eyes and placed her arms up over her head, squeezing the pillows as he pleased her with his tongue. Listening to her soft moans turned him on even more while he continued to pleasure her. She lifted her legs up over his head and arched her back as she placed her hands on his head, running her fingers through his dark, wavy hair, tugging at it slightly. He expertly gave her the release she was so anxiously waiting for, her breathing becoming increasingly louder and more desperate, releasing months' worth of pain and suffering, coming multiple times causing her body to convulse with great magnitude.

He watched as her body shrunk back, and he pulled her up and turned her around. She got on her knees with her back to him, and he took her from behind. It didn't take him long to climax as he increased his rhythm, and when he came, he turned her around and held her close to his heart, giving her a long and gentle kiss on her lips. "Well, good morning to you too!"

"Oh my God," Nicole exclaimed in disbelief, noticing that it was already seven forty-five, which left little time to get ready for work. "I hope you're happy, mister! You're going to make me late for work!" she exclaimed, as she hopped out of bed and headed for the shower.

"Yeah, but it was worth it, wouldn't you say?" Jack laughed as he watched her move gracefully and quickly across the room and into their en-suite. "Do you have a lot of appointments today?" he called out to her as she turned on the shower faucet.

"Probably!" she called back from inside.

He also had a busy day today with work. He had a lot of paperwork to draw up for a new residential area they were building, and they had to meet their deadlines.

In no time, Nicole was out of the shower and in the middle of putting on her makeup. Jack watched her and smiled as she nervously got ready. "Babes, relax, you'll be on time! So, a lady will wait a few minutes for her rollers!" he joked. "What's the big deal? I mean, what else do these old ladies have to do?" he added as he stood by the entrance to the en-suite, watching her as she meticulously applied her mascara, secretly thanking God that he wasn't a woman. Wearing a tie at an occasional function was effort for him.

"Very funny!" she answered, grinning at him, finishing off her makeup application, and proceeding to change. To save some time, she decided to pull her hair up in a neat, high ponytail, which was suitable for the warm weather they were having. She glanced at herself in the mirror, feeling satisfied with what she'd accomplished in such a short time. She quickly moved past him and grunted at the sight of their bed, which still needed to be made. She was meticulous about cleanliness and keeping the house in an orderly fashion, and Jack had been married to her long enough to know that.

"Leave the bed, I'll make it. You go get yourself something to eat, before I really make you late," he said. He couldn't seem to get enough of her now. He could've gone for another round.

"Don't you dare!" she said, running over to him and giving him a quick kiss on the lips. "I love you, and I'll see you later," she said breathlessly.

"I love you too. Have a good one, and don't work too hard!" he answered, but she was already out of the room and downstairs. *Wow, Speedy Gonzales!* he thought. He then jumped in the shower and put his focus on the work that awaited him.

—

It was usually a thirty-minute drive to work, but Nicole managed to make it in twenty. She was just in time for her client, who was getting highlights. The salon was already busy—clients waiting for their stylist to call them to their chair, others in the back getting their hair shampooed, the chatter and laughter that accompanied the client-stylist relationship, and the business phone ringing off the hook. Yeah, it was going to be a busy day alright! Nicole happily greeted everyone and was already cutting her foils, while two of her closest coworkers exchanged looks, noticing the sudden change in Nicole's demeanor. They were aware of Nicole's months of sadness and withdrawal. Oh, she'd tried to hide it, and most of the time she had been successful, but the sadness and emptiness in her eyes said it all.

They gave each other a quick glance, both surprised by Nicole's change in spirit. They shrugged and proceeded with their own clients already waiting in their chairs. Diane was a fellow coworker, tall and slim with blonde hair and green eyes. She was the same age as Nicole, and although they didn't socialize outside of work, they worked extremely well together. Nicole was quite fond of Diane, for she led an interesting life, one filled with a mixture of pain and adventure. She was a single mom of two, and she was a wonderful and busy stylist that everyone adored. She was the one person in the whole salon that Nicole could confide in and feel safe that it wouldn't spread throughout the entire mall.

Nicole had some idle conversation with her client, Stella, while she carefully placed all the appropriate foils on her head. She went to the receptionist's desk and checked the appointment book. It looked like she was going to have a steady day filled with more highlights, cuts, and a couple of colors. She appreciated being steadily busy, for not only did she make more money, but the day flowed faster. She loved her job because it allowed her to get creative, and the interaction she had with each client was very therapeutic for her, especially since her son had died. She couldn't open to her husband since he, too, had suffered a great loss, so being able to talk openly to a handful of clients helped her in her day-to-day. It was a good thing she had her sister, Sara, who was four years older than her. She was also married, and had four-year-old twins, Andrea and Christopher. As she thought about her sister, she realized she hadn't talked to her in a couple of days. With everything that had happened the night before, she had never even got a chance to call her and tell her the wonderful news.

She checked on Stella, whose highlights were still processing, and opened a couple of foils. Nicole decided Stella still needed a few more minutes before she was ready to be rinsed and toned. She grabbed her cell phone from her station and stepped outside of the salon for a bit of privacy. She clicked on Sara's number, and to her disappointment, got her voicemail. She didn't want to give her the news on an answering machine, so she just kept it vague, telling her to call her back when she had the time. She got back to Stella just in time to remove her foils and rinse her hair before applying the appropriate toner, and finally, washing her hair again, finishing her off with a stylish haircut and a blowout. It always gave Nicole great satisfaction when she was able to transform someone's appearance.

"Wow, I love it. Thank you, so much! You just took ten years off me, you know that?" Stella said excitedly, obviously loving her new hairdo. She slipped Nicole a twenty-dollar tip after paying for her service.

Nicole thanked her and went on with her busy day. She wanted to talk to Diane about her pregnancy but didn't get a chance. She didn't just want to blurt it out, and she didn't want the news to leak out just yet because she was afraid it would hurt her clientele. She thought of her parents and made a mental note to call her mom when she got home. Her parents lived in the east end of the city, but her mother had her hands full taking care of her husband. Nicole's dad had suffered a stroke a few years before and had become quite unbearable. He wasn't quite himself, and now he was starting to forget a lot, which worried her and Sara immensely.

The rest of the day was filled with the sounds of chatter, blow-drying, music, and laughter. Periodically, she would check her cell phone to see if she'd missed any incoming calls from Jack. It felt so good to be on the same page again. She knew that he also had a busy day ahead of him, which was probably why he hadn't called her, but that was normal for a Saturday. He was always doing odds and ends on any given Saturday. His secretary was off on the weekends, so he would hold down the fort, return some calls, check on some quotes, or visit some of the locations he was working on. But they had Sundays off to be together. She couldn't wait to see him later, hoping they could make some plans for the rest of the weekend. It was close to closing, and Nicole was pleasantly tired. She sat at her station for a few minutes, welcoming the relief it gave her. Standing all day was hard on her back and her legs.

"Oh my God! What a long day!" Diane said, plopping in her chair and looking just as tired as Nicole felt.

"Tell me about it!" Nicole replied, removing one shoe and massaging her foot. "I think we're going to have a couple more weeks of this, and then it's going to slow down big time," Nicole added, knowing that summer holidays were just around the corner, and everyone went on their vacations or to their cottages. She wished that she was one of them just about now.

"Isn't that the truth!" Diane said in agreement, turning her chair to face her, and leaning forward, obviously wanting to ask her something. "Hey, Nikki, what's up? You've been glowing and smiling from ear to ear today.

Care to share?" she finally asked. She had noticed that Nicole was busy but smiling and buzzing around all day, something she hadn't seen in ages.

Nicole leaned forward even closer, wanting to share her news with Diane, and glanced around to make sure that no one was close enough to hear her, especially Olive. Olive was a nice lady, always pleasant and happy, but she didn't want to share with everyone quite yet. Olive was one of those people that had to know everyone else's business; but Nicole's business was her own. She felt safe enough since Olive was a few feet away talking to her client.

"Are you ready for this?" Nicole asked, and when Diane nodded, Nicole looked around again, and got a little closer to Diane. "I'm pregnant," she said, her voice low enough for only Diane's ears.

"You're kidding! That's great, Nikki!" she yelled, loud enough to get Olive's attention.

"What's great? What happened?" she asked, glancing back and forth from Nicole to Diane, waiting for a reply.

"Oh nothing, Olive. Nicole was just telling me about a trip they might be taking this summer," she said, not wanting to reveal the real reason for her excitement.

"Oh yeah? Where are you going?" Olive asked, not noticing the look of annoyance on her client's face, who probably wondered when she was going to get out of there.

"Oh, they're thinking of going to the Dominican Republic, isn't that right, Nikki?" Diane said, leaving Nicole speechless at her friend's cleverness.

"That's nice! You must be very happy," Olive said, almost forgetting that she had a client in her chair.

"Oh, she is!" Diane responded, glancing at Nicole and smiling from ear to ear. She looked like the cat that swallowed the canary.

Olive's client made a grunting sound, which brought Olive back to what she was doing, and the two girls looked at one another and smiled.

"Congratulations, girlfriend," Diane whispered, giving her a friendly hug before leaving work for the day. Nicole thanked her, and said goodbye to everyone, before she cleared out as well.

6

The drive home was traffic free, which was a great relief to Nicole since she commuted by highway every day. Thoughts of the baby growing inside of her made her heart flutter, and she placed her hand on her abdomen, still in disbelief that she was going to have another baby. Her cell phone rang, interrupting her thoughts, and she was even more delighted to discover that it was Jack calling to see how her day was going. He was in a pleasant mood, but was still at work, and to Nicole's disappointment, was going to be another couple of hours or so. But he promised he'd be home as soon as he finished.

"Alright then, I'll see you later," she said. "I love you," she added.

"I love you, Nicole," Jack replied warmly from the other end. As she hung up, it rang again. The display on her dashboard revealed it was her sister, Sara.

"Hey, sis!" Nicole answered, happy to hear from her. She hadn't seen or talked to Sara in a couple of days now.

"Hey, Nicole! I just got home with the twins, and I got your message. How are you?" she asked, sounding breathless as usual.

"I'm good, I'm just on my way home from work."

"Well, why don't you come over. It's just me and the kids."

"You know what? I just talked to Jack, and he's going to be another couple of hours. Alright, I'm on my way. I have something to share with you," she replied.

"Alright, I'll be waiting. See you in a bit."

As Nicole neared her sister's house, she pulled into a supermarket and picked up a tub of ice cream for the kids. She was having a craving for ice cream, and she knew without a doubt that the kids would be thrilled.

Pulling up to her sister's house, she was captivated by the array of flowers and greenery that her sister had undoubtedly planted. Sara was the one with the green thumb between the two of them, and she enjoyed gardening and getting into the dirt, planning and planting every year. She always impressed everyone with her planting skills and the choice of flowers that she arranged every year; whereas Nicole was the cook and baker, and she was the one to bake a birthday cake or a dessert whenever there was an event. She smiled as she walked up the walkway, noticing that both sides were filled with a beautiful assortment of petunias and impatiens and some other flowers that she didn't even recognize. Everyone in the family joked that Nicole couldn't distinguish between a flower and a weed. She rang the doorbell, and almost immediately the door flew open. Andrea and Christopher rushed into her arms, taking her by surprise.

"Hi, Auntie Nicole! Mom, it's Auntie Nicole!" They were excited to see their aunt, as always, and Nicole was equally thrilled to see them. She hadn't seen them in a few weeks but seeing them now made her realize how much she'd missed them. She hugged them in return, loving the warm welcome they provided.

"Hey munchkins, how are you?" Nicole asked them while they wrestled over the shopping bag containing the ice cream.

"Let go! It's mine!" yelled Christopher, tugging at the bag.

"No it's not! It's for all of us! Isn't it, Auntie Nicole?" shouted Andrea, trying to impress her aunt with her maturity, and frowning at her brother.

"That's right, Andrea," replied Nicole, winking at her niece, acknowledging her voice of reason. She stooped down to their level, catching Andrea sticking out her tongue at her brother. "I brought the ice cream for everyone, but only after your mommy says you can have some, deal?"

"See, I told you!" Andrea responded, and Christopher put his head down.

"Speaking of which, where *is* your mom?" asked Nicole, as she continued her way through the house, observing how immaculate it was.

"Hey, sis, I'm right here!" Sara's voice sounded from behind Nicole, coming downstairs. "Sorry about the kids, they've been at it all day," she said as she approached her younger sister and gave her a warm hug.

"Don't worry about it, for goodness sake! They're kids after all!" Nicole said with a laugh, hugging her back. "I brought some ice cream, although the twins have it now," she replied. "Hey! Where did they go?" she asked, looking around for them.

"Where do you think?" Sara replied, nodding toward the kitchen. "Come with me!" She took her younger sister by the hand and led her toward the kitchen. They laughed in unison at the sight of the twins sitting at the kitchen table with the open box of ice cream between them, looking ready to dig in.

"What did I tell you!" Nicole said, laughing, as she scooped up the box from between them, causing them to sulk and complain that it wasn't fair. "You'll have some ice cream *after* dinner, OK?" she said good-naturedly.

"But—"

"No buts! You know the rules—no snacks or treats until after you've eaten your dinner." Sara said to them pointedly, closing the lid again and placing the frozen treat in the freezer of the refrigerator.

"Oh alright!" they both chimed in together.

It never ceased to amaze Nicole how her sister always seemed to keep it together taking care of two four-year-old's, twenty-four hours a day, seven days a week, with no outside help from anyone. Sara was always the model mother who enjoyed being a stay-at-home mom. She had chosen early on in her marriage to set aside her career and stay home full-time to care for her family. Fortunately, her husband was a chartered accountant, and he made more than a decent salary, which allowed her to stay home and be with the kids.

"You guys, why don't you go in the family room and watch some television. I think your favorite show is about to start," she said, coaxing them.

"*Peppa Pig!*" they both chimed in unison. And with that, they ran into the family room, plopped themselves on the oversized couch, and waited for their favorite program to begin.

"Phew. Come, Nick, let's go out on the deck. We've got thirty minutes of peace," she said, leading her sister outside on the deck. There they had a beautiful patio set for eight people—a glass table and eight chairs with a matching umbrella. To the right of the deck was a large trampoline, which was for the twins, and further down, was a swing set and a slide. In the far corner was Sara's vegetable garden, which was her pride and joy. She had an assortment of tomatoes, cucumbers, and some potted plants with her herbs.

Sara went in the house to fetch some lemonade while Nicole took a seat at the table, admiring her sister's backyard. Sara came back with two tall glasses of lemonade and sat across from her sister.

"So, Nikki, you said you had something you needed to share with me? Good news I hope?" she asked eagerly, curious as to what her sister had to tell her.

Nicole was watching her sister intently, noticing how pretty she was. She was a bit shorter than Nicole but equally attractive, with almond-shaped brown eyes, full lips, a creamy complexion, and dirty blonde hair with blonde highlights throughout.

"I do!" Nicole smiled, making sure she had cemented her sister's attention. "Are you ready for a niece or nephew?" she asked. Nicole watched as her sister's face light up. Sara stood up from her chair to embrace her sister.

"Oh my goodness! That's great, kiddo!" she exclaimed, embracing Nicole warmly. "How far along are you?" She took a step back and gave Nicole the once over.

"Oh, just a couple of months," Nicole told her. "I just found out yesterday."

"That's great, Nikki. I'm so happy for both of you," she said with tears in her eyes. She was truly happy for her younger sister, for she knew what the death of her child a year ago had cost her. She had witnessed firsthand the devastation and grief that had rocked Nicole's entire being, and hearing that they were expecting another child warmed her heart. Sara had been there for Nicole emotionally and physically, driving her to her therapy sessions and allowing her little sister to sob in her arms, knowing there wasn't anything she could do to bring her little boy back. She had become Nicole's rock, and when her nephew had drowned, she had been afraid her sister would never recover. As Sara thought about it, she shuddered at the thought of something happening to one of her kids. Unfortunately, her sister had experienced every parent's worst nightmare. "Have you told Mom and Dad yet," Sara asked.

"No, not yet. I was planning to call Mom today" Nicole replied, thinking that her news would really cheer her mom up. There had been a strong bond between her mother and Jonathan, and when he'd died, a part of her soul had died as well. "I know how unhappy she's been, you know, with Dad and all," she said softly, her eyes starting to get blurry. "It's been so hard for her, especially since Jon—"

"I know, sweetie, I know." Sara hugged her once again. She understood perfectly well. They saw for themselves how their mother had aged since her grandson's death and their dad's stroke. "Tell you what," she continued. "Let's order some pizza, and then we can just chill for a bit, OK?

Some time passed, the two sisters chatting and laughing easily, enjoying each other's company. The twins had finished their pizza and were jumping and playing on the trampoline, giggling and laughing without a care in the world. They had completely forgotten about the ice cream that they were forbidden to eat about two hours before.

"OK you two, settle down," Sara said sternly. "Come over here and sit for a bit while I get us some ice cream!"

"Yeah! Ice cream!" they both shouted with excitement.

The two sisters looked at one another and smiled, thinking that, not so long ago, they had acted the exact same way when their mom gave them a treat. Sara returned with four small bowls of ice cream, and they all ate happily together. Nicole felt elated to be among her family, and she made a mental note to have them over soon.

"Well, sis, I'm going to get going," Nicole said, standing up and stretching.

"You're leaving already?" Sara asked in disappointment.

"Yes, I've really got go. Jack might even be home by now, and I'm exhausted. Correction stuffed and exhausted," she said, stroking her stomach. "Sara, thanks for a wonderful evening. It was so good to see you!" she said sincerely, giving her big sister a hug.

"Anytime, sweetie. You know where we are," Sara replied, walking her sister to the front door. "Say hello to Jack for me. Oh, I can't wait to tell James the great news!"

"Bye, Auntie Nicole!" shouted Andrea from the back of the house.

"Goodbye, munchkins! I love you!" Nicole shouted back as she walked to her car. The two sisters hugged once again before Nicole got into her car and pulled out of the driveway.

She was smiling from ear to ear as she thought about her visit and was anticipating an equally wonderful time with her husband once she got home. She smiled at the thought of him and the night they had just shared. Her whole body tingled at the thought of their morning in bed. They hadn't made passionate love like that in such a long time, and she felt blissfully relieved to connect with her husband once again. She couldn't wait to get home to him now; it hadn't been that long ago that going home was a dark place for her. A house that was once filled with love and laughter had been replaced with silence and loneliness. The worst was the stillness and the emptiness that made it hard for her to breathe at times, causing her to experience severe panic attacks. Now it would be a whole new beginning for both.

She pulled into their driveway next to Jack's truck, thrilled to see that he was home. She shivered with excitement at the prospect of the two of them rekindling their love. She got out of her car and raced inside the house to find Jack sitting in the family room and watching television.

"Hi, Jack, I'm home," she said happily approaching her husband.

"Hey, baby! How was your evening?" he asked her as he stood up to greet his wife, giving her a quick kiss.

"It was good. I went to Sara's for dinner. She says hello and congratulations," she replied, pointing to her belly.

"Come here you," he said huskily, pulling her to him and sitting her on his lap. "How's my baby doing?" he said, smiling as he stroked her abdomen.

"Very well, as you can see. Did you just get home?" she asked, wrapping her arms around his neck.

"Yeah, I just got in not too long before you came in," he answered, planting a kiss on her abdomen. "Hey, Nick, what do you feel like doing tomorrow? The day is ours to enjoy." Jack nuzzled his face in her neck. He couldn't believe how beautiful she looked.

"How about we go to Niagara-on-the-Lake," she answered, feeling excited. She stroked his hair.

"Sounds good to me. We could spend the whole day there, visit a couple of wineries, have lunch, and do whatever." He gently stroked her hair and her face, leaning over and kissing her. His hand moved downward to the front of her shirt, slowly and deliberately unbuttoning her blouse. He placed his hand inside, cupping her breast, feeling it swell in his hand. He smiled up at her as he continued to playfully tease her breast, pinching her nipple. She let out a small sigh, which pleased him, giving him the signal to go on. He placed his lips to her breast, kissing her nipple, teasing, taunting, making her squirm in his arms. She in turn, began to unfasten his belt, and he stood up, with her still in his arms, while she fumbled with the buttons on his shirt. He carried his wife upstairs to their bedroom, where they made love once again. He needed her desperately, and he gave himself to her wholeheartedly. She received him with as much desire as she'd ever known. They finally fell asleep in each other's arms, happy and fulfilled.

—

They awoke at nine o'clock in the morning, took a shower together, dressed, and left for Niagara. It was an hour drive, but fortunately, the QEW was light on traffic—they arrived in no time. They visited one of the wineries, taking pictures and enjoying the beautiful view. They walked hand in hand, stealing kisses as they strolled through the vineyard with its rows and rows of grape vines, so beautifully lined up. It was a glorious day, and the scenery was spectacular. They couldn't have picked a more perfect day, and when they finally left the winery, they drove to the main town. It was filled with restaurants and an assortment of stores. They parked their car and visited little shops, stepping into bakeries that were filled with an assortment of pastries, fudge, and chocolate, all which Nicole desperately craved.

The shops in the small town were quaint and charming. There was a variety of trinkets, clothes, handbags, and souvenirs to please any shopper. Restaurants, coffee shops, and patios were filled with people, and the aromas of grilled calamari and steaks filled their nostrils as they strolled leisurely along the strip, observing the lineup of people waiting outside of ice-cream shops for a cool treat on this particularly warm and sunny day. Feeling hungry, they stopped and had lunch on an outdoor patio, where they shared Caesar salad and grilled calamari. They devoured a basket of garlic bread, and Jack ordered a chilled bottle of white wine. Although Nicole didn't drink any of the wine, she noticed that he managed to polish off the entire bottle by himself. She drank a bottle of carbonated water, and after they finished their entire meal, they decided they would share a dessert, choosing a crème Brulé. When they were finished, they continued to walk along the main street, enjoying the glorious summer's day and taking in everything there was to see.

Having seen enough, they decided they would go to Niagara Falls. They walked to their car and drove another twenty minutes to the falls, where they parked and walked along the strip, enjoying the falls and taking more pictures. They stayed there a while longer, and finally decided they would call it a day and go home. Nicole fell asleep almost immediately once they got back on the highway, and Jack drove home. They couldn't have picked a more suitable day for Niagara, and they were both deliriously happy and tired. This was a whole new chapter for them, and nothing and no one was going to stand in their way of having the life that they so much deserved. The baby they had created together had brought them closer, and they couldn't be happier. As far as Nicole was concerned, they were on top of the world.

CHAPTER

7

"So what do you think?" asked Detective Williams. "Who could've done this?" He appeared pensive and disgusted as he looked down at the unconscious girl lying on the bed. He glanced at his partner for answers. His partner, Steven Fromer, was standing at the foot of the bed, peering down at the young woman who slept peacefully. The two officers were at Credit Valley Hospital. The day before, the woman had been found by a young man who had been out walking his dog. She was found in the park on the ground, face up, her clothes torn from the front. She had been unconscious, barely alive, and she hadn't been wearing anything from the waist down. Her face was bruised beyond recognition—her eyes swollen shut, her lips doubled in size—and both her wrists were severely bruised. Tests confirmed that she had a broken collar bone and several broken ribs. She had been beaten so badly that it was obvious whoever her attacker was had had every intention of killing her. It was a good thing that, just a few yards away from the listless body, a wristlet was found with a few dollars and her driver's license in it, among other random items—a lip gloss, an unused tampon, and a pack of gum. There were also a couple of business cards from a restaurant called The Blue Lagoon.

"I don't know, partner, but I'm sure as hell going to find out," Fromer answered, staring at the woman. According to her driver's license, she was twenty-five years old—the same age as his own daughter. This young woman was someone's child, someone's wife, perhaps. He dealt with crimes of this nature all the time, and it always affected him, but he had a job to do. He couldn't imagine something like this happening to his daughter. He cringed inwardly at the very thought of it. Fromer was going to get to the bottom of this.

This woman's name was Ashley Moore, and they didn't have a whole lot of information to go on. Her wristlet plus a broken cellular phone, an iPhone that had been found a few yards away from where the attack took place. They couldn't question her yet since she was still unconscious. From what the doctor told them, her thighs and legs were severely bruised and cut as well. The doctor was still waiting for the results of the MRI on her brain. She was in intensive care for now, and there was a possibility that there was internal bleeding. "Whoever did this to her beat her to a pulp and left her for dead," Fromer said, shaking his head. He turned to leave. "Come on, let's go check out the bar. Maybe someone can shed some light."

They walked out of the room and closed the door. There was another young officer on duty standing outside of Ashley's room. They had been given strict orders to refuse any visitors at all, except for the nurse and her doctor in charge.

—

That same night, back at the Newman's, Nicole went upstairs to change into her pajamas for the night. As she changed, she caught herself looking in the mirror that stood before her. She smiled at the reflection looking back at her, for she was a woman in love and carrying her husband's baby. She looked at her abdomen a little more closely as she stood there in her bra and panties, still in awe that she was pregnant. It was getting late, and she wanted to get to bed—the next day was a workday for both her and Jack. He had insisted that she go ahead to bed to get her rest, reassuring her that he wouldn't be long. He just wanted to have a drink and watch a little television to unwind before going to bed. His increased drinking had concerned her in the past few months, and she remembered how he'd polished off the entire bottle of wine when they'd had lunch out earlier in the day. For months, she had watched her husband grow more and more distant from her, and it had weighed heavily on their marriage. She'd tried countless times to get him to open to her, or at the very least, accompany her to her therapy sessions, but he'd always refused her, telling her that he didn't need therapy and that he was fine. But he wasn't fine, and deep down, she'd known it. And now, suddenly, he seemed to be back to his normal self, except for his drinking.

"Oh, stop your worrying, girl, you're going to drive yourself crazy," she said out loud to herself in the mirror, and proceeded to change into her pajamas. She went to her bed and grabbed her book, since it always helped her to relax. She tried to read, but surprisingly, she couldn't focus. She slammed her book shut, and she started to feel anxiety setting in, a condition she had experienced countless times since her child's accident. She climbed out of bed and walked toward her bedroom door, opening it quietly. She stood there motionless, listening to the quiet murmur of the television downstairs, and a moment later, the sound of a beer opening, causing her heart to palpitate. She had become all too familiar with that sound over the last few months, and it made her feel extremely uneasy. She thought of going downstairs to try to coax him into coming to bed, but she didn't want to risk getting into an argument with him. Things were finally good between them again, and she feared that it would backfire on her. Every time she'd mentioned his drinking in the past year, he'd always get defensive and very angry. They'd shared such an incredible day together, so she decided that she would leave well enough alone—for now. And with that thought in mind, she turned around, closed the door quietly behind her, and climbed back into bed, feeling apprehension, but that had become her new normal.

—

That evening, Detective Fromer and his partner went to The Blue Lagoon. They needed information about the girl, and the only thing they had to go on was the business card inside her wallet. As they walked in, they noticed how busy it was. They walked past the other patrons and went straight to the bar area. It was dimly lit, and the chatter from the diners and the three huge flat-screen TVs mounted on the wall above the bar area was almost deafening. There was a basketball game in progress, and the sounds of people cheering for their favorite team, along with the occasional boos, was enough to make Fromer want to go home. He could never understand the big hype with these sport bars. They found a small table for two beside the bar, and they took a seat.

"Looks like it's happening tonight, eh?" asked his partner, scoping out the place.

"Oh yeah. I've heard a lot about this place. I've just never checked it out," he answered, looking around, observing the establishment, wondering when a server was going to come to their table.

"How long do you think this is going to take?" asked Detective Williams as one of the waitresses finally took notice of them.

"As long as it takes, partner," Fromer responded. "We've got to question everyone that works here. Maybe someone here knows her, maybe she worked here, who knows," he concluded, getting more comfortable in his chair.

A tall, slim, pretty, blonde waitress approached their table, giving them a warm smile as she took out her notepad and pen from her black apron.

"Hello, my name is Stephanie. Have you two handsome men dined here before?" She asked them in a friendly tone.

Detective Fromer spoke first, turning to look at her. "Yeah, Stephanie is it? We'd like to ask you and a few other people in this establishment a few questions, if that's alright. I'm Detective Fromer, and this is my partner, Detective Williams," he said, motioning to his partner, who nodded to her.

"Um, sure. Let me get this table over there their drinks, and I'll be right back. Can I get you a drink while you wait?" she asked, looking a little uneasy.

"No, thank you. If you don't mind, we just want to talk to you," Detective Fromer said.

"Sure thing!" she replied cheerily. "I'll be right back!" She swiftly left their table and went to retrieve the drinks from the bartender to take over to her other table. In no time at all, she was back at the detectives' table.

"So what can I do for you?" she asked, pulling up a chair from the bar, and feeling thankful for the relief it brought to her legs. It had been a long shift, and she was tired.

Detective Fromer reached into his pocket, producing Ashley's driver's license. "Can you tell me if you can identify this person?" he asked, holding it up to Stephanie and looking at her intently, trying to get a sense of her reaction. "By the way, what's your full name?" he asked, continuing to hold up the driver's license.

"My name is Stephanie—Stephanie Brown," she replied, peering at the picture in front of her. "And yeah, I know her. Her name is Ashley, and she works here. At least she did anyways," she replied sharply. "Not so sure she will be now," she added with assurance, waving one hand in the air.

"Oh yeah? And who's that?" Detective Fromer asked, noting the hint of sarcasm in her voice as he put the license back in his pocket.

"Well, she'd just started working here, not that long ago in fact," she stated, crossing her long shapely legs and moving a hair from her eyes. "She did a disappearing act. Didn't show up to work yesterday or today, not even a phone call or nothing," she added, flippant. "The boss is pretty mad, I can tell you that!" she said with conviction, as though that explained everything. "You know," she added, adjusting her blouse. "It's not like she's needed around here anyway, so I don't understand why he's so pissed!" She tapped her long, blue-colored fingernails on the surface of the table.

The two men glanced at one another, noting that she didn't even ask about her coworker or why two detectives were inquiring about her.

"How long have you worked here Miss—"

"Brown," she cut in smiling from ear to ear, exposing her very straight white teeth. "I've been here, um … let's see … just over four years," she answered cheerfully. "I'm one of the original waitresses here, kind of like Manny's right hand, if you know what I mean." She laughed, crossing one long, shapely leg over the other one, slowly and deliberately, making sure that the two detectives got an adequate view of her legs, emphasizing her black high-heeled shoes.

"When was the last time you saw Miss Moore?" Detective Fromer asked, ignoring her obvious flirting.

"Let's see …" She hesitated, putting her forefinger up to her temple as if to think. "Oh yeah, it was last Friday night, because she was working the same shift as Laurie and me, from one to twelve. But if I recall correctly, she cut out a couple of hours or so earlier," she said, fluttering her fake eyelashes and giving a quick glance to a table of customers trying to get her attention. "Oh, if you don't mind, gentlemen, I've got to get back to work," she said, winking at them both. "Is that all?" she asked, rising from her seat.

"That's alright with us. But if you could point out who Laurie is, we'd like to ask her a few questions as well as your boss—Manny you said?"

"Oh yeah, no problem! Laurie's just split for the night, but she'll be here tomorrow around two o'clock in the afternoon. I could get you Manny if you'd like. He's just in his office."

"Thank you, Miss Brown, that would be very nice," Fromer replied, flashing her a smile.

"Oh, no problem, no problem at all!" she said as she turned around and headed toward the table of customers waving at her.

"What a piece of work!" Detective Williams said, eyeing her. She was bending over a bit too much at another table with a group of men, making sure they got a full view of her bosom.

"Easy, partner! We're here on business, remember?" Fromer laughed. His partner was understandably taken by her—he was single and quite a few years younger than him.

About five minutes later, an older man of about sixty walked over to their table. He wore black slacks and a black silk shirt, which was unbuttoned inappropriately low for a man of his age, exposing a thick, oversized gold chain around his neck that rested on his very hairy chest. He was a stocky man, not very tall, with longish hair colored black, and sporting a diamond-stud earring on his left earlobe. He extended his hand to the two men, which prompted the two detectives to rise and shake his hand.

"Good evening, gentlemen. I'm Manny. I understand you need to talk to me?" he said politely, flashing a set of perfectly white, straight teeth. "Please, sit down," he motioned to them. "Can I get you gentlemen a drink?" he offered, glancing in Stephanie's direction and motioning her over to him with a nod.

"No, thank you, we're good," Detective Fromer replied. He pulled out the license once again from his pocket and showed it to Manny. "We understand that this young woman works here, correct?" he said, eyeing him closely.

"Yeah, she's only been working here a couple of months. She hasn't shown up for work in a couple of days," he replied, glancing at the driver's license and eyeing the detectives carefully. Nervously, he thought of Ashley and the real hot blow job she had once given him after a little coaxing. He hadn't really needed another waitress at the time he hired her, but he liked the idea of having a little variety. Even at fifty-eight, he needed pussy, and he needed it regularly; and what better way to get it. Stephanie was his main girl, but occasionally, he needed a little something extra. He gave his two main girls the best shifts, and he paid them well. He felt himself getting an erection as he thought of the "benefits" of being a successful businessman. It was a win-win situation for everyone involved—especially for him.

Detective Fromer studied Manny as he tried to figure out his angle. Manny was too cool and too polite for his liking. "Well, she's in the hospital in ICU," Fromer said matter-of-factly, watching Manny's expression.

"Oh, really?" he said, his black eyes growing larger. "What happened?" he asked, showing concern for the detective's sake.

"Well, she was savagely beaten and raped and left for dead. She's still unconscious actually," the detective stated, his eyes narrowing toward Manny, watching him closely. "Do you know if she has any family here—parents, siblings, anyone?" he asked, hoping that there was.

"I wouldn't know," Manny replied clearing his throat. "Like I said before, she was new here, a couple of months or so. I don't ask too many questions Detective. I just hire 'em." *And fuck them*, he thought.

"Miss Moore has told us she worked last Friday. Apparently, there was another girl here the same night. Laurie, I believe? We'd like to ask her a few questions," Detective Williams interjected.

"That's fine with me. I could tell her to come here a half hour before her shift begins," Manny offered, already thinking ahead. He'd ask her to come in an hour earlier so he could talk to her first. He wasn't going to take any chances with his chicks. They were good workers and great in bed, and he didn't want any trouble.

Detective Fromer stood up, and his partner followed suit. "Thanks for your time, Manny," he said politely, extending his hand to him. "We'll be seeing you tomorrow then." Manny nodded in agreement, relieved to see them go.

"Sure thing, Detective!" Manny said, managing a fake smile.

—

Stephanie had finished up with her tables and was yearning to go home. It had been a long day again, and she was exhausted. Manny, however, relieved to see the two detectives leave, decided that he needed some tender-loving care. So, as she walked past him, he looked around, making sure that no one was watching, and smacked her lightly on her behind, signaling he needed her to stay a bit longer. Sex always helped him to relieve tension, and since most of the customers had left at this point, he figured he'd get some action before closing the bar. As she turned around to face him, he nodded his head, motioning her to meet him in his office, which was located at the back of the restaurant.

Stephanie wouldn't have minded as much if it was any other night, but tonight she just wanted to go home. She had been working for three solid weeks with no day off, and she was eager to leave. But she knew better than to object to him. He paid her top dollar, which covered her rent and bills and then some.

She answered him with a quick nod before taking off her apron, and walked a few steps behind him toward his office, knowing what was expected of her. She was fully aware of the scenario that was about to take place. He'd be sitting behind his desk with his pants off, and she'd have to sit on his desk facing him and allow him to fondle her any way he pleased until he got aroused. She would then have to get down on her knees and give him a blow job until he was good and ready. Finally, she'd be expected to bend over on his desk and allow him to take her from behind. He would typically smack her buttocks while giving it to her, and when he was ready to ejaculate, he'd forcefully grab her and shove her to the floor on her knees and make her suck him until he'd ejaculate in her mouth. That was the ritual of their employer-employee relationship.

The first year she'd worked for him, she'd felt cheap and dirty; but as time passed, she got used to it, and accepted that it was just part of her job. He did favor her over the other girls—had made her head waitress—and, somehow, that made her feel validated. Her job was secure, the money was excellent, and when she went home, she was a different person. She was able to live a comfortable life in a decent apartment and afford nice things for herself. She walked into the office, which always smelled of stale beer and cigarettes, and sure enough, he was waiting for her.

—

"What do you think, Fromer? This guy seems like a snake," Detective Williams said as he drove out of the parking lot and onto the main road.

"Yeah, tell me about it. I think that there's a lot more to him than meets the eye," Fromer scoffed. "I'm going to head over there a couple of hours earlier, scout the place, and wait for this Laurie girl. I have a feeling that she'll have a little more information about Ashley," he concluded, heading east toward their station.

"Stephanie doesn't seem like she has any use for Ashley. Her animosity toward her is so obvious, wouldn't you say?" Williams asked his older partner.

"Yeah, I noticed that. Usually, a coworker would show *some* concern—ask about her, something. As for Manny, the guy's dirty, I can feel it. But right now, our focus is to find out why Ashley left earlier that night, and how and why she ended up at the park. Did she leave alone or with someone? And if she did leave with someone, did she leave willingly? Or was she threatened? Why would a young girl go to a park in the middle of her work shift? Unless she knew the guy and he turned on her, who knows."

They continued to drive toward the police station, and Fromer was lost in a whirlwind of different scenarios. His shift was over, and he wanted to go home. It was a long and grueling day, and he was tired. These crazy shifts were starting to get to him.

"Well, hopefully we'll get some answers soon," Williams said, as he finally pulled into the parking lot of the police station. "Maybe Laurie will shed some light. And then again, there's Ashley. Hopefully she'll come to and will be able to tell us exactly what took place that night. Unless she doesn't make it," he concluded, as he parked the car and looked toward his older partner.

"Hope you're right, Williams. I guess we'll just have to wait and see. The doctor who's looking after her is supposed to let us know when she comes to. We're going to talk to her first, and I hope that'll be soon. In the meantime, we just must rely on the other waitress," he said, getting out of his car and bidding his partner farewell. It was very late at this point, and he just wanted to go home and get some rest.

8

The next morning was busy as usual. Nicole woke up and noticed that Jack had already left the house. His side of the bed was ruffled, which told her that he had eventually made it upstairs. It had taken her a while to fall asleep the night before, but when she had, she'd fallen into a deep sleep, so much so that she hadn't heard or felt Jack when he'd joined her in bed.

She took a quick shower, changed, and applied her makeup. She quickly made her bed and headed downstairs to have cereal and a coffee. She didn't particularly like Mondays, especially since it was one of the longest shifts she had to work. She worked from ten to seven, and sometimes, when business was slow, the day just dragged on. On the flip side, she got to work with Diane all day, as well as Olive, who worked till three, and her boss Armando. It was on the slow days that she and Diane were able to have a decent conversation, to share and confide in one another. All in all, she worked with good people, and her bosses were easygoing.

The aroma of the coffee brewing filled her nostrils, and as she glanced at the clock, she noticed it was a little early, so she decided she would call her best friend, Emily. She was two years younger than Nicole, and they had been friends since high school. Emily was a receptionist at a dental clinic, and she worked full-time. Nicole hadn't talked to her in a few days, and as she poured herself a cup of steaming hot coffee, she called her best friend. She loved Emily like a sister, and she realized that she hadn't even shared her good news with her yet. Since the death of her little boy, she had come to lean heavily on Emily as well as her sister Sara. If it hadn't been for the two of them, she knew without a doubt that she would've lost her mind and surely would've fallen into a deep depression.

She was elated when Emily finally picked up the receiving end and was thrilled to hear from Nicole, asking her a hundred questions at once. She sounded out of breath as usual—she was probably getting ready to go to work and getting her three-year-old son ready for day care. Her son's name was Christian, and he was a delightful little boy. Emily was happily married, and she was a wonderful wife and mother to her only son. Christian and Jonathan had always played so well together, and she couldn't help but feel her loss just a little bit more when the two girls got together. The two boys resembled one another so much that often, when they were out together in the park or the mall, people would ask if they were siblings. But Nicole loved that little boy dearly, and in a peculiar way, he brought her much-needed comfort.

"Emily, it's been too long, my friend. Besides, there's something I want to share with you!" she exclaimed excitedly, for she couldn't hold her tongue about her pregnancy any longer.

"What gives girl? Tell me!" Emily, in turn, was bursting with excitement.

"Who am I kidding! I thought I'd hold out until I saw you, but I can't, I'm so excited!" she yelled into the phone with glee. "I'm pregnant!"

"Oh my God! Nick, are you serious? That's great news!" Emily shouted into the receiver. "How far along are you? When did you find out?" she asked, one question after another, which was not unusual for her friend. In all the years the girls had known each other, Emily was almost always the more enthusiastic and the more passionate of the two.

"Hey, one question at a time. I'm just over two months pregnant, and I just found out a few days ago. I've been meaning to call you, seriously, but we had a busy weekend. I haven't even told my parents yet!" she explained, taking a quick sip of coffee.

"Oh, Nicole, why not? These are your parents for goodness' sake. I know your mom could use some great news. What's the hold up?" she asked, confused. She was aware of the situation with her parents.

"I know, you're right, Em! Do you want to know the truth?" she asked. "What if I told my mom and dad, and then I was to lose the baby or something went wrong? What would that do to my mom? It would kill her, Em. I mean, well, I don't foresee anything bad happening, but what if it does? I'm scared," she cried. "I'm really scared. I lost Jon—"

"Nick, stop it. Stop blaming yourself once and for all," her friend interrupted sympathetically. "What happened with Jonathan was an accident, and you know that, don't you? I don't want to hear this sort of talk again; do you hear me?" Emily said, trying to end her friend's emotional punishment once and for all. She heard silence on the other end and thought she might be getting through to her best friend. "Nick, are you there?" she asked more softly. She knew her friend all too well. She couldn't really blame her for feeling the way she did. Losing a child was not something you just get over, no matter how much time passed.

"Yeah, I'm here," Nicole answered quietly as she listened to her best friend, wiping some fresh tears that had escaped. "I guess you're right." She stared into her half-empty cup of coffee.

"I know I'm right. Listen to me, Nick. Give your mother the best news ever, and everything will be fine. I promise you. Please, my beautiful friend, I'm pleading with you. Don't think so negatively. If something bad were to happen, it could happen anytime with any of us. Unfortunately, we don't have a crystal ball to foresee the future. Nikki, listen to me, hon. Enjoy the moment, and go with it. Stop being afraid and start living and enjoying! You'll see, you're going to have a healthy and beautiful baby, and everything's going to be fine," she said with conviction.

"I hope you're right. OK, I'll tell her today at some point," Nicole said, already feeling better. Talking to Emily always cheered her up since she was the most positive, most upbeat person that Nicole knew. She was just one of those people that always bounced back no matter what life threw at her.

"That's better! Now cheer up, put your beautiful smile back on your face, and go to work and have an amazing day. I'm going to catch up with you in a day or so. You and I will do lunch or something, alright? Oh, Christian, not the chocolate! Hon, I've got to run. We'll talk soon, OK? Love you!"

"Love you too. Talk to you later," Nicole said, hanging up.

She sat there for a while, absorbing everything that Emily had said to her. She knew in her head that Emily was right, but her heart said differently. As thrilled as Nicole was about the new baby on the way, she was also very much afraid. Up until her son's death, she'd prided herself on being a good mother, and still, she'd lost him. She knew in her head that it had been an accident, but in her heart, she felt she could've prevented it. She worried that something bad was going to happen to this baby too, and it gave her anxiety. Doubting herself as a mother was something she would live with for the rest of her life.

She sipped on her coffee and stared out her kitchen window. She imagined what life would've been like with her little angel if he were still alive. He would've been just over three and a half years old, and he would've been looking forward to being a big brother now. He would've been starting kindergarten in the fall, and their family would've been complete. She pictured her little boy's face, how his crystal-blue eyes scrunched up when he smiled. Fresh tears stung her eyes as she thought about him. She set the coffee cup on the table, closed her eyes, and wrapped her arms around herself tightly, imagining that she was being hugged by her little boy. He had always given her the biggest and most loving hugs, especially when they'd played or after his bedtime story, when he told her how much he loved his mommy. How she missed that! She'd give anything to be with him again. She would never forget her angel—ever.

—

Jack was momentarily lost in thought as he sat at his desk looking over some invoices. This was the season where they were the busiest—too many deadlines to meet, more manpower needed, and a lot of paperwork. It was in the summer season that people hated construction work the most. He often heard the old cliché, "Canada has only two seasons: winter and construction." The roads were often blocked with pylons, which created more volume and traffic and caused many commuters to become more agitated on the road, causing more accidents due to drivers' higher stress levels. People wanted new subdivisions and newly paved roads but were unwilling to understand that they could only work efficiently in the summer and fall months. Once the winter hit, things slowed down big time.

He put his papers aside for a moment and thought about his wife and his baby on the way. He smiled as he thought about how she looked in the early morning while she was asleep. He had woken early, and she hadn't even stirred. She had looked so beautiful and peaceful, and even in her sleep, she looked radiant. He glanced over to the picture frame that was during the mountain of paperwork on his desk. It was a photo of the two of them, taken in the early years of their marriage, before their son was born. They looked so happy and very much in love. He leaned back in his chair and locked his hands together, rocking the chair slightly. Feelings of anger stirred inside of him as he thought of his son and how he had been taken away from him. He knew that accidents happened all the time, but why his son? He had been going to teach him how to ride a bike, catch a baseball, and a thousand other things that fathers did with their sons. He clenched his fists in a ball, wanting desperately to hit something, and hard. *Damn it! Why did he have to die?* A knock on his door interrupted his thoughts, and he quickly resumed his business.

—

It was a typical day for a Monday at the salon, and although Nicole had some appointments lined up, it was nothing she couldn't handle; they were all cuts, no chemicals, which freed her for much of the day to catch up on Diane's events.

"How are you feeling?" Diane asked, leaning forward toward Nicole, not wanting anyone else in the salon to hear. She wasn't sure if her co-worker wanted her news announced just yet.

"Actually, I'm feeling pretty good," she answered in a low voice. "The only thing that I've really noticed is that I'm a bit more tired, that's all." She smiled, resting her hand on her growing baby.

"Anyways, enough about me. What's going on with you? How are things at home?" she asked, changing the subject quickly, as she noticed that Olive had leaned toward them slightly, trying to overhear what the girls were saying.

"Pretty good, I must say. I started the story that I was telling you about. But I think that I should still investigate taking a writer's course. What do you think?" she asked, proceeding to curl her hair.

"I think that's a very good idea, Diane!" Nicole said with excitement. "I know you've got a passion for writing, and I think that taking this course will help you immensely. God girl! Where do you find the time to write with a job and two kids?" she asked incredulously.

"Oh, that's easy! I just pretend that my bathroom doesn't need to be cleaned, and the floors don't need to be washed, and I write, that's how." Diane laughed, leaning back in her chair, and continuing to curl her hair. "Let's face it, girls," she continued, noticing that Olive, as well as her boss and the clients, had tuned into their conversation. "We could be doing the same shit all day, every day. But guess what? It doesn't make a damn difference at the end of the day!" She laughed, and Nicole and Olive laughed in unison, agreeing with her. "Am I appreciated for cooking dinner every day, and cleaning and washing everyone's clothes? No!" Diane answered herself. "So why should I give a crap? I might as well do what God intended me to do, and that is to take care of my passion for becoming the next Danielle Steele, isn't that right?" she asked the rest of the group, having them all in stitches at this point. "I mean, what the hell! Am I only good enough to cook, clean, and transport my kids to and from school? Work all day and then become Madonna in bed at night for Fernando?" she rolled her eyes, throwing her arms up in the air and almost burning herself with the curling iron. "I think *not*." she concluded.

By now she had the entire staff and all the clients in the salon laughing hard at her comical, yet truthful, revelation about all womankind.

"Oh, you women are all the same," Tony, one of her bosses, retorted as he curled his client's hair. "I've got one at home just like you," he said with a chuckle.

"Never mind you!" Nicole scolded her boss warmly. "Everything Diane is saying is absolutely the truth, and you'd better not disagree with me, seeing you're the only male in the salon at the moment," she said pointedly while the rest of the women nodded in agreement, still laughing.

"I wouldn't dare!" he smirked, applying the last curl. "I got to work with all these women." He laughed, knowing all too well he was completely outnumbered.

The rest of the day flowed easily, and it was almost time for Nicole's shift to finish. She thought of calling her mom but decided she would call her from her cell on her way home. Besides, she didn't want to take a chance on anyone overhearing her. Her bosses were great, and she knew she would always have a job there; it was her clients that worried her more. Most of them were wonderful, as they once were when she got pregnant with Jonathan a few years before. There was always a risk of losing some clients while being away on maternity leave, and although many of her clients stayed loyal to her once she returned to work, there were many others that she'd lost—those were the breaks.

An hour later, on her way out, she gave Diane a friendly pat on her shoulder, wishing her a "wonderfully creative evening." In return, Diane winked at her, depositing her equipment into her bag, as she, too, was finished for the day.

"Bye everyone! See you tomorrow!" Nicole called out, putting her purse over her shoulder.

"Bye, Nicole!" her boss called out to her. "And remember, if you can't be good, be careful." He snickered in her direction. It was just like Tony to make statements like that, but the girls loved him.

Pulling out of the parking lot, Nicole retrieved her cell phone from her purse and pressed the speed dial to her parents' house. Her stomach instantly turned to a knot as she waited for her mom to answer. She had been feeling very apprehensive about revealing her news to them, especially to her mom. Finally, there was a click on the other end, and her mother's pleasant voice came on.

"Hello," she said graciously.

"Hi, Mom, it's me, Nicole," she replied, tensing up as she merged onto the highway.

"Hello, dear, how are you?" she said, sounding delighted to hear from her youngest daughter.

"I'm fine, Mom. How are you and Dad doing?" she asked, feeling a little better, but worried for what she'd hear about her father.

"I'm alright, Nicole. As for your father, well, let's just say that things are a little crazed around here. One minute he's acting normal, and the next he flies off the handle over something I say or something trivial. He forgets a lot, and he gets very angry. Frankly, I don't know what to do," she said, feeling like she might've said too much. She was not the kind of woman who burdened her children with her problems since they had their own families to take care of.

"Oh, Mom, I don't know what to say," she said sympathetically. "Have you thought about taking him to see the doctor, perhaps mentioning to him that his memory isn't good? Mom, if you want, I could make the appointment, and we could take him together if you think it'll help?" she offered, feeling sorry for her mom.

"No, honey, that's alright. You have enough on your plate. I have made an appointment for him, so hopefully they can figure out what's going on with him," she in a low tone. "So how are you, honey? What's going on with you? I haven't heard from you in a while. Is everything with you and Jack alright?" she asked, concerned for her youngest daughter.

"Yes, Mom, we're fine," she answered reassuringly. "Actually, I just wanted to let you know that you're going to be grandparents again," she said, feeling somewhat relieved as she let out her breath.

"Oh, Nicole, that's wonderful news! I'm so thrilled for both of you!" her mom cried with excitement. "How far along are you, dear?"

"I'm just a little over two months, and Jack and I are thrilled, Mom.

Listen, let me talk to Jack, and we'll plan a barbecue at our house, OK? I'd like to have Sara and her clan as well, you know, sort of like a celebration! Do you think that you and Dad will be able to make it?" she asked, sounding hopeful. "It would mean so much to the both of us!" she added excitedly. She hadn't seen her parents for a while, and she really missed them.

"That sounds wonderful, Nicole. You call me with the details, and we'll be there. I can't wait to tell your father the news. I just know he'll be delighted," she said, elated for her daughter and son-in-law; they had been through so much, and she was thrilled that they were expecting another child.

Nicole smiled at the prospect of having a barbeque with all her family surrounding her. She just had to run the idea by Jack, although she was confident it wouldn't be a problem. One thing about Jack was that he loved to entertain, and he loved her family. His parents and his brother lived in Vancouver, and his older sister lived in Florida, so her family had become his family from day one. His parents had moved there after Jonathan died. Jack had always felt like they'd abandoned him and Nicole at a time where they needed them the most. Even the phone calls had diminished, calling their son only on holidays.

Nicole felt so relieved after hanging up with her mother. *Well, that wasn't so bad*, she thought to herself. She hoped to God that everything would be alright with the baby, because if something bad were to happen, her mother would surely die of a broken heart.

In the meantime, Jack had called his wife to let her know that he was on his way home. They decided that they would just stay in, have a bite to eat, and just chill in their backyard. Nicole pushed all the negative thoughts away and replaced them with positive ones, giving her energy as she thought about the baby that was growing inside of her and her deep love for her husband. It had taken a while for things to fall back into place, but ultimately, everything had worked out. She couldn't have been happier than she felt at this precise moment.

9

Detective Fromer made sure he got up bright and early Monday morning. He went through his usual routine and then had a cup of coffee with a couple of cigarettes and a slice of marble cake that his wife had baked the day before. He read the morning paper, grabbed a shower, and waited anxiously for twelve o' clock; that was the time he'd decided he would go to The Blue Lagoon to wait for Laurie, the waitress, to come in to start her shift at the restaurant. Even though Manny had told him to go in around one thirty, he thought it would be better to throw him off track and surprise the bastard. There was something sketchy about him. He seemed too superficial for his taste, and the guy wore too much jewelry. In all the years he had been on the force, he always trusted his instinct, and where this guy was concerned, his gut was telling him that Manny was doing a hell of a lot more than just running a bar.

—

Manny was also busy trying to call Laurie. He'd called her several times already, but he kept getting her voicemail. "Where are you, bitch!" he roared, slamming his cell on his desk. It was almost noon, and she wasn't answering. He was in a foul mood, and he didn't need this shit right now. He knew the suit would be coming in around one thirty, and he needed to warn her to keep her trap shut. He needed to be nice about it, didn't want to scare her or off or anything. He just didn't like it when cops came sniffing around his joint. He decided he would make one last attempt to call her, and as he did, he watched the newest waitress that he'd hired a couple of days ago come into the bar. She was by far the youngest of the girls he had on staff.

As he listened to Laurie's voicemail once again, he became more and more agitated, but his eyes never left Cindy. She was putting her apron around her waist, ready to begin her shift. She was eighteen years old and very cute. Although he hadn't made a move on her yet, he knew it would only be a matter of time, but he had to be careful; that's how he operated. They came in inquiring about a job, with their fancy resumes, which he politely pretended to be interested in. He would "interview" them, asking the obvious questions pertaining to work, and if they were young, naive, and pretty enough, they were hired. The resumes went directly into the garbage, for he wasn't interested in where they went to school or how much experience they had. The girls got paid well, particularly Laurie and Stephanie. They pretty much did what they wanted if the customers were happy, and their boss was "happy." Most of the girls that came to him were from broken homes. He'd heard it all, from running from their stepdads or alcoholic mothers to how they simply didn't want to follow house rules and were determined to "make it" on their own. Yeah, he had it made alright! Life was good, business was booming, and his cock was satisfied. The occasional drugs that he obtained and sold didn't hurt either.

Again, he tried to call Laurie on her cell, and once again, it went to her voicemail. He slammed the phone down again, swearing under his breath. He got up from his chair and paced around his office, thinking he needed to get ahold of her before the suit did. He glanced down at his gold watch and swore out loud when he noticed that it was now after noon and still no sign of Laurie. She was due to come in at around two, but he desperately needed to talk to her. It infuriated him that he couldn't get hold of her.

——

Detective Fromer made himself comfortable at a table close to the entrance of the restaurant. He ordered himself a coffee and looked around, familiarizing himself with the place again. There were two girls' waitressing, and he had asked a young blonde waitress, that went by the name of Cindy, if she would be kind enough to let him know when Laurie came in to work. Cindy seemed quite young, and he wondered if she was even old enough to work there. He took notice that Stephanie wasn't working that day, unless she was coming in with Laurie. It was possible.

He thanked the young waitress when she brought him his coffee, and he politely asked her how old she was. Cindy hesitated for a moment; then nervously told him she was twenty-one. She quickly exited, making her way to the other waitress, who had just taken an order from a young couple. She whispered something in her ear, sparking the other waitress to look in his direction.

He took a sip from his steaming hot coffee. He suspected that both were underage and wondered all the while where Manny was. There was no way that he'd have two young girls open the place on their own.

Suddenly, Manny appeared, walking out of the office toward the front of the bar coming practically face-to-face with Detective Fromer. He was momentarily stunned when he spotted the detective sitting at a table in the front. *Fuck!* he thought. What was he doing here so early? He'd told the son of a bitch to come around one thirty, but here he was! He pasted on a happy face, pretending to be glad to see him.

"Well hello again, Detective!" he exclaimed, extending his hand for a handshake. "How nice to see you again." He continued with his fake welcome, making sure he didn't remind Fromer of the time they had agreed upon, to not raise suspicion.

"Good afternoon, Manny. Nice to see you too," Fromer replied, just as insincere. "I hope you don't mind. I was in the area and decided to come in and have a coffee. Hang around here a little," he said, flashing one of his super-phony smiles at him. He picked up his mug, his eyes never leaving Manny's face.

"Oh, no problem. Enjoy your coffee," he said, silently cursing him with his pasty smile. *Like hell he happened to be in area!* he thought. "Can I get you anything else? Perhaps a slice of pecan pie to go with the coffee?" he offered, wishing Fromer would just leave his premises.

"The coffee's great on its own," he said, sensing Manny's growing agitation and loving every minute of it.

"So, is there any news about Ashley? Did you guys find out who did that to her?" he asked, putting both his hands in his pocket.

Detective Fromer hesitated before answering him, taking a long sip from his coffee. "No, not yet," he replied. "But you'd better believe I'm going to find out," he said, watching him intently.

"Well, I hope you find out soon. She was a pretty good worker around here," Manny replied, almost sounding genuine.

"Yeah, so you said. I just wonder why she'd leave work early. Would you know anything about that?" he asked, straightening himself up in his chair.

"I wouldn't know, buddy. I was in my office with a mountain of paperwork," Manny said, recalling that night perfectly. He'd been in his office alright, getting it on with one of the girls after smoking a couple of joints. He hadn't cared that she'd left and was assaulted and was in the hospital with critical injuries.

"So you mentioned that Laurie starts working at two?" Detective Fromer asked, glancing down at his watch. He wondered how much more small talk he could take.

"Yeah, it shouldn't be much longer," Manny said, losing his patience with the suit.

"No problem, man. I'm in no hurry. Please don't let me hold you up.

You go ahead and do what you need to do. I need to make a few phone calls anyways," he told him, giving him the green light to get lost.

"Alright then. I'll leave you alone. I'm just going to be around," he said, taking the subtle hint to leave. He turned and walked back toward his office, glancing around at the two girls and nodding to them, motioning them to go into his office. He needed to remind them gently not to reveal their real ages and to do their job as professionally as possible.

In the meantime, Detective Fromer made a quick call to the hospital to inquire about the girl. He needed to speak to her before anyone else did. He found out that she was still unconscious, but out of the woods. He felt immediate relief, first and foremost because he felt sorry for her, second, because without her testimony, they'd have almost nothing to go on. He made sure that she was still under watch and that no one other than the doctor or nurse went in to see her. It surprised him, however, that not one person had even tried to visit her.

After hanging up with the cop on duty at the hospital, he scratched his head and thought for a minute. He retrieved the driver's license from his pocket and looked at it carefully. *She was a pretty girl*, he thought to himself, thinking that the young woman lying in the hospital bed looked nothing like the woman in the photograph. He felt a strong need to solve this case, for this young woman had been savagely beaten and raped and left for dead. He needed to talk to Ashley as soon as she came to. She was the key to solving this case.

Before he knew it, it was nearing one forty. He watched as some patrons came in the establishment. It seemed slow. It was, however, only Monday afternoon. By evening, he was sure the place picked up, as most restaurant/bars did. Cindy approached him and asked him if he wanted a refill. He declined politely, and waited patiently for Laurie to come in.

"Um, Cindy is it?" he asked as she turned to leave. "I was wondering if you would be so kind as to let me know when Laurie comes in. I just need to speak to her for a few minutes," he reminded her, still watching the door.

"Sure, no problem. Oh, there she is now!" Cindy exclaimed

innocently, pointing to another young woman who had just entered the restaurant.

Detective Fromer looked toward the door as a young woman walked in—a pretty girl, average in height. He had to admit, Manny's waitresses were all very beautiful women. She walked over to the back of the restaurant and hung up her sweater. He stood up, and walked in her direction, and as she turned around, he extended his hand to her, taking her by surprise.

"Hello, I'm Detective Fromer, and I was wondering if I could have a few words with you. Are you Laurie?" he asked politely.

"Um, yes. Why do you ask?" She looked perplexed.

"I'm sorry, please don't be alarmed. I just wanted to have a word with you if that would be alright." She nodded. "Here, let's have a seat over here where we could have some privacy," Fromer continued as he escorted her to a nearby table where they seated themselves. Laurie looked nervously around for her boss, wondering what was going on.

"What's your last name, Laurie?" he asked.

"Jefferson—Laurie Jefferson. Umm, I'm sorry, but could you please just tell me what this is all about?" she asked, feeling uneasy and getting fidgety in her chair, totally unprepared for this unexpected conversation.

"Miss Jefferson, I understand that you were working last Friday evening with a young woman by the name of Ashley Moore. Am I correct?" he asked.

"Yes, as a matter of fact, I was. What's happened? Is it Ashley? Because she didn't show up to work on Saturday or on Sunday," she stated, alarmed.

"Yes, I know. She's in the hospital, Miss Jefferson," he said, noticing her eyes widen in surprise. "I understand that she left before her shift was up. Am I correct?" he asked.

"Yeah, she was waiting on this guy, and it looked like they hit it off. Next thing I know, she asked if I would cover her because she wanted to leave with him. What happened to her? Is she alright?" she asked, genuinely concerned for her coworker. She had only known her for a couple of months, but they had hit it off from the beginning. They had become fast friends and discovered they both shared a dislike for Stephanie and their boss.

"Well, she's not doing very well, I'm afraid. She was assaulted and is in the hospital with life threatening injuries. He watched Laurie's eyes widen in horror. "Whatever you can tell us would be of great help. It seems that you saw her last. Did she tell you where she was going with this man?" the detective pressed on.

"Oh my God! No. No, she didn't," Laurie responded, bewildered but what she'd just heard. She held her face with both hands, trying desperately to recall her conversation with Ashley that night, however brief it had been. "She just told me that this guy was hot, and she was hoping to get to know him better by the end of the night," she continued. "Oh God! Is she going to be alright?" she asked in shock. "Do you think he did this to her?"

"We don't know yet, Miss Jefferson. That's what we're trying to find out. Do you remember what the guy looked like?" he asked.

It took her a little while to respond. She looked in a daze, trying to recall something about him. "Yeah, he was a tall guy, pretty solid. He didn't look like the office type if you know what I mean," she stated, remembering that night vividly. "He had dark, curly hair and was a good-looking guy in a tough and rugged sort of way. I remember he was sitting over there at the end of the bar for about an hour or so." Laurie pointed in the direction of the bar. "I don't remember exactly because it was busy that night. He looked like a nice enough guy. I don't know," she said, feeling apprehension creeping in. She was afraid of possibly getting an innocent man in trouble. But was he innocent? She certainly didn't know.

"Has he been here before?" he asked, pressing on.

"Yeah, actually, I have seen him here before. He's come in a few times, and he always sits at the bar alone. Never at a table," she recalled. "He looked a little shy at first, but Ashley looked kind of interested in him, otherwise I don't think that she would've went anywhere with him." Her head was spinning as she thought about that evening.

"Did she look like she was forced to leave with him?" he asked.

"No, not at all. As a matter of fact, while I was clearing a table, I just happened to glance in their direction, and he looked like he was about to leave. It was Ashley that kind of persuaded him to hang around and wait for her. She was into him. When they did finally leave together, he had his arm around her waist. That's the last time I saw her," she concluded, putting her head down, feeling a twinge of guilt take over her. If she hadn't agreed to let her cut out early, Ashley wouldn't be fighting for her life right now.

"I take it you didn't catch his name?" he questioned again.

"No, I didn't," Laurie responded, lifting her head to face the detective. "But in the past when he'd come in, he'd usually always come in around the same time, have a few beers, and leave. Shit! I wish I would've said something to her before she left," she added angrily. "You know, she only worked here for a couple of months or so, but I really liked her. We worked well together," she said genuinely.

"Would you happen to remember approximately what time it was when she cleared out from here?" he asked.

"Oh my goodness, it must've been around eight or so," she answered, shaking her head. "I really don't remember exactly. Like I said, it was busy that night, and I had my hands full with my tables, and a few of hers. I hope she's going to be OK," she said again.

"I hope so as well, Miss Jefferson. Is the bartender—"

"Phil. His name is Phil, and he's usually here every night after five," she interrupted.

"Thank you, Miss Jefferson. You were most helpful," Fromer said, rising from his seat. He reached inside his pocket and handed her his business card. She took the card from him, looking at it. "If you remember anything else, please don't hesitate to call me," he said with a nod, letting her know that the interrogation was over—for now.

"No problem. Goodbye," Laurie said to him. She watched him turn and walk out. She just stood there for a moment with the business card in her hand, and she glanced at it one more time before depositing it inside one of the pockets of the black apron that was tied snugly around her tiny waist.

When she turned around to proceed with work, she noticed Manny standing just a few feet away from her, watching her and looking very displeased. She stood there frozen for a moment. After what seemed like forever, he turned on his heel and walked back in the direction of his office. Laurie took a deep breath and proceeded to get to work. She always felt uneasy around him, and she didn't like the way he was glaring at her just now, although she knew that she didn't do anything wrong.

She had been working at The Blue Lagoon for the past two years, and almost from the beginning of her employment there, he had come out and expressed what he wanted and expected for her to work for him. She felt she had no choice in the matter. She'd been thrown out of her house when she was sixteen, and she had a little sister that she cared for, so she desperately needed a job that paid well. If that meant that she'd have to occasionally give Manny a blow job, as much as it repulsed her to her core, or to sit for him while he fondled her, well then so be it. It sickened her to allow him to put his old penis in her mouth, but it really was no different from what she'd had to endure from her stepdad. At least she got paid well, and thankfully, it wasn't too often that she had to do anything. All the waitresses knew that it was Stephanie that Manny screwed around with most. She was his playmate, and although Stephanie never actually admitted what was going on, it was obvious to the rest of them that she was the preferred one.

As she checked the schedule for the following week, she felt immediate relief when she realized that she would be working with Stephanie. That meant that she was off the hook as far as her having to service Manny—Stephanie would cover that department.

All the girls knew that Manny was a scum bag, but at least he took care of them financially. Most of the time when she was summoned to his office, she would fulfill her deed, and he, in turn, would slip her an extra hundred bucks for "being a good girl." Well, a job was a job, and that was the only way she could justify what she did to survive.

CHAPTER

10

Nicole stretched out her long shapely legs on one of the recliners outside in their backyard. It was a beautiful early evening, and Jack was firing up the barbeque. He was going to grill a couple of steaks, corn on the cob, and some pita bread. He'd had a long day but was satisfied with the progress that he and his men had made. So far, they were meeting their deadlines, and work was in full swing. He had ordered his wife to relax and enjoy the evening, and from what he observed, she was doing just that. Jack looked at her and momentarily got a vision of another barbeque, only that one had also included his son. Nicole had been lying on the same chair, with Jonathan playing around her, while Jack grilled the burgers. Mother and son were singing the alphabet together while Jack looked on with pride. He had only missed two letters out of the whole alphabet. She had been a good mother to him—correction, a great mother—so what happened? How could she *not* have noticed him leave her sight even for just one moment? Jonathan was a tenacious two-year-old, and everyone who'd known him knew that.

"Honey, are you alright?" Nicole asked, looking at him with concern. He had put the steaks on the grill and had forgotten about them, not realizing that he had been staring at his wife.

"What? Yeah, I'm fine, why do you ask?" he asked, shaking his head back to reality. He turned the steaks before they burned.

"I was just telling you how hungry I am, and you looked like you were a million miles away," she said with concern in her eyes.

"I'm fine, really," Jack replied, taking a long swig from his beer. It was a hot day, and the cold beer felt soothing as it went down.

"Anyway, Jack, I just wanted to run something by you," she said, changing the subject. "I've talked to my mom—and by the way, I told her about the baby, and she's thrilled for us. I've sort of invited my parents to come over one day soon for a family barbeque, and I wanted to include Sara and James with the twins, and Emily, her husband, Alex, with Christian. Sort of like a celebration. What do you think?" she asked excitedly.

"Sure babe, that sounds great! How about this Sunday?" Jack asked as he turned the corn, making sure that they browned evenly on both sides.

"Oh, that's great! I'll let them all know tomorrow. It'll be so much fun. We haven't done anything like this in so long!" Nicole exclaimed. "I mean—well, not since Jonathan died that is," she said, her voice barely audible, but loud enough that Jack heard her.

"Why do you always have to bring him up!" he burst out, jolting her in surprise. "Can't you just let it go for once!" He slammed the tongs he was holding onto the side of the barbecue, shocking Nicole in fear, causing her stomach to turn upside down. "Do you see *me* bringing him up all the time?" he yelled, his face turning dark with anger. "I mean for the love of God, Nicole, let it finally *go*!" Jack slammed his fist on the side of the barbecue.

Nicole's eyes instantly filled up with tears at his sudden outburst. She could barely speak. She just sat, paralyzed, staring at the man she loved but not recognizing who he was at that moment. It had never been clearer to her how much losing their son had affected her husband. Jack had appeared so strong, and it seemed like he was moving on from the magnitude of their loss; but it was obvious to her that, inwardly, he was in an enormous amount of pain. The truth was the deep scars of their loss were still so fresh and raw. He had never wanted to talk about the accident, but he clearly had monumental emotions bottled up inside. It was just a matter of time until it all came out with such force, revealing his broken heart as well as his anger. It scared her to see him like this.

After Jonathan's funeral, both her and Jack had recoiled into their own space, into their own cocoon, with their broken hearts and shattered dreams. They had never really dealt with their loss together. Nicole had gone to therapy, and she'd had her sister, Sara, and best friend, Emily, to lean on, but Jack had had no one. It was too much for her to bear. She sat up from her recliner and looked out into space, not knowing what to say to him. Being able to communicate was essential to dealing with the enormity of their loss. All along, she thought she was alone with the pain that she suspected would never fully heal, and it saddened her to realize that it didn't matter if they had multiple babies, the emptiness that hovered over them would always exist. If they were to heal, they had to grieve, together, and it infuriated Nicole to know that she couldn't even say her deceased son's name without manifesting an explosion.

Shortly after, they wordlessly sat down to eat at the patio table she had so lovingly set. As hungry as they had both been earlier, they just picked at their food in silence, each trying desperately to make small talk—to fill the awkward silence in the air between them—but with no success. The mood had altered. Nicole felt empathetic toward him, but didn't know how to reach him, or what to say for that matter. She suspected that she was expected to never to talk about their little boy ever again, to act like he never existed; but that was impossible because he did exist, and he was everything to both. She hoped that, in time, he'd see that and seek help, just as she had.

Jack, on the other hand, felt ashamed of his outburst and surprised that he'd reacted the way that he had. He sheepishly looked up at his wife, who clearly wasn't all that interested in eating, and watched her pick at her food. He felt so guilty for blowing up at her like that, and his heart broke in two at the situation they were in. He tried to comprehend what had happened, but couldn't, which was why he had disengaged from his wife for so long. He never meant to hurt her. He simply didn't know how to deal with the constant ache that he felt in his heart.

As the evening wore on, it was evident that both had lost their appetites, and when Nicole cleared the table with much of their dinner still on their plates, Jack continued to sit outside and drink his beer in silence. She noticed he was on his third beer now, but she didn't dare say anything to him about it. She decided to leave it alone and go to bed early, perhaps read a little, if for no other reason than to distract her from overthinking the horrendous evening they had just experienced. She quietly said good night to him, and when she turned to leave, he stood up, walked over to her, and kissed her on her forehead.

"Good night, baby. I love you," he said simply, kissing her again, this time on her lips. "I'll be up soon." Nicole nodded, turned, and went in the house and up to bed.

—

The rest of the week flew by so quickly it hardly seemed possible to Nicole that it was practically the end of the work week. It was the same routine every day: go to work, come home, have dinner, and go to bed. Neither Nicole nor Jack mentioned what had happened the previous Monday evening. They acted like nothing had transpired between them, although she received a delivery of beautiful red roses at the salon.

She had been in the middle of a haircut when her roses arrived, and her bosses wanted to have some fun with her and tease her a little. After she'd finished with her client, she read the little pink card that was attached to the bouquet. As she read it, her eyes welled up with tears. He had simply written, "I love you, and I hope you forgive me." She was moved by Jack's gesture, and it lifted her spirits.

"Well, you must've been a really good girl last night!" Tony snickered, smiling his wicked smile. He always loved to tease the girls, particularly Nicole because she always had a comeback.

"Either that, or he's feeling guilty about something!" Armando called out as he approached the front of the salon with a clear vase that they kept in the back and smiling from ear to ear. "I know—I'm a man. A guy doesn't normally send flowers to his wife unless it's her birthday, or he needs to apologize for something he's done," he said philosophically. "That's just how it is." He placed the empty vase on the front desk.

"Well, I disagree!" Diane interrupted. "You guys are living in the stone ages. It's not uncommon for a man to send flowers to his loved one for no reason at all. That's what makes it so romantic," she said as she cashed out a client. "Isn't that right, Suzie?" she asked her client, who was in the middle of paying her.

"I don't know about that, Diane," she said, laughing. "I tend to agree with the guys on this one." I've been married and divorced twice, and I can tell you this much: a man is a man. They're all dogs in one form or another. A man doesn't send his woman flowers unless he wants something, or he's guilty of something. That's what I think," she said with conviction.

"Nicole, come on. I need you on my side," pronounced Diane, as she gave her coworker a friendly shove to the side. "Tell them they're wrong. Your guy sent you these gorgeous flowers because he just wanted to say, 'I love you,' right?" She looked at her imploringly.

"That's right, Diane. He does love me, and he just wanted to be nice and make my day," Nicole replied, managing a smile; but deep inside, she knew the others were right. Jack did feel guilty about Monday, otherwise he wouldn't have sent them. It had been several years since she'd received flowers from Jack for no apparent reason. Back in the day, when they were dating, he'd sent her flowers often, especially if they'd had a fight or if she was having a bad day, but that was eons ago.

"Bull shit!" Tony countered. "First of all, no one said that your husband doesn't love you. I've been married for over forty-five years, and I can tell you this much: if I were to send my wife flowers for no reason at all, she'd have a heart attack. I'm telling you, the guy's guilty of something," he said, winking at Nicole.

"Well, be that as it may, the point is I got flowers and you didn't, so there!" Nicole said, raising her eyebrows and winking back at him. "Now I just need to fill up this vase with water," she said cheerfully, taking the vase with the flowers and heading to the back of the salon to the empty sinks.

"Carmen, what do you think?" Diane asked Carmen, her other boss, the quieter one of the three. "Please tell me that you've sent flowers to your wife without any reason." Diane wanted to prove something to the other two bosses.

"I think it's none of our business," he replied. "I really couldn't care less as to *why* she received flowers from her husband. They're beautiful, and she's thrilled about it, so who cares!" he said, chuckling. "All I know is that her husband will be one lucky fellow by the end of the day." They all agreed. "And to answer your question, Diane, I haven't sent my wife flowers for no reason. But maybe our generation is different from yours. You happy now?" He winked at her, and she moaned in return, and they all laughed.

Diane finally caught up with Nicole, who was in the middle of arranging her roses. She was the only one in the shop who knew about Nicole's pregnancy, and she was positive that her pregnancy was the reason for her receiving them.

"Hey, Nicole, by the way, those are beautiful!" she said, feeling a bit envious. How she wished Fernando would do something like that for her. "Please tell me, just for argument sake, that he sent you these flowers 'just because.' I don't know. I mean, I know I'm a single mom with a boyfriend, but I guess I'm just a hopeless romantic. Tell me I'm right," she said, laughing.

"I don't want to burst your bubble, my friend, but they're right, you know. Here, read the card he had attached," Nicole said to her, pulling out the envelope from her pocket and giving it to Diane. "I trust you won't say anything," she said, watching Diane as she quickly read it.

"Damn! What did he do? If you don't mind me asking." Diane kept a watch for anyone listening. There always seemed to be someone around, particularly Olive, who was watching them from her station.

Nicole gave her a quick rundown of what had happened the previous

Monday. She also confided in her about Jack's incapability of dealing with their son's loss. "I'm telling you, Di, it's more than I can take sometimes. I'm not even allowed to bring up *our* child to him because he freaks out," she said, feeling a lump build in her throat.

"Oh, hon, I'm so sorry. I feel for you, and for Jack. Obviously, the guy needs help. He figures if he doesn't talk about it, then maybe it didn't happen. Do you know what I mean? My ex was like that too. Whenever we had a problem, he wouldn't want to talk about it, and he'd think that our problems would just disappear—sweep it under the carpet, and poof! No problems!" Seeing that Nicole was starting to get upset, Diane picked up her tone a little. "Listen, everything's going to be fine. If you ever need to talk, you know you can always call me, day or night. Just try to see things through his eyes," she continued, giving him the benefit of the doubt. "He's obviously hurting bad, so just leave it alone for now, OK?" she said, giving her good friend a warm hug. "Come on, let's see if we can keep these old geezers out of trouble." She laughed jokingly, entwined her arm around Nicole's, and approached the front as they both laughed.

"What's so funny?" asked Olive as she finally finished her roller set on one of her clients. Watching the two younger girls giggling and talking among themselves delayed her work, and her client didn't look too happy about it. The two girls just looked at one another and giggled.

11

*B*ack at the station, Detective Fromer sat at his desk in a daze as he thought about all the information he'd gathered from Laurie. This case wouldn't get too far without hearing from Ashley, and for now, he had to wait. He thought about the guy in question and wondered if it was really him that had raped and assaulted the girl. He could've been a stalker for all they knew. Maybe that's why he'd visited The Blue Lagoon several times—maybe he had his eye on the girl, and that night, he decided to act. Fromer just wished that he had more to go on. He sat back in his chair, with his one hand on his temple and the other tapping his desk. Maybe it wasn't him but someone else. Perhaps Ashley had an ex-boyfriend that wanted revenge. After all, it wasn't a crime to go out after work for a couple of beers—Fromer did. This suspect sounded like just a regular guy who just needed to unwind after work before heading home, like just a regular Joe Blow. Or was he? That's what Fromer needed to find out.

Earlier in the day, he'd received a call from the hospital and spoke to the doctor in charge of Ashley. Apparently, she was coming around slowly but wasn't quite ready to speak to anyone. He made sure to re-mind the officer on duty that no one was to enter her room, except of course the doctor and the nurses. She was awake but still too weak to communicate with anyone, so he figured he'd give her a couple more days to regain her strength and recuperate. He needed her to be strong enough to talk to him. Hopefully, she'd be able to shed some light on what happened that night. There was already a bulletin on the news, basically describing what happened to the girl and how she was found at the park—date, time, and location. The bulletin also asked anyone who was in the area or had any information about what happened to contact the police. Any person that called was reassured that their name would remain anonymous to protect their identity. It was just a waiting game now. Hopefully, someone would come forward. He also needed to check out the construction companies around the vicinity.

—

Jack was waiting for his wife to come home. He knew she was on her way, because they had talked briefly earlier, and he was relieved to hear her sound happy and relaxed toward him. He loved his wife, and he didn't want to hurt her any more than he already had. He was so grateful for having her in his life, and he was so glad he'd thought of sending the arrangement of flowers to her work. He hadn't done anything like that in years, and he almost felt like he was courting her again. He made a mental note to himself to do little things like that for her more often. He simply had to get his anger in check—he just didn't know how.

Nicole unlocked the door, and when she walked into their home and saw him rise from the La-Z-Boy chair to greet her, she couldn't help but to run into his arms and kiss him feverishly. How she loved this man! They kissed for a long time, lovingly and intimately, and after some time, he picked her up and carried her upstairs where he made love to her.

CHAPTER

12

The Blue Lagoon was in full swing by evening, and Manny had all his girls working, ready to take on the usual Friday night business. Stephanie, his head waitress, was the first to be there, wearing her usual short, tight skirt; and tonight, she was dressed a little more boldly, wearing an extremely low-cut, black, see-through blouse that would have any man at her knees. Truth be told, she was the most beautiful of all the girls, and as well, had the most experience. Manny had instructed her to wear something really daring, and she did just that. He knew that she was the most obedient of all and told her that the tips would be more generous if she presented herself as a little sexier. All the girls were to wear black with high heels and short skirts. Manny wore black tight pants and a black silk shirt, unbuttoned enough to reveal his hairy chest.

He noticed Stephanie and Laurie talking around the bar area, and he overheard Ashley's name in the conversation. He walked over to the two girls as Laurie filled Stephanie in on all the details of their coworker being attacked and how she was left to die. Laurie mentioned that she wanted to go and visit Ashley in the hospital, and that's when Manny intervened.

"Hey, Laurie!" he said loud enough to make her jolt. "I don't want any of you girls visiting her, is that clear?" he warned while he gently put his hand on Stephanie's behind.

"But why not?" asked Laurie in confusion. She genuinely felt sorry for Ashley and wanted to see her friend. "What's the problem if we did? It wouldn't be on work time," she stated in disbelief. How could he have the audacity to control what they did outside work?

"Well, I just don't think that it's a very good idea, that's all. I think we should let her recuperate and see what happens. From my understanding, there are no visitors allowed in anyway," Manny answered in a gentler tone.

"Oh," Laurie replied meekly. "Well maybe we could send her some flowers or something, from all of us," she added, delighted about her idea.

"Sure! We could do that. Now how about we get back to work, eh?" Manny said, smacking Laurie on her behind. "And you," He turned to Stephanie, "I think we need to 'talk' in my office," he said, low enough for her ears only, skimming his large sausage-like fingers over her upper arm. "There's some things we need to go over, if you know what I mean?" He placed his hand on the back of her waist and led her toward his office in the back of the bar. Stefanie turned toward Laurie, who was already at a nearby table, taking an order. She kept her head up, and proceeded to the office with Manny, knowing fully what they needed "to talk about."

Laurie and the other girls noticed their boss and Stephanie walking toward his office, and they glanced at one another but didn't say a word. They just kept quiet about the two of them, for they knew better than to gossip and jeopardize their job. Laurie almost felt sorry for Stephanie as she watched her being led to the back room, where the door closed behind them. She was certain that it wasn't business they were discussing. She was aware what Manny wanted, and she was grateful that it wasn't her having to have sex with him. It was mostly Stephanie he preferred on the nights he needed sex. Only Stephanie didn't look too pleased to go, and it appeared she wasn't her usual self either. She seemed more quiet, more subdued. It was over an hour later when Stephanie finally emerged from the corridor, and she wordlessly proceeded with work, grabbing a drink menu, and greeting a young couple who had just entered. She looked pale, as well a little distracted, but Laurie decided it would be best not to say anything because it really wasn't any of her business.

—

Stephanie tried to focus on being in her usual friendly waitress mode, but she simply couldn't concentrate. She was more than a little upset, and she'd told Manny so. She hadn't been feeling well in the past few days and felt nauseated for much of the time. She couldn't keep her food down and felt extremely tired. She was working crazy hours and barely had any time for herself. She suspected that she might be pregnant, since on more than a couple of occasions, Manny had had intercourse with her and didn't pull out in time. When she'd freaked out about it, he reassured her that he'd had a vasectomy years ago and had insisted that she not worry. But she was worried. A baby was not something she needed right now.

Tonight, was no different. His wanting to "talk" to her wasn't talk at all. She'd managed to gather her nerve and explain to Manny that, although she still wanted to work for him, she wasn't interested in having sex with him anymore. It had taken all the courage she could muster to express herself, and she'd thought she was being heard. She'd felt, at first, that he was listening to her, but then, without any warning, he'd roughly grabbed a handful of her hair and shoved her to the floor on her knees. Then he'd unzipped his pants and whipped out his erect penis, and before she'd known what was happening, his hand had been on the back of her head, where he'd forcefully thrust himself inside her mouth, making her gag profusely. He hadn't seemed to care, as he'd continued to ram himself viciously inside her mouth, increasing his thrusts until he'd ejaculated inside of her mouth, causing her to choke on his semen, which got all over her face.

Stephanie had been dumbfounded. She'd tried to get up from her kneeling position, but her legs wouldn't comply, and she'd leaned back in a seated position, wiping his semen off her face with her bare arm. She'd looked up at Manny with tears in her eyes, feeling hurt and humiliated at what had just taken place. She'd felt like a piece of property, *his* property, to do with whatever he wanted, whenever he wanted. She'd opened her mouth to say something to him but couldn't. The shock and degradation that she felt disgusted her to the core. Her tear-filled, horrified eyes had gazed into his, which were filled with satisfaction and control, and she'd leaned her head forward in defeat.

He on the other hand, hadn't been quite done with her. He was angry with her for having the audacity to assume that she could tell *him* how it was going to be, and to prove his point further, he'd grabbed her by one arm and pulled her up violently while she stumbled to get on her feet. Manny had roughly placed his large, greedy hand inside her low-cut blouse, taking possession of her breast and sucking on it roughly, causing her to cry out in pain as he bit hard on her nipple, making it bleed slightly. It had been a "don't mess with me" message, and for the first time in all the years since she'd known and worked for him, she had been truly frightened.

She had been doing sexual favors for him for several years, but this was the first time that he had displayed so much power and had been so dangerously forceful with her. She couldn't talk to anyone about this, for she had been giving in to him for so long. Anyone with half a brain wouldn't take her seriously. She couldn't talk to the girls at work, and she didn't have any close friends or family either. Going to the police was futile because what could she possibly say to them? That she had been willingly having sex with her boss for the past few years, and that suddenly, he'd forced her to give him oral sex? They would laugh in her face! She was his whore, and it was her fault for allowing herself to get used like that.

When she had first started working for him, she had been in her late teens, and the attention that he'd given her flattered her, knowing that an older man found her attractive. He'd given her the shifts and money she'd needed and more, but it hadn't occurred to her that everything had a price. And what a price! Now she was stuck, and there was no way out. She felt confused because in the past, on a couple of occasions while fondling her, he had mentioned that if she were "a good girl," he would make her a silent partner, promising her the moon and the stars and telling her that he'd always take care of her financial needs as long as she complied with his sexual demands. At the time, it hadn't seemed so terrible because, inwardly, she'd had a small crush on him.

Tonight, Manny had lifted his head up from her, and given her a quick kiss on her quivering lips and a smack on her behind. "I take it that we understand each other?" he'd asked, zipping himself up. She'd nodded to him slowly in agreement, feeling dirty and sore.

"Now get yourself cleaned up and get back to work," he'd added. And with that, he'd turned on his heel and walked over to his desk, giving her a quick wink before seating himself, dismissing her with his hand. Suddenly, she'd had the urge to vomit. She'd quickly exited his office and run into the ladies' washroom, where she barely made it to the toilet. She'd pulled her hair back, leaned forward, and vomited.

There was no way out for her. This was the price she would pay for being his sexual slave, and it was all her fault.

—

The young woman lying in the hospital bed had finally gained consciousness but was still unable to open her eyes or speak clearly. All that came out of her swollen mouth was a murmur. The two nurses that looked after her couldn't believe how dreadful her face looked. The swelling had come down a bit, and the cuts and bruises on her body were starting to heal; her broken ribs were on the mend, but her face was another story altogether. The good news was that the test results had come back, and there was no brain damage or internal bleeding. All she really needed now was time to recuperate and let her body heal. She had been beaten badly, but in time, her body would heal. As for her emotional well-being, that was left to be seen. She had endured a horrific and heinous crime, and the effect it would have on her emotional stability worried the doctor and the main nurse that was assigned to her. She was so fragile, and when her doctor tried to get Ashley to speak, she only responded with a tear that rolled down her face.

They had done a rape kit on her and discovered that she was, in fact, raped; there was also quite a bit of tearing in her genital area. Unfortunately, there was no semen found, since the monster who had brutally raped her was a step ahead and had worn a condom during the attack. It was also revealed that she had been choked—going by the redness around her neck—perhaps from a handkerchief or a scarf. Both her wrists were badly bruised, and her lips were double their size. She had deep cuts to her head, and both her legs were severely bruised.

The doctor had already made a call to Detective Fromer informing him of Ashley's medical update, for he was aware of how anxious Fromer was to talk to the young woman. No one was allowed to talk to her until the detective saw her first. The doctor did tell him that it would probably be another day or so before Ashley would talk and considering everything that she had endured during the attack, he wondered about her state of mind. He had seen this before, and unfortunately, it was something that, no matter how many years passed and how much therapy the victim went to, the brutal beating and rape were something she would never really get over. It was just something that the victim had to live with.

—

Jorge Cartagena had just finished his shift as a cab driver and was grateful to be home with his wife and boys. Every Friday night was pizza night. He had already devoured a few slices, and he was washing it down with a cold beer while his boys were play fighting around him, nearly knocking over his beer from the coffee table.

"Hey, come on! Can't you see I'm trying to watch something?" he yelled, startling them.

"But, Daddy, we just want to play!" said the older of the bunch.

"We wanna watch a video!" whined the younger one.

"Well, too bad, isn't it?" responded Jorge, irritated, as he took another bite from his pizza. "What does a guy have to do to get some peace around here?" he asked, taking a gulp from his beer.

"Come on, Jorge. They're just kids," replied Maria, who had just emerged from the kitchen, all sweaty from cleaning up. "Why don't you go into our room and watch whatever you want, and let them watch a video," she continued as she plopped herself on the couch across from him, stroking her big pregnant belly. "Please, Jorge. It's been a long day, and I just want them to settle down," she urged him.

"Alright, alright, I'll go," he said, standing up, tickling his boys one by one, making them laugh hysterically.

"Jorge, please don't get them hyper!" she begged, flinging her arms up in the air with exasperation.

"OK, OK, I'm leaving. But first …" and then he let out a loud burp, which amused everyone except his wife, who shook her head and rolled her eyes in disgust.

"Was that really necessary? And then you wonder why they behave the way they do," she said in frustration. She was simply too tired to argue with him.

Jorge walked over to his very pregnant wife and gave her a quick kiss on the top of her head, laughing at himself as he exited the family room, and made his way down the hall to their bedroom.

He grabbed the remote control, turned on the small television set that was sitting on top of his wife's dresser, and propped himself on the bed, surfing through channels. He found the news, and he shifted into a more comfortable position as he listened to the weather report. The heat wasn't letting up, and apparently, they were going to be in for a really hot summer, which pleased him since the winters were so long. Various other news came up: a missing dog with a five-thousand-dollar reward for anyone who found him, a fire in the east end of the city, a serious collision that killed three people, and a variety of other current events. A news bulletin was presented that described a situation that happened a week ago, where a young woman in her mid-twenties was found at

Marie Curtis Park. Apparently, she had been brutally beaten, sexually assaulted, and left for dead. They went on to say that she was currently in the hospital under police supervision and was now in stable condition but still unable to communicate with anyone. They also went on to say that if anyone happened to have been in the area or seen anything, they should come forward to the police.

Jorge sat up as he narrowed his eyes and scratched his bald head. He remembered that he had driven to that park at the end of his shift on the same day of the alleged attack. He scratched his head again. When he had arrived at the park, there had been no one around—no children on the playground, nobody walking their dogs, no joggers, absolutely no one—except for a parked black pickup truck. He sat on the edge of his bed and recalled a man and a woman arguing in the distance. They had been yelling at one another, and although he couldn't make out what they were saying, it had looked intense. The man had yelled at her, too, and that was when she'd slapped him. He clearly remembered that image very well. He shuddered as he thought of how he'd driven away, dismissing the situation, thinking that it wasn't his business to intervene or to even stick around and see what was going to happen next. After all, couples argue all the time, so why would this be any different? Although the slap that he'd witnessed her give him could've made the guy she was arguing with very angry—angry enough to strike back at her. Things could've progressed and made the guy lose it completely on her. But to savagely beat and rape her? Could this just be a coincidence? Was this the same woman the news reporter was talking about? And why hadn't he done something when he was there?

"Son of a bitch!" he said out loud as he bolted from the bed and paced the floor of his room. Suddenly, he remembered that when he'd been pulling out from the parking lot, he'd noticed that the pickup truck had a personalized plate. Normally he wouldn't notice other people's license plates, especially in his line of business, but when they were personalized, it was automatic for him to read them. He tried to remember the plate; he recalled saying it out loud to himself. It started with an "N," and for now, that was all he could remember. He thought about calling the police, but he wanted to have all his facts straight.

He paced the small bedroom, trying to put the pieces together. But what if it wasn't the same woman that the police were inquiring about? What he'd witnessed between those two people could've been just an innocent altercation, and who was he to get involved with that? But what if it wasn't? He couldn't live with himself if she, in fact, was the same woman that was beaten and raped.

As these thoughts rolled through his brain, he tried very hard to think of the name on the plate, and suddenly, it came to him— "NEWMAN." That was it! He went over to the phone that was on his bedside table and dialed the police department.

CHAPTER

13

The plans were finally set for Sunday. Nicole had already invited her parents, who were thrilled to visit their youngest daughter. It had been a while since they had gone anywhere, her mom informed her daughter. She needed a change of scenery, since the only place she and her husband were going lately was the doctor's office, and even that was sometimes a challenge. Her father's condition had worsened somewhat: he was getting more and more forgetful, and his anger had heightened as well. From what her mother told Nicole, his moodiness was over the top, feeling happy and content one minute, and angry and hostile the next. Nicole sympathized with her father but with her mother even more so. Growing up, she always remembered her mom to be even-tempered and patient, and now, having to live with his beginning stages of dementia along with the effects of the stroke he had suffered just a few short years ago was starting to wear her down. She had confided to her daughter that the death of her grandson and now dealing with her husband's deteriorating mind were finally starting to get to her. Nicole and Sara always agreed that their mother was a strong woman and that her strength and faith in God would get her through it.

Nicole was thrilled that Sara, her husband, James, and their twins had accepted their invitation to the barbeque, as well as her best friend, Emily, and her little boy, Christian. Her husband, Alex, couldn't make it because he was away on business, but having Emily present meant so much to Nicole. She was certain that the kids would have a blast, as they always did when they got together. It had been a long time since the chatter of children filled her house, and she anticipated a wonderful day ahead. Even Sara was looking forward to seeing her parents—she hadn't seen them in weeks.

Nicole and Jack went shopping together, gathering everything they needed for the barbeque and making sure they had enough food. It had been a busy day for her at the salon earlier in the day, and she was exhausted. Jack had also had a busy day at work, and they both turned in early for the night.

—

The phone call they received at the police station proved to be interesting. Detective Fromer was home having dinner with his wife when he received a call from the station. The officer gave him a quick summary of the phone call pertaining to the assault and beating of the young woman. Fromer left a disappointed but accepting wife at the kitchen table and made his way to the station, where Jorge Cartagena was to meet with him. At first, Jorge had been hesitant to go to the police station but was reassured by the police that any information he had would be greatly appreciated, and that his name, for now, would remain anonymous.

During his meeting with Jorge, Fromer listened to everything Jorge claimed he witnessed on the night in question, recording him the entire time. He seemed to be telling the truth—as Fromer listened to the man, Jorge's eyes never wavered from the detective. In all his years on the force, he had learned that eye contact and body language were significant in determining the likelihood of whether a witness were truthful or not. If they fidgeted and seemed significantly restless, or avoided eye contact when questioned, it was usually a sign that they were lying. This didn't seem to be the case with Jorge Cartagena.

Fromer took down all of Jorge's details in case they needed him to identify the suspect. In the meantime, he made sure to do a background check on Jorge, just to make sure he didn't have a criminal record of any sort. Fromer also checked out the taxi dispatch where Jorge was employed. It was on record that Jorge had received a call to go to that park, and the person hadn't shown up.

Detective Fromer was hopeful that this information gave them something to go on, and that it would, hopefully, lead to an arrest. On the other hand, it could very well be a bust. It wasn't unusual for two people to engage in an argument in a public place.

While at the police station, Fromer received a call from the doctor that oversaw Ashley. She had recently regained consciousness, and when she was asked if she was strong enough to have a visitor, she had simply nodded. Her eyes were still swollen shut, but she seemed willing to listen. Detective Fromer hoped that she would be able to shed some light on what happened.

He left the station and made his way to the hospital. He was anxious to talk to the girl and see if she could give him *any* clue as to who did this to her. Was it in fact this Newman guy? Or was it someone else? Was it possible that Newman attacked her? Or did he leave her there, and someone else had shown up and done the deed? That was what he had to find out. So far, all he really knew was that, at some point in the evening, she and the man in question had met at the bar where she worked, been attracted to one another (enough so that they left together) and ended up at Marie Curtis Park—hardly enough evidence to go and arrest the guy. Fromer most definitely would get to the bottom of this.

He quietly entered Ashley's room. The young woman was lying on the bed with a light pink blanket covering the bottom half of her body. He took a couple of steps toward her, observing how painfully different she looked from the picture on her driver's license. Her doctor had warned him before entering her room that she still wasn't in any condition to really communicate with anyone, and that she still needed time to mend. Her eyes were still swollen and very bruised, and her neck was bluish in color. He shuddered as he thought about what this young lady had endured. She was conscious at the very least, and he hoped that she would be able to somehow answer some of his questions. The doctor warned him to take it easy on her given the state she was in. He approached her bed slowly and wondered if she was awake or not. He pulled a chair next to her bed and seated himself. He stared at her for a few minutes, noticing that she hadn't flinched at his arrival. He wasn't sure if she was even aware that someone was there with her. He felt instantly compassionate toward this young woman, who happened to be the same age as his daughter. He was told that, up until this moment, no one appeared to want to visit her, and he wondered if she had any family or close friends. He decided he would just go for it and talk to her.

"Ashley?" he said gently, looking at her face. She flinched her eyelids ever so softly, trying to open her eyes. "Ashley, my name is Steven Fromer, and I'm a detective." Again, her eyelids fluttered. "I understand you can't talk to me right now, but I thought that maybe I could talk to you, and you could just listen," he continued, pulling his chair closer to her. "Ashley, I know you probably feel like crap right now, but I'm here to try and help you, if you'll let me, that is," he said sympathetically. She didn't move this time.

"First of all, what happened to you was terrible and brutal. I don't want you to be afraid of me, OK? You're safe now, and nothing and no one will hurt you again, do you understand?" he asked gently, wincing at a tear that started to roll from her right eye. His heart went out to her, but he had to go on. "Ashley, do you know who did this to you?" he asked her softly, taking one of her hands and placing it in his own, being gentle so he didn't scare her. "If you do, could you please squeeze my hand?" He waited for a response. There was none. Just as he was about to continue, she let out a moan, and for a moment, he wasn't sure if she was in pain, or if she was trying to communicate with him. She started to turn her head toward his direction and then moaned again. It was obvious to him that she was in distress. He let go of her hand and stood up just as the nurse entered the room and headed straight to her patient. She had been caring for her for the past week, and she didn't want her patient to get herself upset or excited.

"I'm sorry, but I think you need to leave now, Mr. Fromer," she said to him in a stern voice as she stroked her patient's hair.

"Detective Fromer," he corrected, as if his title would make a difference to her.

"Very well then, Detective Fromer," she corrected. "I'm going to have to ask you to leave now. I don't want Miss Moore getting upset. She's just regained consciousness, and she needs to take it easy," she said, adjusting Ashley's blanket.

"Yes, I understand, but if I could just have a couple more minutes with her. I promise you, I'm not here to upset her—"

"Well, then I'm sure you can understand my position, Detective Fromer," she interrupted, leaning over to her patient, adjusting the blanket once again. "You'll just have to come back another time when Miss Moore is feeling better." She stood straight up and faced Fromer from across the bed. He sensed she was a no-nonsense kind of woman, and it was best if he left—for now anyway. She was obviously very protective of the young woman, and he respected that she was just doing her job and looking out for her patient. Under the circumstances, he would've done the same thing, so he gave her a quick nod and left the room. However, he would be back in a couple more days, and that was a promise. Tomorrow was a new day, and he was going to pay Mr. Jack Newman a little visit.

CHAPTER

14

Nicole got out of bed that Sunday morning bright and early. The birds outside were chirping cheerily, the sky was baby blue with not a single cloud, and she was in great spirits as she thought of the day ahead. Jack was still in bed sleeping, and she quietly went downstairs to the kitchen to make some coffee. The mere thought of her family and friends visiting them elated her. The house finally felt alive, and she was part of the living.

She peeled some potatoes for the potato salad she was going to prepare for the barbecue and placed them in a bowl with some cold water for later. Then she whipped out her mixer and all her ingredients to make some muffins for the little ones. She decided to do half blueberry and half chocolate chip. All kids loved muffins, and she already had some ice cream for them in her freezer. She rolled up her sleeves and got to work. An hour and a half later, she couldn't believe what she had accomplished. The muffins were done, the meat was marinated and waiting to be grilled, and her potato salad was prepared and in the fridge. She'd also made a huge Caesar salad and her famous dressing for it. All that was left to do was cut up and spice her vegetables for the grill. She was in the middle of cleaning up the kitchen when she felt Jack's strong arms circle her waist, which nearly scared her to pieces.

"Well, good morning, Martha Stewart," he said, nuzzling his head on her shoulder and planting warm kisses on her neck.

"Jack, you scared me!" Nicole cried out, loving the way his kisses on her neck made her feel.

"You know, it really turns me on to see you in the kitchen, and half naked," he said, untying her apron from the back and moving his hands to the front of the pink teddy she had worn to bed.

"You are insatiable, you know that?" she laughed, sensing what he wanted as he continued to fondle her underneath her camisole and rubbed up against her from behind. Jack leaned into her against the sink, where Nicole dropped the dish, she had been washing. She turned around to face him as he removed her matching short bottoms, sidling up to her. Before she knew what was happening, he had her breasts out of her camisole. He put one to his mouth, licking and sucking on her nipple, and squeezing the other with his hand. He then lifted her up and entered her, causing her to cry out in sheer ecstasy. Their sex life had always been full of spontaneity, and this was no exception. He bent his dark head to her awaiting lips as he skillfully manipulated his tongue inside her mouth, searching for hers, tasting it, owning it. He thrust himself inside her, gently at first, and then with a fierce power that had them both panting with desire, rocking her up and down his shaft, each wave more mind-blowing than the last. They exploded together in bliss. Then Jack slid her down slowly and held her close to his chest, their hearts beating as one, leaving them both exhilarated and grinning with delight.

"I hope that was as good for you as it was for me," he said, smiling from ear to ear.

"I love you, Mr. Newman," Nicole said, her heart still beating a million miles per minute.

"I love you too, Mrs. Newman," he said, planting a warm kiss on her lips. "Now, I'm starving! What's to eat?" He looked around the kitchen.

"Why don't I make us some eggs to hold us over till later, and I'll make you a coffee. I already had one while I prepared. I don't think I should be drinking another coffee with the pregnancy and all."

"Good girl," Jack said, helping himself to a muffin that was still cooling on the counter.

"Hey, you! Those are for the kids!" Nicole laughed as she watched him shove a whole muffin in his mouth.

"Mm, these are amazingly good! Babe, you must have one," he coaxed.

"No, thank you! Since I'm going to get as big as a house, I think I should at least try to eat more sensibly," she said, caressing her abdomen.

"Oh, come on! You'll always be sexy to me, pregnant or not," he said, finishing off the muffin and bending down and planting a kiss on her pregnant belly. "Come on now! Our baby wants it!" He laughed, grabbing another muffin, and sticking a piece of it in her mouth before she could protest.

The next few hours flew by as they prepared for their family and friends to arrive. Jack had put some beers and soft drinks in the cooler outside with ice. Nicole finished up what she needed to do and ran upstairs to take a quick shower. Everyone was due to arrive within a half an hour, and she was so excited she could hardly stand it. She had told everyone to come by two o'clock, and knowing her mother, they'd be the first to arrive. She got dressed, settling on a simple baby-blue tank top and white capris. She applied a light coat of mascara and some lip gloss, pulled her long hair up in a ponytail, and went downstairs just in time to answer the door.

Her parents were the first to arrive, coming in with a cake, a pasta salad, and a bouquet of assorted flowers. Nicole was so overjoyed to see them both. She let them in, getting the hugs and kisses out of the way. A few moments later, Sara, James, and the twins arrived, followed by Emily, and to her surprise, her husband, Alex, with their son, Christian. Apparently, Alex got home sooner than he thought, and it pleased Nicole even more. The house was filled with chatter and laughter as everyone greeted one another. The men were already in the backyard, talking business and sports, standing around the barbeque while Jack put the steaks and burgers and chicken breasts on the grill.

She couldn't help but smile as she looked around her, feeling a sense of peace as well as euphoria as she listened to the sounds of the three children playing together. It was music to her ears as she watched them running around the backyard. All the people that mattered the most to her in her life were right here in her home, and it delighted her to the core of her being.

"Nicole, just look at you! You're beaming, my friend!" Emily said excitedly as she gave her friend a warm hug.

"I'm so happy," she sniffed, her eyes welling up in tears. "It's just seeing you all here, together in my home, makes me so very happy!" Nicole said, wiping a tear.

"And why shouldn't you be happy, sis?" Sara said as she helped herself to some veggies and dip. "James and I are so thrilled for you and Jack," she added, leaning in toward her younger sister and planting a kiss on her cheek. "I can't wait to meet my niece or nephew!" she said, glassy-eyed.

"Oh, darling! You look absolutely radiant!" Noreen, said as she embraced her younger daughter, and joined the rest of the girls. "Your father and I couldn't be happier," she said, patting Nicole's abdomen lightly.

"Thanks, Mom!" Nicole said cheerfully. "Thank you all for everything!" she said, looking at the trio of women who were her constant support. "I wouldn't be here today if it weren't for the three of you," she added warmly. "I love you all so freaking much!" She laughed, and the rest of the ladies laughed along with her.

The rest of the day went without a hitch. The men caught up with their own news, and the children played joyfully outside while the women helped set up on the patio, bringing out all the delicious food, adding all the barbecued meat that Jack had grilled. It was a gorgeous day, and everything was going as planned. They all ate, and things settled down. Nicole was busy in the kitchen putting the coffee on when her doorbell rang. Wondering who it could be, she walked to the front of her house and opened the door. Two tall men, dressed casually, stood before her, taking her by surprise. Instantly, she thought they were solicitors trying to sell her something, and for a second, she was annoyed that they'd have the audacity to bother people on a Sunday.

"Good afternoon, is this the Newman residence?" asked the taller of the two.

"Yes, yes it is," she replied quizzically. "Can I help you with something?" She started to feel a little uneasy and looked toward the back of the house, trying to make it obvious that she wasn't alone in case they were up to no good, although she was certain that they could hear the commotion that was happening in their backyard.

"Hi, my name is Detective Fromer, and this is my partner Detective Williams. We were wondering if we could have a few words with Mr. Jack Newman," the detective said, looking serious.

"Um, I'm his wife. Could you please tell me what this is all about?" she asked wide-eyed, feeling her heart rate increasing.

"Mrs. Newman, if you'd please get us your husband. We just need to ask him a few questions. It's rather imperative that we speak to him," the other detective said, avoiding her question.

"Well, it's not really a good time—we sort of have guests over right now. Could you just leave your number, and he'll call you? Or maybe you could come another time?" she responded nervously, feeling apprehension rising within her.

"I'm sorry, Mrs. Newman, but we really need to speak to him right now. This can't wait a moment longer, and if your husband cooperates, then this shouldn't take too long," he said all businesslike.

15

Recognizing that she didn't have much of a choice, she motioned for them to enter her foyer, asking them to wait there until she called her husband. They did, sensing her vulnerability and panic.

Nicole suddenly felt overwrought with anxiety as she went outside to call her husband. She didn't want to cause a commotion, so she walked over to him where he was sitting with the other guys, enjoying a beer. He immediately saw something was wrong by the worried look on her face. She was practically hyperventilating as she told him that she needed him inside. He stood up instantly and followed her back in the house, quietly asking her if she was alright. When she didn't answer him, he knew something was wrong. As they entered the kitchen, away from their guests, she told him rapidly that there were two detectives waiting in their foyer that needed to talk to him.

"Jack, why would two detectives want to talk to you? What's happened? What's this all about?" she asked, her voice rising with panic.

"Well, how the hell would I know!" he responded, wondering himself what this was all about. "Nikki, please, babe, calm down will you? It's probably nothing. Just go back outside to our guests so that they're not wondering where we went," he said more gently.

"No, Jack! I want to hear what this is all about," Nicole whispered loudly. Seeing that he had no choice, Jack allowed her to lead him to the foyer, where he was met by two strangers.

"Jack Newman?" asked Detective Fromer, eyeing him carefully.

"Yes, I'm Jack Newman," Jack replied, feeling confused as to why these two clowns were in his house. "What's this all about, gentlemen?" he asked, trying to keep his cool.

"Mr. Newman, I'm Detective Fromer, and this is my partner Detective Williams," Fromer said, motioning toward his partner. The other detective nodded. "Is there somewhere we could go and sit down, Mr. Newman? We need to ask you a few questions."

"Listen, man, we've got company in our backyard. What's this all about?" he asked, putting his arm protectively around his wife's waist.

"I understand—your lovely wife already told us. This is rather important, Mr. Newman, so if you'll cooperate with us, then this shouldn't take too long. Now, we could either talk right here in your foyer, or we could step outside on the front porch. Or if you'd rather, we could just go down to the police station. Either way, we're not leaving here until we question you. Do you understand?" Fromer said sternly.

Jack looked from the detective to his wife, who stood there wild-eyed, and back to the detective. Understanding that he had no choice in the matter, he decided to cooperate with them.

"OK, let's get this over with, shall we?" he said, leading them into the living room, where all four took a seat on the couches facing one another, his wife barely sitting at the edge of her seat.

"You know, I don't appreciate you coming to my home—I repeat *my* home—on a Sunday afternoon, upsetting my wife, and taking us away from our company," Jack said, feeling extremely irritated as he glanced to his left at Nicole, whose face was ashen. He put his arm protectively around her waist to comfort her as he listened to the detective.

"Mr. Newman, we understand the inconvenience we've imposed on you today, but we're just trying to do our job. Now, just calm down and allow me to ask you a few questions, please," Fromer said with some impatience, feeling like he needed a cigarette at this point. He reached into his pocket and pulled out Ashley's driver's license, leaning closer to Jack as he handed it to him. "Mr. Newman, can you identify this woman?" he asked, observing Jack's face turn white.

"I—I don't know," he stammered as he tried to compose himself, his wife leaning over with him to get a good look at the picture. "Am I supposed to know her?" he asked, handing him back the license card and clearing his throat. Nicole looked over to her husband and back to the detective, who watched the couple carefully.

"I believe you do," he stated. "Where were you a week ago Friday evening, Mr. Newman?" Detective Fromer asked.

"Um … oh yeah, I had to go to a residential area to give a quote, and then I came home," he replied, shifting himself on the couch, trying to stay cool for Nicole's sake but feeling like the shit was about to hit the fan, and that there was nothing he could do to get out of this awkward situation.

Knowing that Jack was omitting a very important piece of information, Fromer continued. "Do you know a bar called The Blue Lagoon, Mr. Newman?" the detective asked, his eyes never leaving Jack's, imagining how awkward he must be feeling with his innocent wife sitting next to him.

Jack fidgeted while he ran a hand through his dark, wavy hair before he answered. "Yeah, I know the place. I've been there a few times for a beer. Why?" he asked, waiting for the axe to fall on him.

"This young lady, Ashley Moore, works there as a waitress," Detective Williams said, pointing to the driver's license. He observed Jack's expression and, seeing that he was playing innocent, he continued. "Did you or did you not go to that bar that evening, Mr. Newman?" he asked, his impatience growing as he waited for a truthful response so he could get to the point.

"Yeah, I think I remember going in for a beer or two. Why? Is that a crime?" Jack asked testily, rubbing his hands together in front of him nervously.

"No, not at all," Williams answered very politely. "Did you and Miss Moore get acquainted that evening?" he pressed.

"Yeah, we talked for a while. Why?" Jack snapped, running his hand through his hair once again and shifting his gaze over to his wife, who just sat motionless beside him.

"How long were you there for, Mr. Newman?" Williams asked.

"Jesus, I don't know, not very long! Do you mind getting to the point detective. As I've told you before, we've got company in the backyard who are probably wondering where the hell we are!" Jack said, practically screaming at him.

"Don't worry, I'm getting there," the younger detective snapped back at him. "Did you or did you not leave the establishment with Miss Moore? And before you answer that, Mr. Newman, know that we have a couple of sources who told us that you did," he said, keeping his voice calm and courteous.

Jack went to open his mouth to protest, but found he had no words. He felt trapped as he turned to look at his pregnant wife who was glaring at him, waiting to hear what he had to say. The two detectives sat across from them watching him intently. "Look, I've had just about enough of this cat-and-mouse game! Either you get to the point or get out of my house!" Jack said, standing up, getting more and more angry by the minute.

"Well, it seems that you and Miss Moore got a little friendly at the bar and decided to leave the establishment to get to know one another a better—isn't that right, Mr. Newman?" Williams continued, feeling empathetic toward Jack's wife, who looked back and forth between her husband and the detectives, her face filled with disbelief and confusion. "You were seen by someone at Marie Curtis Park having a heated argument with Miss Moore who ended up slapping you. Isn't that right, Mr. Newman?" he said, going for the kill. "What went down between the two of you? What were you arguing about to make her slap you?"

Jack looked speechless as he listened to the detective describe what happened that night—the night he thought he'd put behind him forever.

"Mr. Newman, Miss Moore was found the next day at the park—raped, beaten to a pulp, and left for dead. You think you could be straight with us and tell us what happened?" Fromer said as he rose from the couch, his partner following.

Jack started to shake all over. He was dumbfounded. He turned to look at his wife, who looked speechless, holding her hands together and looking up at him in disbelief with tear-filled eyes.

"Shit! What are you saying, man? That I did that to her!" Jack shouted, finding his voice as he stood up to face the detectives. "I could never do such a thing. You've got to believe me," he pleaded, more so to his wife than to the detectives, who just stood in front of him, allowing him to explain.

"So you *were* at the park with her. Mr. Newman, why don't you sit down and calmly tell us what happened," Fromer said, seating himself once again, motioning to Jack to do the same.

"Nothing happened, damn it! Nothing!" he shouted at them. "I went to the bar for a couple of beers, shot the shit with the bartender, Phil I think his name is. This Ashley girl was talking to me, and she seemed friendly—"

"She was so friendly, you decided to take her for a swing at the park," Detective Williams interrupted sarcastically, grinning at him.

"What were you doing with her?" Fromer asked. "What was the argument about?"

"Listen, guys, you have to believe me!" Jack said, more to his wife. "Yes, we went to the park together, but we just talked. Nothing happened, I swear to God!" He pleaded with Nicole, as he bent down to her level, taking both her icy cold hands into his own. She didn't say anything. "Remember when you called me, Nikki, and I talked to you and told you I was coming home really soon?" he continued, looking into her eyes that were filled with tears and betrayal. "Yes, I was with her at the park, but nothing happened! I swear to you! We kissed a little, and when I told her that we needed to stop and that I needed to go home, she freaked out!" He let go of Nicole's hands and stood up to face the two detectives. "She stormed out of my truck after I offered to take her home, and I followed her by foot. I didn't want to leave her alone at the park, but she just freaked out. She didn't take well to my rejection, and that was when she slapped me, so I finally left. I swear to all of you, I never beat her or raped her. You've got to believe me!" he implored.

"Why would you take a perfect stranger to the park, Jack?" Nicole finally spoke, standing up to face him. "You weren't at home. You weren't at work, because I called and spoke to your secretary, which tells me you were fooling around. You couldn't stand to be at home with me, so you found yourself a bitch you just met?" she shouted at him angrily.

"Nikki, you're right!" he pleaded with her. "Things were so tense at home. I admit it—I hated being home. And I did kiss her, but I swear to you that's where it ended. Nothing happened, baby. I've never cheated on you. You must believe me!" he begged, as he tried to embrace her, but she wouldn't let him. "When I realized what I was doing, I stopped before anything happened!" He felt like a trapped animal. "I swear to you, detective!" he said as he turned away from his wife toward the detectives. "I never beat or raped her! Someone else did this to her, and I'm getting blamed for this!" he shouted.

"You mean my phone call stopped you!" Nicole shouted bitterly from behind him, causing him to turn around and face her.

"No! Nicole, I love you! Please. You've got to believe me when I tell you that I would never do anything to hurt you," he pleaded as he took her face with both his hands and tried to kiss her.

"Don't touch me!" she cried, breaking away from his grip. She quickly wiped the tears that escaped.

Jack was taken aback, and he released her. He looked at the detectives. "I'm telling you the truth! I was with her at the park. We kissed, we argued, and then I left. End of story. Is Ashley—"

"Dead?" Detective Fromer interrupted. "No, Mr. Newman, she's very much alive. She's now in stable condition, but seriously hurt."

"Well, thank God for that! She'll tell you then—what happened I mean!" Jack said, relief sweeping over him.

"Mr. Newman, it'll be a couple more days before she's able to talk to us. Until then, we don't want you leaving the city, or country for that matter, until you hear from us again. Is that understood?" Fromer ordered. Jack nodded. "Now, we need to search your truck. I believe that's your truck in the driveway?" he asked, flashing a warrant to Jack.

"Yeah, that's the one," Jack answered. "It's unlocked."

"That's fine, Mr. Newman. Now, we shouldn't be too long. Therefore, you're free to carry on as you wish. Just remember what I said," Detective Fromer warned. "Thanks again for your cooperation." And with that, the detectives turned around and walked out the front door to the driveway, where Jack's black pickup truck was parked.

"Sure. Anytime, asshole," Jack growled under his breath as he shut the door behind them. He watched from the door's window as they approached his truck. He turned around to face Nicole, who was standing motionless, her face buried in her hands. With trepidation, he went to his wife and reached for her. Suddenly, without warning, she shot out her hand and slapped him hard in the face, shocking him.

"You son of a bitch, I hate you! You hear me? I hate you!" she shouted at him, her blue eyes blazing at him. "How could you do this to me? How could you jeopardize everything we have?" she demanded, her eyes shooting daggers at him. She continued shouting at him, causing everyone from the backyard to come running into the house, her mother running to her daughter's side. "You lied to me! The whole time, you were lying to me!" Nicole repeated, her whole body shaking with fury. "I want you out of this house, you hear me?" she screamed in his face.

"Nicole, please! You can't believe that I would do something so horrible! My God, what kind of a monster do you think I am?" Jack shouted back, embarrassed by all the spectators that were standing around them with looks of confusion and horror on their faces. His mother-in-law was trying to calm her daughter, but Nicole was belligerent.

"I don't know for sure what you did or didn't do with her. I guess I'll just have to wait and see like everyone else. But one thing I'm certain of is you took a woman you *just* met to the park to make out with her! You wanted to fuck her because you certainly weren't getting anything from me, now, were you?" she screamed at the top of her lungs, shocking her family and friends, who were unfortunate enough to hear all the ugly details.

"Nicole, that's not true! I didn't do anything. I swear on Jonathan's grave!" Jack pleaded.

Her face turned ashen as his words cut into her soul. She flung herself from her mother's embrace toward her husband in fury. "How *dare* you use our son's name! You *never* mention our son's name, and you freak when I mention him at all. And now, suddenly, you have the nerve to swear on my dead son's grave?" she spat at him with tears streaming down her face. She suddenly felt weak and faint.

"Stop this, Nikki! Please! Think of our baby that's growing inside of you!" he begged her, and as he approached her, she collapsed in her mother's arms, her sister running to her side.

"Nicole—"

"Jack, please!" Noreen shouted at him as she tried to hold her daughter up. "Just leave her alone now. Can't you see she's fainted?"

Sara helped her mother move Nicole to the safety of the couch, where they lay her down gently. Emily rushed in with a glass of water and was already putting it to her friend's lips, along with a wet cloth to her forehead.

"Noreen, I can't just leave her! She needs to understand—" Jack started to explain, feeling helpless.

"Buddy, I think you should leave. Just for a little while anyway. Or at the very least, until your wife calms down," James said, feeling a little sorry for his brother-in-law, but staying loyal to his wife's sister. The three women were huddled protectively around Nicole, urging her to open her eyes and talk to them.

Feeling completely helpless, Jack felt he had no choice but to leave the house. *His* house, leaving behind *his* wife! He just shook his head, glancing over at his wife, who had already opened her eyes and was slowly sitting up. The women stood around Nicole, creating a barricade, talking to her and making sure that she was alright. It would've been impossible for Jack to get to her now, even if he tried. All Jack knew for the moment was that the detectives believed that he might be responsible for the rape and beating of Ashley, and that his wife felt betrayed by him.

Jack turned to face his brother-in-law and Alex, who just stood there awkwardly. He glanced over to his father-in-law, who shook his head and made his way to the family room, leaving Jack in confusion and defeat. He bowed his head, turned around, and dutifully walked out of the house that, less than twenty minutes ago, had been filled with laughter and joy. Jack didn't have a clue as to where he would go, but he felt hopeful that, with some time, everything would fall into place; everything would be back to normal again. But would it?

Jack felt torn and empty as he walked out into the sunshine in the middle of the afternoon. He just started walking with no destination in mind. Thankfully, he had his wallet on him, so he figured he'd probably hail a cab and check into the nearest motel for the night. The two detectives had just finished searching his truck, and they nodded at him as they made their way to their car, reminding him again not to go very far in case they needed to talk to him. He said a few words to them, and they responded with a nod as they got into their car.

Jack stood there for a few minutes as he watched them drive away down the street. He shook his head at the recent turn of events that had blown up in his face. He felt confident that as soon as the detectives talked to Ashley, she'd explain to them exactly what had happened and clear him of any wrongdoing. At least he hoped so. He couldn't understand how he'd gotten mixed up in this whole mess. He clenched his fists as he thought of the girl and how she'd slapped him. How dare she! She could cost him his marriage. There was no way in hell that he was going to let that happen. He knew he had his work cut out for him with Nicole. That was an entirely different matter altogether. For now, he'd have to give her the space that she needed.

—

After Jack left the house, Nicole sobbed like a small child in her mother's arms, while her mother stroked her younger daughter's hair, telling her softly that everything was going to be alright. Her heart was breaking, and the pain of feeling betrayed was overwhelming. Sara and Emily sat next to them while Noreen consoled her daughter.

After some time, Sara cleaned up from the barbeque, making sure everything was spic and span, while Emily kept an eye on the three children, who continued playing on the trampoline, undisturbed by what had just transpired with the adults. They were all excited to be together again, and they laughed and played with exuberance, giving no sign of slowing down. The men drank beer outside while keeping an eye on the kids, making sure that no one got hurt, discussing the unfortunate confrontation they'd witnessed between the couple.

Soon they would all leave except for Sara. They felt that Nicole shouldn't be alone in her condition, and her sister should stay the night with her. Her mother wanted desperately to stay and comfort her daughter, but Sara insisted that she leave because she had enough on her plate with their father to tend to. Sara reassured her mother that she would stay the night with Nicole and make sure she was alright. Emily and Alex offered to take Sara's twins back to their house to spend the rest of the day and night with their son, since they played so well together, giving Sara peace of mind while she stayed with her sister, and allowing James to go to work and not worry about the kids. It was all figured out, and once again, everyone was completely supportive to Nicole's needs. They were sympathetic toward the couple and told Nicole that they hoped that everything would work itself out, and that it was just a hurdle that they had to get over, reminding Nicole how much love they shared, especially with their unborn baby on its way. The kids were ecstatic when they heard they'd be having a sleepover, and everyone said their goodbyes to Nicole, leaving her feeling grateful for her family and friends, who had never let her down.

"Honey, we're here for you, anytime, alright?" Noreen said gently to her daughter, with tears in her eyes. She kissed Nicole and regretfully took her husband, who at this point was confused, and went home.

Nicole just nodded at them, her eyes brimming with tears. This day was certainly not like anything she had imagined.

They all left, leaving the two sisters behind. Sara immediately locked the doors, armed the house, and put the kettle on. She was going to make hot chocolate for the two of them, and then they could sit down and talk. She glanced at Nicole, who just sat there, rolled up in a ball on the couch. Sara prepared two mugs and poured the steaming hot water into the mugs, added some marshmallows, and took them over to the family room where her younger sister sat, placing the hot mugs on the glass coffee table. Sara watched her sister as she plopped herself on the couch next to her, not wanting to disturb her. Nicole stared into space, deep in thought. Sara's heart broke for her, and she wondered what she was going to say to her. From what she gathered from the earlier escapade; she knew it didn't look good for her brother-in-law. She hadn't stayed behind to rehash it all but, rather, to simply be there for her as she'd always been in the past. Being the older sibling came with more responsibility—being the role model and, of course, always being the protective older sister so no one could hurt her younger sibling. Although, as they grew up and became adults, Sara learned rather quickly that, as much as she tried, it was sometimes futile.

"Hot chocolate with marshmallows always put a little smile on your face when we were kids," Sara said as she handed the hot beverage to Nicole, who was lost in her thoughts. She took it from her sister's hands, and after some hesitation, put it to her lips and carefully took a sip.

"Thanks, sis," was all Nicole could muster. She felt so grateful for her sister, who was continuously her rock and support.

"Anytime, kiddo," Sara replied, taking a sip from her own mug. A little smile broke out on Nicole's face as she pointed to her own mouth, indicating the little white mustache that the cocoa left on Sara's upper lip. Sara, in turn, pointed to her own upper lip, showing that Nicole had the same, causing the girls to giggle. Sara knew that it was most likely they'd have a long night; but she was prepared for it.

—

Earlier, the two detectives had taken notice that Jack had left the Newman house, and they'd given him one last warning about trying to flee. Jack had been furious with the detectives, telling them that if anything were to happen to his unborn child, he'd hold them personally responsible for the unnecessary stress that they were inflicting on their lives. He also went on to tell them that, in time, they'd get the answers from Ashley, and that he'd be cleared from the mess; and that, thanks to them, his wife had thrown him out of his own house. The detectives had responded by nodding, acknowledging that they'd heard him, before driving off, leaving Jack standing there.

"Man, I wouldn't want to be in his shoes!" Detective Williams scoffed.

"Well, we don't know for sure that it was him. Let's not forget, buddy, the guy may very well be telling the truth, "Replied Detective Fromer as he drove away from the house.

"Yeah well, it sure looks that way to me man! You know what they say: if it looks like a duck, walks like a duck, quacks like a duck—"

"I know, I know, it's a duck!" Detective Fromer interrupted. "Look, we'll have the DNA samples in right away, and hopefully, we'll get some answers, but until Miss Moore can actually tell us in her own words that he raped and beat her, we have nothing. The fact that she was in his truck and at the park with him is not enough to arrest the guy. I'm telling you, man, something in my gut tells me the guy is innocent. He may or may not be a cheater, but that's a different matter altogether. We need to find out if he's the bastard that landed her in the hospital."

He was quite a few years older than his partner and had more years of experience. He had seen a lot in his years, and sometimes, what was perceived to be one thing proved otherwise in the end. Detective Williams shrugged, and they drove together in silence.

16

The Blue Lagoon wasn't very busy on a Sunday evening, and yet Laurie was instructed by Manny to stay till the end and close the bar with Stephanie. She had noticed how unusually quiet Stephanie had become in the past couple of days, and it concerned her, since her coworker was usually upbeat with everyone. She was usually always smiling, and even flirtatious, with some of the customers, but lately, she looked sullen and pale. A couple of times, Laurie had noticed that Stephanie had rushed to the lady's washroom, and when she had returned, her face was white as a sheet. When Laurie had asked her if she was alright, she simply told her that she had probably caught a bug and couldn't get rid of it. Tonight however, she looked deathly pale, and Laurie was concerned that she wouldn't make it till closing.

"Steph, are you alright?" Laurie asked her—they both happened to be picking up a drink order at the bar at the same time.

"Yeah, I'm fine," Stephanie answered, putting on a fake smile just as Manny walked in the front door, causing both girls to look in his direction. He winked at them both as he walked past them in the direction of his office. Stephanie's face instantly changed. She made her way to her table with the drink order.

Laurie shrugged. She went to her table and set down the drinks for a young couple she was waiting on. She didn't know what was going on with Stephanie, but whatever it was, it couldn't be good. She seemed more nervous by the minute, but she obviously didn't want to talk about it with her, so she carried on with her business.

Manny was in excellent spirits as he sat in his chair with both his feet on the desk. He had just smoked a joint, and the buzz it gave him had started to take effect. He had also just scored some cocaine from "Freddie," his man, and he couldn't wait to get his hands on it. He figured he'd sell the majority of it, make a profit, and still have some left over for himself to indulge in. Yeah, life was good, and it was only going to get better. All that was missing now was a willing and juicy pussy—well, juicy at least!

He glanced at the clock, and it was nearing ten o'clock. From what he noticed, the place was kind of slow, and his girls were handling it quite well. He smiled as he thought of his two top waitresses. They were so efficient the place practically ran itself. He quickly sprouted to his feet, and popped his head out the office, just in time to see Laurie's table leaving. Stephanie had been a pain in his ass lately, complaining that she wasn't feeling well and whining all the time, and he was getting tired of it. He gave Laurie a quick wave, motioning her to go in and see him. He was getting a hard on, and he needed some tender loving care.

Laurie reluctantly walked down the corridor to his office and stood at the entrance while her boss sat behind his desk. He motioned her to enter and close the door behind her, which she did. She sensed that he wanted some action from her, and it had been a while since he'd needed her for anything sexual. She just stood there by the door, feeling intimidated by this powerful man. A man who, financially, took very good care of her needs and wants, but at a high price.

"Hey, I don't bite you know!" he snickered at her. "How was business tonight?" he asked for sake of conversation as he leaned back in his chair and unzipped his pants.

"It was OK—nothing earth-shattering," she responded quietly. "I really should get out there and give Steffy a hand, since she's all alone and all," she said, hoping he'd let her go. She wasn't in the mood for Manny's sexual escapades. A thought suddenly occurred to her that she thought might persuade him.

"Oh, I'm sure Steffy's alright. And besides, it's been quite a while—you and I should get reacquainted, wouldn't you say?" he responded, pulling out his cock out, ready for action. *She isn't going to get away that easy*, he thought to himself.

"Umm—Manny, I've sort of got my period," she said timidly. "I'm really heavy," she added, hoping against hope he'd just let her get out of there.

"You got your friend, eh?" he said annoyance starting to set in. He needed a good fuck, and she was on the rag! One thing he couldn't stand being a bloody pussy. Juicy was one thing, but bloody was just gross. He sat up in his chair. He may not be able to fuck her, but she sure would be alright to give him a good blow job, period or no period. "Get over here!" he demanded.

"But I just told you—"

"I know what you told me," he interrupted. "So you've got your period. So, what! How about you get your little ass over here and let me feel you a little. Your mouth doesn't have a period, does it?" he asked her wickedly.

"Well, no—"

"Come on, sugar, times a wasting," he commanded. He smiled slyly as she approached him slowly. He couldn't wait to get his hands on her young tits. One thing he hated from older women were sagging tits, not to mention dry pussies. He always did prefer the younger ones. That was the major reason why he'd left his wife eons ago; she was going through menopause and wasn't at all interested in sex, not to mention the fact that she found oral sex repulsive. She was a damn good cook though! Too bad she was so frigid. With Elaine, it was always the same old missionary style, and he'd gotten tired of her quick, which was why his marriage only lasted a few years. She had caught him cheating on her numerous times, so him leaving her saved her the trouble of filing for divorce. He'd never loved her anyhow, he'd just married her because she was still a virgin at thirty, and she had some money. Now this one seemed to be giving him a hard time.

Laurie went by his side as he commanded her, and she stood there nervously, her heart pounding so hard she thought he could hear it. Without a word, Manny clumsily unbuttoned her black blouse, revealing a black-lace, push-up bra. She took a deep breath and flinched as he placed his hands on her swelling breasts and fondled them. Then, with one quick movement, he pulled her breasts out of her restraining bra one by one, and he squeezed and pinched them hard. She shuddered, as he leaned forward and sucked on her nipples, softly at first and then rougher, until she cried out in pain. The truth was, she was expecting her period, and her breasts were extremely sensitive. He was getting more and more aroused, making him hard as a rock, and he shoved her to the floor on her knees between his legs and roughly placed his penis in her mouth, instructing her to suck on him as hard and as deep as possible. She obediently did as she was told, and as she sucked on his penis, he leaned back in his chair, savoring the arousal she was giving him as he got harder and harder. He held her head roughly in his hands and guided her head up and down his shaft, loving the power he felt.

Stephanie's table had just cashed out, and she noticed that Laurie hadn't returned yet from Manny's office. She felt sick at the thought of him forcing her to do the same things she herself had been forced to do in the last four years. Laurie was newer at the establishment, and Stephanie felt bad for her. Even though none of the girls discussed what went on with their boss, it was apparent that Manny was getting it on with most of them, or at the very least, with Laurie and herself. She didn't want Laurie to get pregnant like she had just found out she was, and she felt a little protective of her, so she decided she would surprise them in the office and, hopefully, stop him in his tracks.

She removed her apron and marched to the office. When she opened the door, she realized it was too late. Laurie was on her knees on the floor between his legs giving him oral sex. Laurie suddenly stopped what she was doing as she welcomed the surprise intrusion from Stephanie, causing her to feel a mixture of embarrassment as well as relief.

Manny, however, was annoyed with Stephanie's rude interruption, as he wasn't far from ejaculating. "Well, look who decided to join us!" he snickered, thinking why not have the benefit of both girls. "Please, Stephanie, come in and close the door behind you! You could help finish me off, since your little friend here seems to have her nasty period. Get over here and lift your skirt. I think I want to come by giving it to you!" he laughed.

The two girls looked at one another, knowing that they didn't have much of a choice. It was either do what he requested or lose everything. Stephanie took a deep breath as she lifted her short skirt, exposing her thong, which just drove Manny insane, and she walked over to where Laurie was stooped. Laurie went to stand up, thinking she was done, but Manny grabbed her by her wrist and lowered her down again, putting Laurie in a state of panic.

"I've got a better idea, girls! How about you," he commanded to Laurie, "giving Stephanie some tongue, while I watch a little!" he continued, as the two girls looked at him with horror. "It really turns me on to see two girls doing it!" he said, as both girls felt like they were going to be sick to their stomachs. "Do it!" he yelled at them both. The girls made no move to do what was asked from him, for this was above and beyond what they'd ever had to do. "I said do it now! Move it, Laurie! Start giving her tongue!" he demanded, grabbing Stephanie roughly by her wrist and clearing his desk with one swift move. He pushed her in a lying position on the desk.

Laurie wanted to scream, but nothing came out of her mouth. There'd been something about Manny that she feared ever since she'd started working for him, but she felt she had no choice. Stephanie, on the other hand, froze, as she felt like she was in the beginning of a nightmare—only this wasn't a dream; it was very real.

Manny roughly shoved Laurie's head down as he impatiently spread Stephanie's legs apart roughly, exposing her lacy white thong. He then went into his shirt pocket and took out a small white packet. He dipped his forefinger in it and rubbed some of it on Stephanie's genitals. Laurie started to cry, but Stephanie remained there, frozen with fear with her legs wide open. She thought momentarily of kicking him in the face with her heels and making a run for the door, but she found she couldn't. In the four years she'd worked for him, he'd controlled her every move, and she knew that he would make her pay in the worst way. She subconsciously decided she would remove herself from this horrible nightmare that was about to take place.

Laurie, on the other hand, couldn't believe what he was asking her to do. Giving him the occasional blow job was bad enough but giving oral sex to another woman with cocaine on her was over the top. She felt sleazy and sick to her stomach, and her mind was racing as she tried desperately to figure a way out of this disgusting act. All kinds of things went through her mind, like how she'd gotten herself into a place like this, and why the hell she hadn't gotten out when he first asked her for sexual favors. But where would she go? She had no one in this big ugly world.

Manny smiled wickedly at them both, getting more and more aroused as he put some white powder on his erect penis. He grabbed the back of Laurie's hair and forced her to go down on him first, which made her choke on the white powder—she'd never done any sort of drugs before in her life. After a couple of minutes of sucking him, he guided her head toward Stephanie, who just lay in a zombie-like state with her eyes closed. Mentally, she had placed herself in a better place: a place where there was no evil; a place where she felt she belonged and was loved. In the meantime, Laurie did what she was told, finding that the white powder made her more compliant, and gave Stephanie oral sex, feeling numb and fearful yet excited at the same time. She did the best she could, since she'd never had sex with another woman before. Manny was having the time of his life. This was better than he'd anticipated. He fondled Laurie's behind as he watched the two girls, getting more and more turned on. He had watched thousands of porn videos in his time, with women doing it with multiple people, but this was the ultimate high for him.

He continued to watch Laurie, noting that she looked like she was enjoying herself, and after just a few more minutes, he couldn't take it anymore. He was going to explode, so he grabbed Laurie by the back of her hair and roughly pulled her away from Stephanie, shoving Laurie to the side. He quickly moved in between Stephanie's open legs and savagely entered her, pushing himself in as hard as he could, moaning and grunting as he shoved his way in and out of her repeatedly, causing Stephanie to come out of her trance and cry out in pain. He didn't care as he continued to drive into her with powerful force, letting her know without a doubt that he owned her; and when he finally ejaculated, he grunted and moaned like a wild animal as Stephanie just lay there, listless and in shock at what had just transpired.

Stephanie couldn't even cry. She tried to but found she couldn't. She felt completely used, and her body went numb. Her mind was fully aware that she had just been savagely raped and forced to have sex with a woman, but everything inside her just shut down. She didn't have the energy to get up from the hard desk. She tried to move but couldn't. She wanted to die, as she felt she could no longer live with herself anymore. This was, by far, the worst that Manny had ever done to her. It was the ultimate, most degrading act she'd ever had to do, and she felt completely worthless and more alone than she had ever felt in her entire life.

Manny, on the other hand, was proud of himself. He zipped himself up and motioned a speechless and dazed Laurie to leave. He needed to close the bar and meet up with Freddie, who wasn't too happy about having to wait for his money.

Laurie stood there for a moment, trying to absorb the enormity of what had just taken place, and finally realized that she should leave. She glanced over to Stephanie, who was still sprawled on the desk with her legs apart and her eyes half closed. A part of Laurie wanted to reach over to her and help her, but fear took over her as she quickly glanced back to Manny, who was getting a package from a safe nearby. She buttoned herself up and scurried out of the office, wanting to get as far away as possible.

After Laurie walked out of the office, Stephanie slowly got up to a sitting position on the desk, feeling like she'd just been hit by a freight train. Her whole body ached, and her head was throbbing. She looked over to her immediate right, where Manny was standing by the file cabinet with an open safe, counting a full handful of money. She stood up slowly and wearily, feeling her legs buckle beneath her as numbness took over. She grabbed onto the end of the desk and, with all the strength she could muster, pulled herself up again, praying that she'd be able to stand up. The fact that Manny was oblivious to her was a relief as she slowly walked away from the desk, taking one last glance at her boss, and walked out of the office.

She anticipated going home and taking an extra-long shower in hopes of removing all evidence of the filth that had just invaded her body and mind. The emptiness and repulsion that she felt inside overwhelmed her, as she had no one to go home to except her cat. This was truly the lowest point in her life, and at that precise moment, she promised herself that somehow, someday, she'd make Manny pay for what he'd done to her. There was no way in hell that a monster like that would use her any way he wanted and get away with it. No way.

CHAPTER

17

A couple of days after the fiasco at the Newman's, Sara finally left her sister and went home to her husband and children. Nicole had reassured her that she was alright, feeling guilty for taking her away from her family once again. Jack had made numerous attempts to call her, but Nicole never picked up the phone. Noreen had called, concerned for her daughter, but she reassured her mother that she was feeling better, not wanting to cause her anymore unnecessary anxiety. It was a difficult time for Nicole, but she'd had some time to absorb everything that had gone down that Sunday afternoon.

Although Sara supported her sister, she tried to shed some light on the situation from an objective point of view, which irritated Nicole at first, but Nicole also understood what Sara was getting at. She helped Nicole to realize that, in all the years she and Jack had been married, he'd never cheated on her, and that his family came first.

Sara pointed out that, although what Jack did with the girl was wrong and unlike him, he'd thankfully had enough sense to leave before it really turned ugly. She reminded her little sister that if her brother-in-law had been going to have sex with Ashley, he'd have done it, whether Nicole had called him or not. In the beginning, Nicole was irate with her sister, but she finally realized she was talking sense. Sara also reminded her little sister that Jack was not the kind of man to do anything so brutal to anyone—referring to the beating and rape of the girl—and in her heart, Nicole knew she was right. She admitted to Sara that she had never believed that he was responsible for the heinous crime that was inflicted on the young woman. She was, however, very hurt and angry with her husband for risking their marriage for a fling with a stranger. It still left a bitter taste, knowing that he'd almost cheated on her.

They had sat up that Sunday night until early morning talking things out and having her sister with her provided great comfort for her. However, Nicole was still hurt by Jack's actions and furious with him for putting himself and her in this compromising position. Now he had the detectives on him, and until there was solid proof that he wasn't the guy who beat and raped the young woman, everything was in chaos. She had lost trust in him, and most importantly, she felt betrayed, and as far as she was concerned, that was the most fundamental ingredient to a safe and secure marriage. She knew in her heart that he loved her, but she wasn't sure if she'd ever be able to get past this. There was no denying that she loved him with everything in her and was carrying his baby, which made it more difficult for her.

She had taken the day off that Monday and resumed work on Tuesday, trying to keep things light with everyone at the salon. She hadn't even told Diane what had transpired for fear of breaking down in tears and causing a commotion with everyone she worked with. She decided that, for now, she'd just hang low and concentrate on taking care of herself and her unborn child. She was afraid for what the future held for them. What would happen to their marriage? Would the young woman clear Jack's name when she finally spoke to the detective? And if she did tell the detectives that it was someone else, would Nicole be able to forgive Jack or trust him in the future? Would their baby grow up without a father if he was sent to jail, and how would she be able to handle it? After losing Jonathan, she'd thought that the worst had happened to them, but the situation they were in currently was also incredibly painful. She had a lot to think about, and she had to keep herself busy.

Emily had also called her several times, concerned for her friend, and they'd chatting easily on the telephone. Nicole understood how busy everyone was, and she appreciated the support she received. She hadn't decided yet what she was going to do about Jack or their marriage.

She did wonder about the young woman that was in the hospital. If she could only see her, perhaps ask her a few questions; but she knew that it would be out of the question. Why would this other woman have any desire to talk to her, especially about Jack? Nicole was strangely curious about this young woman that had captured her husband's attention. What was it about her that had attracted him enough that he'd taken her to a nearby park and made out with her? Was she beautiful? Was she promiscuous? What was it about her that had driven her husband, her man, to reach out to another woman? Were they having an affair? Was Jack telling her the whole truth? Was it possible that she was responsible for driving him into another woman's arms? Had she become so emotionally closed off that he couldn't stand to be home with her? Was that why he came home later and later? So many unanswered questions that drove her crazy when she let her mind drift away. No! They had lost their child, and she was devastated and perhaps unhinged, but she did the best that she could under the circumstances. And she'd never sought out another man. He should've been with her, sharing their grief together.

As Detective Fromer entered Ashley's room, he noticed immediately how very different she looked from the last time he'd seen her just a few days before. It amazed him how much better she looked to him, and he realized how very right the nurse had been to send him away when she had. Ashley was sitting up in her bed, her eyes were open, and the bruising and swelling had almost diminished. She looked a million times better. She was watching television from across the room, and she immediately turned in his direction, acknowledging his presence, her hazel eyes expressing both surprise and confusion.

"Hello Ashley," he said warmly, as he approached her slowly. "I'm Detective Fromer," he added, not sure if she'd recognize his voice.

"Hi" was all she said, not taking her eyes off him.

"I just wanted to talk to you for a few minutes, if that's alright," he said, noticing how very pretty she was now that her face didn't look so distorted. "May I sit down?"

"Sure," Ashley said simply, covering herself up to her waist with a light-pink sheet.

Detective Fromer took a seat on the chair that was next to the bed. "Ashley, I don't know if you remember me at all. I was here a few days ago." He paused, waiting for acknowledgment but getting none, so he went on. "You weren't up for talking, but I can see now how much better you look," he said, trying to sound positive. "First of all, how are you feeling?"

"Like crap," she answered. "That's how I feel—like I've been hit by a train." She turned her head the other way, toward the window. "How do you think I feel?" she said more to herself than to him.

"I'm so sorry for everything you've endured. I really am. What happened to you was malicious and inhuman, and you are very lucky to be alive, young lady," he said warmly.

"You'd think, eh? You think I was *lucky*?" she asked as she turned to face him, her eyes displaying hurt and anger. "You think I was lucky, Detective? How do you figure that?" she asked, her eyes welling up with tears. "I don't think I'm lucky to be alive! I prayed for death, Detective, and instead, I must live with this pain in my heart and the memory of everything for the rest of my pathetic life!" she said, wiping the tears angrily that had already escaped.

Detective Fromer felt an enormous amount of sympathy for her as he watched her. She was young enough to be his daughter, and it pained him to the core to see this young woman talk so negatively. "I understand why you'd feel that way, Ashley, but you're young, and with time and support from your family, you'll get through this," he said philosophically.

She shook her head in disagreement, looking down at her hands. "I don't think so. I can't sleep, because every time I close my eyes, I relive it. I can't concentrate on anything. And I don't have any family, at least no one who'd give a damn," she said, her voice trembling. "I don't want to hear about therapy, because I've heard it before from the nurses. And I don't want to talk about this anymore, if that's OK with you," she said, looking away from him.

She was rightfully angry and in a great amount of pain, but he had to press on, assessing the fact that the longer she withheld information, the longer it would take to move on with the investigation. "Ashley," he said, taking her trembling, cold hands into his own. "Look at me, please," he said gently, causing her to look up into his caring and fatherly eyes. "I know you have a long road ahead of you—I realize that. I also know that what happened to you has altered your life forever, and it's never going to be the same. But thank God you *are* alive, and you have a second chance to live your life," he continued as another fresh flow of tears escaped her eyes. He let go of one of her hands and reached over to the Kleenex box that was on the side table next to her, pulled out a tissue, and gently wiped her cheeks. "Ashley, you must have some family, someone you could go to, someone you could lean on," he continued. "But first you have to tell me exactly what happened that night. Who did this to you? I'm trying to help you, and I can't do that if you don't tell me who's responsible for this," he said, looking at her intensely.

She instantly pushed his hand away from her face and shook her head violently, as if to erase the painful memory of it all. "No! I can't!" she cried helplessly, burying her face in her hands.

"Yes, you can," he encouraged. "Do you know this person, Ashley? Was it a stranger who raped and beat you? Who was it?" he urged, hoping she'd answer him.

"I can't say! Please, leave me alone!" she cried. "I'm confused—I don't know! Please! Leave me alone!" she cried.

"Ashley, please—"

"No! Leave me alone!" she cried, as fresh tears flowed. "Please don't make me remember! Please let me be!" she cried hysterically.

At this point, Detective Fromer had no choice but to respect her wishes and leave the room. He wasn't happy about it, but he had no choice. There was no point in pressing her any further when she was obviously in a bad state of mind. He turned to leave, and when he got to the door, he turned around to look at her. She was curled up in a ball, her knees up to her chest, her arms wrapped tightly around her legs, with her eyes shut tight, and she was rocking back and forth. *Poor girl*, he thought to himself. It was then that the realization hit him. This was a delicate matter, and it would take a lot of patience on his part—and time. He needed to give her another day or so. Somehow, he needed to find a way to get her to trust him enough to open up to him.

Fromer walked out to the elevator of the hospital. He would give her some time. Ashley obviously needed extensive therapy to come to terms with everything. It frustrated him to think that all she needed to do was give him a name or describe him. His hands were tied until then. He had received the results of the DNA test from Jack's truck, and it confirmed that she was in fact in his truck—her fingerprints were practically all over—but that wasn't enough to go on. All it proved was that she had been there, and Jack had already told them that when they'd questioned him. He couldn't arrest the guy for making out with her in his truck! It all boiled down to Ashley's statement. She was the one with the key to solving this case.

—

Jack had made several attempts to contact his wife, but she didn't give him a chance to talk to her. She wouldn't even pick up the phone. He had checked into a little motel just a few kilometers away from home, and he was desperate to go back to the house, but his brother-in-law had advised him to give his wife the space that she desperately needed. They had talked on the telephone extensively when Sara was with Nicole, and Jack had confided to him about everything, including his feelings around the sudden death of his little boy and the strain in caused in their marriage. He opened up about the anger he'd tried to mask since losing his child while in the care of his wife, but also the sudden joy and love he felt since finding out about his wife's pregnancy. He also confided to James the details of his encounter with Ashley and his attraction to her. He pleaded to his only ally that his brief acquaintance with the young woman was halted when he came to his senses; he had not allowed anything further to happen because of the love that he felt for his wife.

He shared with him how he felt like a piece of shit for hurting his wife the way he had, but that he wasn't about to take the blame for something he didn't do. Making out with another woman was wrong, and he would spend the rest of his life making it up to Nicole; but raping and beating a woman? That was another matter altogether, and he was damned if he was going to do time for someone else's crime. It angered him to think that his wife could even think such a thing of him; but could he really blame her? The truth was his behavior in the past year, especially that night, had been so out of character for him. When James had asked him how he really felt about the baby on the way, Jack told him he was thrilled about it.

When Jack had described how he'd felt about the loss of Jonathan, he'd broken down and sobbed like a small child into the receiver, making it difficult for James to understand him. He had never really allowed himself to feel the loss and to grieve for his little boy. He had kept it all bottled up inside: the anger, the hurt, the incredible pain that he had been certain would kill him. Even at Jonathan's funeral everyone had thought how odd it had been that Jack hadn't displayed any emotion.

Now he was a suspect for a heinous crime, and his pregnant wife had no desire to speak to him. Even going to work was a struggle for him. How long would he have to wait for some news? Any news! When was Ashley going to clear his name? He needed to go home, and soon, and he expressed his concerns to James, telling him that the longer he stayed away, the more guilty he would feel when he looked into his wife's eyes. James had been supportive toward Jack, but it was a complicated situation for all of them. When Jack had asked James if he believed him, there had been a short pause; but then James had told Jack that he did believe him. Now Jack had to convince Nicole that his marriage meant more to him than anything else. He had to stay positive and continue to try and make amends.

—

A few days had gone by since the perverse sexual escapade that Manny had orchestrated, and Stephanie had done a no-show at work. Manny called her several times, both at home and on her cell, but all he got was her voicemail. *Where could the bitch be?* he thought. It wasn't like her to just not show up at work. She hadn't even called in sick. By Wednesday, he was fuming, and Laurie and the other girls just did their job and stayed out of his way. They made sure to go in earlier, do their side work, be nice to the customers, and basically run the restaurant. Manny spent much of his time in his office, usually on the phone with Freddie, his drug dealer, or the suppliers who continually hounded him for money. He was starting to get careless with the business, and even though the girls ran the restaurant like clockwork, his increasing need to get high was taking over and clouding his judgment.

Laurie had been increasingly edgy since that Sunday night, and she made even more of an effort to stay out of his way and do her job. She was truly afraid of him and what he was capable of. She thought about giving him notice and leaving; but where would she go? She contemplated getting a regular job, waitressing in a restaurant, or working in retail at a Wal-Mart, but in truth, she was painfully aware of the lack of income she'd make in comparison to what she brought home now. She knew that she lacked the skills to do much of anything else, and she had no support from family or even friends. She was alone in the world, and she silently accepted her fate and decided that she would keep working for Manny—for now anyways.

Stephanie had received all the messages that Manny had left her, but she didn't care anymore. After she'd gone home that Sunday evening, she'd stood under the hot shower for what seemed like hours as she'd manically scrubbed at the evilness that had invaded her body. She'd scrubbed to the point where she was practically raw, all the while crying hysterically. She had decided that night that she had to terminate her pregnancy. It sickened her to her core to know that a part of Manny was growing inside of her. The very next day, she booked herself an appointment with her doctor and told her that she couldn't, and wouldn't, bring a baby into this world. The doctor gave her the usual song and dance about the repercussions as well as other options, such as giving her baby up for adoption, but Stephanie was adamant. She was going to have an abortion even if it meant that she got rid of it herself! She practically shouted at her doctor, telling her that it was her choice, and that she wanted it done as soon as possible.

Fate must have been on her side, because there had been an opening the very next morning due to a cancellation. She was scheduled to have the abortion, and she couldn't wait. The whole procedure felt daunting to an extent, but she was determined to go through with it. Bringing an unwanted child that belonged to the monster that she had come to loathe was unimaginable to her. In just a few hours it would all be over. Then she would decide what her next step was going to be. She needed to make a major change in her life, and leaving The Blue Lagoon was one of them. There was no way she'd ever put up with Manny and his perversion anymore. No way.

CHAPTER

18

*B*ack at the salon, Nicole tried her best to keep up her spirits. It wasn't as hard as she thought it would be, since everyone she worked with was a character. Two of her bosses were sitting in the back, talking among themselves in Italian, which usually meant that it concerned the business. Diane was busy applying foils on one of her most annoying customers, and it looked like Diane was ready to belt her. Olive was being her usual nosey self, not wanting to miss anything, looking in every direction except in the direction of her client, who was sitting in Olive's chair. Carmen, the quiet boss, was in the middle of a haircut, and his client looked like he was having a morning power nap. Yeah, all in all, it looked like it was going to be a fine day.

Jack had called her on her cell phone that morning during her drive to work, and she'd found she couldn't resist the urge to talk to him. Nicole had finally picked up her cell after a few rings and listened to what he had to say. Her heart physically hurt after he told her that he loved her. He told her that it wasn't him that raped and beat the girl and expressed deep regret for even doing what he did with her. He was practically in tears as he pleaded with her to forgive him, which made her want to reach out to him. She was still angry and hurt, but the truth of the matter was she still loved him. They decided they would meet up at their house after work and talk things out. She agreed that they had gone through too much to give up on their marriage now, and that they needed to find a way to get past this.

A few hours into work, Nicole got a client for a color and a cut. As she mixed up the formula, she glanced over to her client, Betty. From the minute Betty had walked in, she hadn't stopped talking. Nicole wasn't in the mood for her today; it seemed like every time Betty came in for an appointment, she was always going through some dramatic times and needed to express it to Nicole, and to everyone else who happened to be in earshot. Nicole loved her job, and she loved being able to express herself creatively, not to mention the amount of freedom the job gave her. She appreciated the one-on-one interaction she had with her clients, and she relished the connection she had with most of them, but the self-centered, non-stop chatty ones were sometimes difficult to manage. Betty was, in her opinion, the typical drama queen, and Nicole had no use for it today. She had a lot on her mind and was anxiously anticipating seeing her husband and talking to him. If she had to be honest with herself, she missed him terribly, and she longed to see him and hear what he had to say.

"Hey, Nikki! What's up?" Diane asked her, breaking Nicole's train of thought as she stirred the combination of the color and peroxide in the color bowl.

Diane leaned closer to Nicole for fear of being heard. "I'm sorry about Hurricane Betty," she whispered, making Nicole laugh at her keen description of the client. Everyone in the salon had done Betty's hair in the past, and it was well known how difficult it was getting through a service with her incessant talking. Nicole carefully applied the color to Betty's roots, nodding and making courteous sounds as Betty chatted away, completely unaware of her surroundings or who was listening to her. When she finally and thankfully finished applying the color, she excused herself to her client and went to the back of the salon, where the sinks and shampoo chairs were placed strategically, to remove her gloves and wash her hands. Diane was right behind her. "Are you alright?" she asked Nicole, leaning in toward her.

"I'm good," Nicole stated simply as she finished washing her hands and reached up above her to grab a clean towel from the white cabinet that ran across all four shampoo basins. "I'm fine, hon, really." She folded the towel and placed it beside the large shampoo and conditioner bottles. "I'm just a little tired I guess," she said vaguely, not willing to disclose the recent events that had taken place and risk anyone at the salon knowing her situation. As close as she was with her coworker, certain things were to be kept private, and other than her family and closest friend, the emotional torment she was experiencing needed to be kept away from her place of work.

"Yes, of course, hon. I understand. I remember all too well what it was like to be pregnant," she said matter-of-factly. "And hormonal!" she added.

"What is this, girls, a conference?" One of their bosses interrupted as he approached the back of the salon. "Come on, Diane, you have someone in your chair waiting for a haircut. Chop chop!" He laughed.

The two girls both glanced over to Diane's station, where an obese man in his fifties had somehow managed to heave himself in her hydraulic chair. Diane and Nicole gave each other a knowing look. This one always managed to relieve gas while getting his haircut. They both burst out laughing, causing everyone around them to stop and stare at them. It looked like the day was going to be a very interesting one.

—

Jack was counting the hours and couldn't wait to finish up with work so he could finally go home. His home! Not the cheap motel he had been staying at, but home to his wife. The thought of that comforted him. He'd felt an enormous amount of relief since the conversation he'd had with his wife earlier that day. He felt that if he had her in his corner, he could get through anything, even this absurd craziness with Ashley. He wondered when he would hear from the detective. Surely, he'd have some answers by now. He took it as a positive sign—he knew that if he were to be formally charged, they would've done it by now. He needed to be cleared from the mess he was in. Nicole seemed more forgiving toward him, but he knew he was still in hot water concerning the girl.

He still couldn't believe that Ashley had been beaten and raped. Jack wondered how soon after he'd left her there that the attack had happened. Who could've done that to her? The park had been secluded; he hadn't seen a single soul, which is why he had insisted on taking her home, or at the very least, waiting with her for the stupid taxi that didn't even end up showing up. He wondered if Ashley had talked to the detective yet and what she would say to him. She had been furious with Jack after he'd rejected her, so furious that she'd slapped him. A thought suddenly occurred to him: what if she told the cops that he was responsible for the attack just to get back at him? Then what? He also knew that if he wanted to keep his ass out of jail then he'd better stay the hell away from her. He thought about calling the detective to inquire about her but decided against it. *No news is good news*, he thought. He glanced at the time, finished up some things in the office, and headed for home.

CHAPTER

19

Once the detective left her room, Ashley broke down sobbing, allowing the waterfall of tears to flow easily as she rocked herself back and forth. The physical pain that she had initially felt when she'd come out of consciousness was slowly starting to heal. Her swelling had come down, and the bruises were a faint yellow in color, but the pain she felt inside her heart and in her soul was excruciating. She felt like any shred of trust she had in anyone or any bit of worthiness she felt for herself was ripped from her soul. The emptiness she felt seared inside her very core. The memory of the rape was so clear in her mind: the way he'd grabbed her unexpectedly from behind and thrown her to the ground. She recalled fighting back with everything in her, kicking and clawing, but he had been strong and powerful. He had forced himself on her; the weight of his body had held her down on the cold ground while he'd torn her blouse open, roughly pulled up her skirt, and forced himself inside of her. He had continued to plow into her, all the while covering her mouth with his hand, preventing her from screaming for help. There had been no one around to help her, and she had finally surrendered to the violent invasion of her body.

Somehow, she was able to detach herself from the cruel assault that he'd inflicted on her, thinking that if she just took her mind to a better place, then it wouldn't be so horrific. He would just take what he wanted, like every other man had, and then leave her alone. But that's not how it happened at all. After he had raped her, he'd started hitting her, throwing punches to her face, her body, her head, and kicking her until she lost consciousness. The first few punches she'd received were hard and extremely painful, and the kicks to her ribs seared through her body like knives, but after what seemed like an eternity, she'd felt nothing. She remembered thinking that this was the day that she was going to die. As a matter of fact, she'd prayed for it as he had continued to kick her lifeless body that had been crumbled in a heap on the ground. She had been certain that death would take her away from all the abuse that she'd suffered over the years, and that somehow, she'd be transformed to another life—a life worth living and free of pain, where she'd soar in the blue skies, like an eagle.

Ashley tried very hard to remember the man who had assaulted her to near death, but she simply couldn't. All she could remember was that he had been very tall with a big build, and he had been wearing a black ski mask. She had tried to see his eyes, but everything had happened so fast that she hadn't stood a chance. He hadn't said one word to her during the assault.

The tears continued to flow, like an endless waterfall, and when the nurse came in to check on her, Ashley was beyond consoling. The nurse ran to her side without a word and took her in her arms while Ashley cried like she'd never cried before, her body shaking so violently it tore the nurse's heart out. It seemed like time stood still as she held her for hours.

—

A couple more days went by, and Stephanie was at home recovering. She was experiencing period-like bleeding and cramps, and she felt a little tired, but terminating the pregnancy gave her enormous relief. Her voicemail was filled to the max with messages from Manny, asking her where the hell she was and why her ass wasn't at work where it belonged. Her answering machine was full of similar messages from him; he sounded powerful and intimidating as though he were right there in her apartment. She knew that she had to face him sooner or later, but she preferred later. Truthfully, she was terrified of him. She thought about calling him and telling him that she'd moved and gotten employment somewhere else, but she was certain that wherever she went, he'd be sure to find her. She wanted desperately to report him to the authorities but didn't have the courage to do so. How could she possibly explain the sexual activities that had gone on when she'd participated? No, she hadn't done it willingly, but all the same, she'd gone along with everything; and not just on one occasion but for the past four years! The humiliation that she felt about the recent occasion was far more than she could bear, and she couldn't imagine telling anyone, let alone the police. She hadn't technically been forced into it, she could've just told him off and walked out on him right there and then, but she'd been terrified—of him and what he'd do. The fact that someone had that kind of power over her, to take part in such a repulsive act, was mind-blowing. She decided that she would take a long luxurious bath, and hopefully, she'd come up with some answers.

—

He angrily slammed his cell phone down so hard; it practically fell off the desk. Manny was not used to being ignored, and after several more attempts at calling Stephanie, it was obvious to him that it was exactly what she was doing. It had been a whole week since she had gone into work, and it infuriated him. The bitch was clearly up to something, and he didn't like it one bit. He had already hooked up with Freddie after receiving a stash of cocaine, which appeased him; but Freddie wasn't too pleased with him, since Manny already owed him so much more for other "small favors" Freddie had done for him, and Freddie had told Manny so. But Manny was confident that he'd get the money soon. However, he would need the girls to start doing more than just waitress. It was going to be a tough one for him since most of the girls that worked for him were underage, and the only two who could really help him out were Laurie and Stephanie.

He decided that those two would be enough to service anyone in the back room for some extra cash; only most of the cash would go to him. He had some connections—an assortment of men that needed some tender loving care, both single and married, old and young, and some rich dudes who just had more money than they knew what to do with it. It had been so easy for him to get Laurie and Stephanie to do what they'd done, so he decided that it wouldn't be that difficult to get his two main girls to "take care" of the men that needed sex. He smiled wickedly to himself as he thought about his plan. How perfect would that be? Business would carry on as usual, and there would be some extra cash on the side, with the help from the girls, of course! Why wouldn't they comply? They practically had sex among themselves, and for his benefit! God that had been something. He got an instant erection just thinking about it. It didn't take much except to threaten them a little. He felt confident that they'd go along with it, with a little help from some nose candy that had just been delivered. He opened his safe and carefully placed the small package of white powder in it.

He would have to spruce up the back room if he was going to have any activities going on, perhaps adding a large, oversized couch that could accommodate a group of two—or three. He'd pay the two girls some extra cash, a commission so to speak, depending on how many guys they fucked. He lit up a joint and thought about it. "Oh yeah!" he sneered out loud. Business would most definitely start looking up, and then he could finally get Freddie off his back, especially if he let him have a freebie with one of the girls occasionally. All he had to do was give a little white "candy" to the girls, help them get into it, and everything would just fall into place. He put his feet on his desk and crossed one foot over the other, inhaling the joint nice and slow, feeling the buzz take effect.

CHAPTER

20

*H*er cell phone was ringing just as Nicole was just getting into her car. Somehow her female intuition told her that it was Emily. Her best friend knew exactly when her shift was up, and when she glanced down at her call display, Nicole smiled, as it was, in fact, Emily. She clicked "on" as she started her car.

"Hey, Emily, I knew it was you!" she greeted her best friend.

"Hello, my friend! And how are you today?" Emily asked in her usual cheery voice.

"I'm alright. Really, I'm OK, I don't want you to worry," she replied, pulling out of the parking lot, away from work.

"Are you really, Nikki? I hope you're not just saying that. Listen, what are you doing tonight? Because I was hoping you'd come over, and you and I could catch a movie or something. Alex is taking Christian to Chuck E. Cheese, and I thought you and I could spend some time together. What do you say?" she asked enthusiastically. Emily's cheery voice filled Nicole's car through the speakers of her Bluetooth.

"Oh, hon, I'd love to, but I'm going to have to take a rain check.

I'm on my way home right now. Jack and I are meeting at home. We're going to talk tonight," she confided in her friend as she made a left turn from The East Mall and merged onto HWY 427.

"Oh, I see things have progressed! When did this all happen? Has he been cleared from all that shit he's being accused of?" she asked in surprise.

"Well, no, not really. Not yet anyway. Listen, Em, you know as well as I do that Jack could never do such a thing. *That* I know for sure. Now I'm not saying that what he did was right, not by a long shot. But we can't sort anything out if we don't talk, right?" Nicole asked, wanting to be validated. "Emily, we talked this morning briefly, and he apologized profusely. What can I tell you, I love him, you know that" she continued.

"I know you do, Nikki. I also never believed that Jack could do such a vicious thing to anyone. But can you tell me from the bottom of your heart that what took place with her in his truck is OK with you?" Emily asked, concerned for her friend. "I mean, I know what you're saying, really I do, but make sure you get him to really open up to you about *why* he would even jeopardize your marriage the way that he did," she said, thinking to herself that if it had been Alex who had made out with another woman, she'd have pulled a Lorena Bobbitt on him. She had no use for shit like that, but she didn't express that to her friend.

"I know, I know, Emily you're right. There *is* no excuse for that, I know that. But I must hear him out regardless, do you know what I mean? I'm carrying his child, Emily! We have a second chance, and I don't want to lose him now!" she said, her eyes welling up in tears, causing her vision to blur.

"I understand, my friend," she replied sympathetically. "Listen, you're driving, and you're pregnant, so I'm going to let you go—for *now* that is! You know that whatever you decide to do, I'll always be there for you. I love you, and even that stupid husband of yours." She laughed. "No, seriously though, I do think the world of both of you, and I hope for both your sakes, *and* the baby's, that you guys work this out. So good luck tonight, and I'll be waiting to hear from you, OK?" She laughed lightly. "I love you, and whatever you do, *don't* sell yourself short, you hear me?" she exclaimed.

Nicole wiped a single tear that escaped and laughed. "I hear you, chief!" She was thankful for her longtime friend, who always seemed to make her feel a thousand pounds lighter. "I'll call you soon, I promise. Oh and, Em—"

"You're welcome!" Emily answered her, already knowing what Nicole was going to say. And with that, they hung up.

As Nicole approached her exit, she felt her stomach do a couple of somersaults. Her heart was pounding, and her anticipation was accelerating as she got off the highway. Within just five minutes or so, she'd be home to face her husband. She hoped and prayed that her instincts about him were right, because she wasn't sure how much more she could take at this point.

21

*D*etective Fromer was getting more and more nervous, and he lit up another cigarette. Every time he had a lot on his mind, he smoked like a chimney, which got on his wife's nerves. She was a clean fanatic, and the smell of his cigarettes made her batty. He was thinking about Ashley and how he'd left her. She had clearly been distraught. He'd hoped that he'd get somewhere with her that evening, but it hadn't worked out the way he'd wanted. He had to see her again, even if she hated him for it, which bothered him even more. The last thing he wanted to do was hurt her, but it was imperative that he talk to her very soon while everything was still fresh in her mind. The longer she stalled, the longer it would take him to make an arrest.

—

When Nicole arrived at her house, she wasn't sure if Jack was there or not. When she entered the house and walked toward the kitchen, she was both surprised and apprehensive to see that Jack was already there, sitting on the couch in the family room. He stood up immediately when he saw her, and for a moment she wanted desperately to run into his arms and forget everything that had happened, but she knew she couldn't do that. She had to think with her brain and not just with her heart. Even though she was expecting him, she froze in her tracks.

"Hi," he said, smiling at her warmly.

"Hi," she responded, noticing how well he looked. She figured he had probably just taken a shower, because he smelled of aftershave, and he was dressed in khaki shorts and a white polo shirt.

"You're looking good. How are you feeling?" Jack asked, not sure if he should approach her or not. He wasn't entirely sure of anything anymore, but his insides were urging him to take her in his arms and lavish her with kisses.

"I'm good, you know—considering," Nicole responded, not being able to take her eyes off him. Her heart was beating so hard, she thought it would explode. "How are you?" she added, taking a few steps toward him.

"I'm glad to be home again," Jack said, taking a step toward her. "I miss you, Nikki," he added, observing her carefully.

"I miss you too," she said softly, taking another step toward him, trying everything in her power not to seem too anxious. "Have you eaten anything?" she asked, as her stomach made a silent rumble, a reminder that she hadn't eaten anything since breakfast.

"No, actually, I haven't been eating much these days. Are you hungry? We could order in some pizza if you want," he offered. "And talk of course."

"That sounds great! You call and order while I go upstairs to change, if you don't mind," she said, wanting to get out of her work clothes.

Jack ordered the pizza while Nicole scurried upstairs to change. It didn't take long for her to change into a lavender-jersey pantsuit and return, sitting on the love seat across from him. They sat there for an awkward moment, not sure where to begin, when Jack decided he would go first.

"Listen, Nicole … I know what I did was wrong," he began, getting right to the point. He figured there was no point in stalling since he just wanted to get this conversation over with. He felt bad enough without making it long and torturous for both. "Where do I begin?" he asked, putting his hand through his dark hair, the way he always did when he was bothered by something.

"How about from the beginning," Nicole responded quietly, feeling her insides turn. "How about you tell me how you could pick up a random girl and then take her to a secluded park to do God knows what with her," she said in an even tone, fearing what he had to say.

"First of all, Nicole, let me explain something that I've thought about these last few days. I've racked my brain to shreds asking myself the same thing, and the only conclusion that I can come up with is that I felt lost." Nicole frowned at him, but Jack continued. "This past year and a half, well, since Jonathan died, a part of me died too. I know how difficult it was for you as well, and I'm not taking that away from you, I swear!" He paused and looked at his wife, whose eyes were glued on him, listening intently. "I just felt like he was ripped from me, you know what I mean. I felt like I was cheated somehow. At the same time, I was trying desperately to be the supportive husband because I saw what it did to you as well." She looked up at him, her eyes brimming with tears. "I couldn't face you, Nikki. I couldn't look at you for the longest time. Every time I looked at you, I saw Jonathan. He had your crystal blue eyes, and it hurt like hell when I saw you because you were a painful reminder of what I lost … what we lost!" he corrected as he got up from the couch and went to sit beside her. She let out a sigh, but he continued. "Nicole, I guess a small part of me blamed you," he said, facing his wife, who looked up at him with hurt in her eyes. "Oh God! I know the accident wasn't your fault—I know that! I guess I needed to blame someone so badly for taking my son away from me," he concluded softly, feeling like a weight had been lifted off his chest.

Nicole wiped the tears that she couldn't restrain and took a deep breath, her eyes penetrating his. "You *do* know that it was an accident, don't you? I would *never* ever hurt my child, and—"

"Baby, I *know* it was an accident!" Jack interrupted. "Of course it was an accident! God knows, you were a great mother, and that's why it hurts so damn much. It shouldn't have happened. He should be here, with us." He said, leaning forward, taking her hands into his. I stayed away from you because it killed me to be home. This was a home where there was so much happiness, and then, in a blink of an eye, there was nothing but emptiness and sorrow. You had become nothing more than a painful reminder, and that's why I'd go out after work almost every night. I needed an escape. Before Jonathan died, I couldn't wait to come home," he said, as he stood up from the couch, and walked across to the mantel, where the photograph of his son still stood in its silver frame. He picked it up and held it in his hands while Nicole looked on. "I'd finish work and literally run out of there to come home to you," he said softly, staring down at the picture, carefully studying it, like he had never seen it before. "And to our son," he said in a choked voice. He stroked the outline of the little boy that was smiling back at him, causing him to tear up. It was much more difficult than he had thought, but he had to go on. This was do or die.

Jack looked up from the photograph and across to the same crystal blue eyes that he'd loved for so long. "Nicole, I used to come home to the smell of baked cookies and the sound of your singing or humming in the kitchen while you prepared dinner, and the little guy just running around and wanting me to put him on my shoulders and play hide-and-seek … and then there was nothing. This house went from being full of laughter and love to emptiness and pain. I still have a hard time being home sometimes. Everything's changed so much," he concluded, his voice barely a whisper.

"Well, of course everything changed, Jack! We lost our child for God's sake! Do you think it was easy for me? I blame myself every day! Every single day since he died, I think about him and how I could've prevented it!" Nicole shouted, more to herself than to him, as she rose from the couch and walked across to him, taking the picture frame from his hand. She traced the outline of her smiling boy's face with tears running down her cheeks. "I was careless, Jack, and that's why you punished me! You punished me for my carelessness by being absent. I know it wasn't intentional, Jack. I know that. But, why on earth did you do what you did with this girl? I don't understand. Please help me to understand," she pleaded, facing him, her heart ripping in two.

His hazel eyes bore into hers as he contemplated his answer carefully, not wanting to hurt her. "I didn't plan on it, Nicole, you have to believe me when I tell you that. I went to the bar like I had so many times before. I was there just shooting the shit with the bartender, and she was just there," he replied, like that explained everything.

"What were you doing with her, and how long did you know her, Jack?" she asked.

"I had never seen her before that day, honest. She was friendly, and I felt comfortable. I felt like a man! You and I had been living like strangers for the past year. We weren't even having sex anymore!" he said angrily.

"No, thanks to you!" she shot back. "You were never home to have sex with me. Is that it, Jack? You just needed another woman to make you feel like a man?" she shouted, her anger getting the best of her.

"Yes. I guess I had forgotten what it felt like to be needed—or wanted. It was wrong … I know that. I wasn't thinking, Nick. I admit it, I was totally wrong," he said, gently taking her by her shoulders and bringing her closer to him.

"No, you weren't thinking. Not with your head anyway," she said angrily. "I needed you too! I needed to be held and comforted in my darkest hours, and you were never home! You had become a workaholic, coming home later and later. You consciously made the decision, day after day, to be absent from home—and from me," she said to him, looking right through him as she recalled all the days and months she'd spent at home alone, the many nights he wouldn't even go up to their bedroom. "But you decided that you needed someone fresh, young, and exciting, isn't that right?" she said angrily, glaring up at him, seeing his whole body stiffen.

"No! It's not like that. She was just someone that didn't have anything to do with the emptiness I felt inside. She was just an escape from a dark hole I felt I was living in. I had forgotten who I was or what purpose I had. I swear to you, from the bottom of my heart … I wasn't looking for anything!" he pleaded, wanting to take his wife in his arms right there and then. His desire for her mounted as he looked down at her. "Nicole, I love you. I've always loved you. And I'll never stop loving you," he said, practically crying.

"So she was just a distraction then … a young and pretty distraction, right?" Nicole asked him testily. "How far *did* you go with her?" Her heart was thumping so loudly; she figured the neighbors could hear it.

"Nicole, stop it! We're not getting anywhere by rehashing all of this!" Jack shouted at her. I swear to God, nothing, and I mean nothing happened! We kissed, and that's it!" he said in frustration as he continued to plead his case.

"Oh no?" she replied, lifting her head to meet his eyes just inches away. "So, you just kissed? Is that what you want me to believe?" she shouted at him, her voice breaking. "Did you want her, Jack? Tell me! Did she turn you on?" she yelled in hysteria. "tell me, Jack! Did you want to fuck her?" And suddenly, his mouth was on her trembling lips as he kissed her hungrily, taking her in his arms and claiming her mouth, her lips, searching and possessing her tongue. She tried to fight him off, but he continued to kiss her feverishly, wanting her, wanting to end the madness. Jack kissed her with a yearning he'd never felt before, and suddenly, her arms were around his neck, holding him tightly, as she kissed him back in desperation and desire. Nicole clutched onto him as she let herself go, and he picked her up effortlessly and carried her to the couch, laying her down gently.

He quickly and expertly unbuttoned the top of her blouse and started kissing her neck and then went back to her awaiting lips. Nicole moaned with pleasure as Jack removed her top and bent his dark head to her cleavage, caressing her swelling breasts, one by one, as she allowed herself to be taken by the force of the passion, they felt for each other. She was breathless as he unbuttoned his pants and helped her remove hers. He kissed her more softly, caressing every inch of her body as he expertly unfastened her bra, exposing her breasts, kissing and licking her nipples, teasingly sucking on them, tantalizing them, as she moaned in sheer ecstasy. He moved his lips further down to her stomach, her abdomen, kissing every inch of her body, making it his. He spread her legs gently, and she complied, as he softly kissed the inside of her thighs, then moved to the center of her, gently teasing her, making her moan with desire. All the built-up anger and frustration that had suppressed them quickly vanished and was replaced with love and devotion. Nicole gave herself to him, letting go of the hurt and doubt that she'd felt for him just moments ago. At this very moment, all they felt was an intense need to be together, and in the end, when it was all over, Jack enveloped her in his arms, Nicole's head on his chest, her leg crossed over his, breathless and overcome with love and satisfaction. The love they felt for one another hadn't altered, and their lovemaking proved that.

"What the hell just happened?" Nicole asked, smiling at him, stroking his chest.

"Baby, I love you, and I don't ever want you to forget it, you hear?" Jack said, smiling back at her, trying to recover from what had just transpired.

"I love you too, Jack! But we still haven't ironed out everything," she replied, half wishing that they hadn't gotten carried away like they had. It clouded her judgment, and she needed a clear mind to sort everything out.

"Oh for heaven's sake, Nikki, what's there to iron out? I thought we sorted everything out already. I was as honest as I could be. I didn't have sex with the girl, nor did I beat or rape her. What the hell else am I supposed to do, confess to the Pope?" he said as he sat up.

The doorbell suddenly interrupted their discussion, making Nicole sit up as well. "It must be the pizza we ordered," Nicole said, springing up from the couch, trying to put her clothes back on.

"Baby relax—I'll get it," he replied, already putting his pants back on and heading for the front door. Sure enough, it was the pizza-delivery guy, and after Jack paid him, he returned to the family room with the pizza. "Smells good doesn't it?" he said, setting it down on the coffee table while Nicole retrieved two plates and some napkins from the kitchen.

"I'm starving! I feel like I haven't eaten in days!" Nicole said, picking up a slice, and taking a bite.

"Yeah, well I hope you can try to remember that you've got our baby to feed too," Jack said, poking her lightly on her abdomen and then taking a bite from his slice. "Let's just have a nice dinner shall we?" he asked in hopes of putting all negative energy behind them. "OK?" He gave her a loving smile.

"OK," she replied, smiling back at him, wondering if they would ever completely get things back on track.

CHAPTER

22

She had contemplated what to do next, but she hadn't come up with a plan, not yet anyway. The bath had helped her to relax a bit, but Stephanie couldn't decide what to do about Manny and work. She was feeling a little edgy about seeing him, and she realized that the longer she waited to deal with him, the harder it would be on her. She wasn't kidding herself. She knew without a doubt that he was pissed with her, since she had not returned any of his messages. She was afraid, and she was alone. She wondered about Laurie. Had she returned to work, and if so, how was he with her? How was she with him? The sleazy image of what they had done still haunted her, and she was unsure and afraid of how to handle it. Should she be worried about her safety? Hell yes! She got into her bed and pulled the covers over her, feeling scared and alone. Maybe tomorrow she'd go to her work and tell him that she was just sick or something, hoping he'd understand. Then, she decided, she would probably quit. What could he possibly do to her? She'd figure out something, but in the meantime, she needed to get some sleep. Exhaustion overtook her.

———

As Fromer walked down the hall toward Ashley's room, he was met with the nurse on duty, Ashley's overprotective nurse.

"Good evening, Detective!" the nurse said pleasantly as she walked over to him.

"Good evening to you too!" he replied just as pleasantly. "I'm here to see Miss Moore," he commented, making his way toward Ashley's room, the nurse right behind him.

"I can see that, Detective, but I'm going to ask that you do not, I repeat, *do not* upset her. She was just given a sedative, and she doesn't need to get herself all worked up now," she said sternly.

"I'm not here to upset her. I'm here to do my job, if you'll let me. Now please, if you'll excuse me, I'm going to ask that you give me a few minutes alone with her," Fromer said as he turned to face her. "I understand you care about Miss Moore, and it might surprise you to know that I care about her too. But I need to do my job, you understand?" he said, turning away from her, not waiting for a response as he let himself into Ashley's room, causing the nurse to sigh with exasperation.

As Fromer walked in, he noticed Ashley sitting up in bed, her eyes on the television set that sat across from her bed on a small chest, the volume on low. There was a solemn look about her as she gazed at the television with a blank look on her face. He wasn't sure if she even realized that there was anyone in her room because she just continued to stare obliviously at the screen. He closed the door softly behind him and proceeded to walk toward her as he cleared his throat to catch her attention. That was when she turned to face him, her eyes watching him as he sat himself on the chair beside her bed.

"Hello, Ashley," he said softly. She blinked as if to acknowledge his presence. "How are you feeling this evening," he asked, wondering if she was too out of it to even have a conversation with him.

"OK, I guess," she replied sadly. "Are you here to question me again?"

"Ashley, I hope you can believe me when I tell you that I'm not here to upset you. I'm simply here for some answers," Fromer stated gently. He leaned his body closer toward her. She just nodded in response. "Do you think you can help me out, kiddo?" he asked her gently.

"I can try. But things are still hazy to me. I don't want to get anyone in trouble," Ashley responded quietly. He couldn't believe it! She was recovering from a brutal beating and rape, and she was concerned about getting this bastard into trouble?

"Alright then. How about you tell me what you do remember, starting from when you were at work. I understand you were working, and you met a gentleman at the bar. You two started chatting, and you ended up leaving the restaurant with him, am I right?" Fromer asked her point blank.

"Yes. I met this guy that I was interested in, and we sort of started talking and stuff," Ashley said, recalling the events of that horrible night. Fromer nodded, giving her the OK to continue. "Well, he sort of gave me the impression that he was interested in me too. So, I left work earlier." She paused, staring straight ahead. "We ended up at the park not too far from my work," she continued.

"Was it Marie Curtis Park," he interjected, wanting to make sure that he had all his facts right.

"Yes. It was. We got there, and we—" Ashley paused, and Detective Fromer waited for her to continue. He wondered if she simply couldn't remember or didn't want to remember. "Well, we made out for a little while," she said with embarrassment.

"Where did you two 'make out' so to speak?" he asked.

"In the parking lot, in his truck," she replied simply. "We were sort of all over each other, and then—" she stopped dead in midsentence, looking confused.

"And then what, Ashley? What happened after that?" Fromer pressed, waiting for her to go on.

"I don't remember exactly," she said quietly. This is where I have a hard time remembering the details. I remember he and I were arguing—"

"What were you arguing about, Ashley?" he asked, trying to keep her on track and focused.

Ashley thought for a moment. "I don't remember why we were arguing. We were outside, and I remember that I was angry, and I slapped him," she said, recalling the anger that she had felt but not being able to remember the reason.

"Why did you and him get out of the truck if you two were making out? Did you argue while still in the truck?"

"I don't remember. I remember we were making out, and then I remember being outside and arguing. I remember slapping him." Ashley paused and frowned. "Beyond that, I remember being thrown to the ground," she said as her lips started to quiver and her eyes welled up with tears. Suddenly, she wrapped her arms around herself and started to rock slowly back and forth. Her voice was barely audible when she finally spoke again. "He tore my blouse open," she whispered, "and I tried to scream for help." She started to rock faster as the tears slid down her cheeks. "I couldn't scream because his hand was covering my mouth," she continued as she relived that painful night. "He hit me hard in the face and then pulled up my skirt," she cried as she spoke. "His body was big and strong, and he was on top of me, and I couldn't breathe. I was sure I was going to die! He undid his belt, and I tried to kick, but he was too strong. I tried to scream when he took his hand off my mouth, but there was no one around. He held my arms over my head with his hand, and he punched me repeatedly. He just kept punching me, and after a few punches, I didn't feel anything and that was when he raped me. I felt numb, like it was a bad dream, and when he finished raping me, he started to kick me in the ribs and my legs. I tried to get my cell phone, but I don't remember why I didn't have it. I must've lost consciousness because the next thing I remember is waking up in the hospital." She stopped rocking herself and looked straight ahead.

Fromer couldn't help but to stare at the young woman who had just poured her heart out to him as she relived that fateful evening. He thought it was a miracle that she was alive.

"Ashley, is the man that you met at the bar the same man that you were arguing with?" he asked, wanting confirmation of her story. Ashley nodded as she wiped a tear that trickled down her cheek. "Do you, at any time, remember that man from the bar leaving you at the park?" he asked, trying to fill in the blanks.

"No, I honestly don't remember," she said in frustration. "I told you everything that I could. Please! That's all I can remember," she said, running her hands through her short bob. "Do you think this is easy for me? It's not, Detective, I can tell you that," she said.

"So you're saying that you don't remember if the man that you were arguing with is the same man who attacked you?" he asked, standing up from his chair and pacing the floor while scratching his head.

"No," she answered quietly. "I'm not sure if the man who attacked me is the same man that I was with in the truck. I told you; I remember arguing with that guy, but I can't recall why we were arguing." She dragged her hands through her hair in frustration. "I don't remember anything until I was forced to the ground."

"You said he covered your mouth with his hand, is that right?" Fromer asked, turning around again to face her.

"Yes, that's right."

"Were your eyes covered as well? Did he blindfold you? Is that why you don't remember who he was?" he asked, probing her.

"No! I told you; I remember seeing him unbuckle his belt to his pants … Wait a minute!" She exclaimed as she turned her body to face him. He was wearing a black ski mask! I couldn't see his eyes. I tried to, but I couldn't. I'm sorry, I know I'm not being much help here. I just want to get out of here and try to get on with my life!" she cried, shaking her head in exasperation.

"Where are your parents, Ashley?" Fromer asked the question that had been on his mind since this whole ordeal had happened.

"My parents want nothing to do with me, Detective," she sighed. "I really don't want to talk about them right now, if you don't mind," she said, so quietly he could barely hear her.

"Do you have any siblings?" he asked, sitting down beside her again.

"No. I'm an only child," she replied with indifference.

"Do you have an aunt, an uncle, grandparents, anyone at all?" Fromer asked, hoping she had someone close to her. She'd need family around her, especially after she was released from the hospital, which by the look of her, he gauged would be soon. Her exterior wounds looked to have healed, although her emotional state was another story. That, he thought with sureness, would take years to overcome.

"You know what, Detective? Like I said before, I don't have anyone. Please, can you just let it go?" Ashley answered, looking straight at him with a look of annoyance. "Besides, why do you care?"

"Why do I care?" he asked her incredulously. "Maybe because you're going to be released from the hospital soon enough, and you need to have someone close to you, don't you think?" he asked, concerned for her safety.

"Detective, I've been on my own for a number of years now, and I've been doing quite alright, you know. I don't need anyone to take care of me," she said with defiance.

Detective Fromer couldn't argue her point. "I'm just trying to help," he said in defeat, not knowing what else to say to her. She just listened to him in silence. "Anyway, get some rest. And if you can remember anything else, and I mean *anything*, please call me, OK?" he said, looking right at her. Ashley just nodded in agreement. Fromer didn't know what else to say to her, so he turned around and walked out of her room.

Leaving the hospital, he decided he would make his way to The Blue Lagoon and pay Manny a little visit. Something about that guy just didn't sit right with him. He'd felt it in his gut from the minute he'd met him. It was bizarre to him that Manny hadn't bothered to visit the girl in the hospital. After all, she was one of his employees, and the girl almost lost her life. He wanted to check out the happenings at the bar. He pulled out his cell phone and called his wife to let her know he'd be home a little later. He didn't like to worry her unnecessarily, and after he hung up with her, he made his way to the bar.

Detective Fromer pulled up into the parking lot at The Blue Lagoon and sat in his car as he recapped the story Ashley had given him: She was working when she met Jack Newman. There was an obvious attraction between them, and they chatted it up a bit and then left the establishment together. They ended up going to Marie Curtis Park, which was just a few minutes away, where they made out in his truck in the parking lot. She doesn't remember getting out of his truck, but she remembers slapping him for some reason. After that, she blanks out again, and the next thing she recalls is that a tall, well-built man with a black ski mask throws her to the ground, rapes her, and then beats her to the point of unconsciousness. After that, nil—she wakes up in the hospital.

He scratched his head with one hand, thinking of Jack Newman's story. His story was much the same, except that he received a phone call from his wife, which prompted him to stop what he was doing with her and go home, which infuriated Ashley. Then, at that point, she stepped out of his truck while he called a cab to take her home, which she angrily declined. In the meantime, they argued, and she slapped him (which is when the cab driver must've arrived and witnessed the slap, unbeknownst to Jack and Ashley). The cab driver witnessed the two together arguing, didn't think too much of it, and left the park. There were no other witnesses at the park to confirm if Jack had left her alone at the park like he claimed he had. Ashley didn't remember why she got out of the truck or if Jack left her. Then there's this guy—who has the same build as Jack and is wearing a black ski mask—who rapes and beats her.

Fromer contemplated everything as he tapped his fingers nervously on his steering wheel. He wondered at how coincidental the similarities were between Jack and the man who raped and beat Ashley, and if there were, in fact, two different men. At the same time, the DNA proved that Ashley's fingerprints were all over the truck, where they were getting "friendly," so to speak, but Jack had already confirmed that when Fromer had questioned him. The examination that was done on Ashley proved that she had been raped, but no semen was found in her vagina. The bastard was certainly prepared, that was for sure. Ashley couldn't identify the rapist because he had been wearing a black ski mask. Aside from her blanking out on a couple of occasions, all the evidence pointed to Jack Newman, since the cab driver didn't see anyone else at the park except for Ashley and Jack.

But then again, he thought, why on earth would Jack bother to call for a cab if he intended on attacking the young woman? Why would he incriminate himself if he was, in fact, her attacker? Was it possible that during their argument things had gotten so out of control that he had gotten very angry and attacked her? Perhaps it was never his intention to hurt her, but instead, he simply lost it after she slapped him and went crazy? Things like this happen all the time, unfortunately, where there's a lover's spat, and a perfectly normal guy with no police record just snaps. The police had checked the time of the call he'd received from his wife, and some time had passed from the phone call to the time he'd gotten home. And what would he have done with the black ski mask? All Fromer knew now was that things looked grim for Jack, especially since there was no one to collaborate his story, and there were no other suspects. For now, it seemed like Jack was the prime suspect.

23

*I*t was nearing eleven o'clock when Detective Fromer walked into The Blue Lagoon. He noticed that there were a few people still at the bar having drinks and a couple of tables over to one side with people drinking and conversing. He made his way to the end of the bar, seating himself in a position where he had full view of the whole bar. There were two waitresses working on the floor, and both looked quite young. He looked around, noticing there was no sign of the owner; maybe he was in his office again. One of the girls noticed him and hurriedly walked over.

"Can I get you something," she asked in a friendly tone.

"Yeah, I'd like a beer please," he answered. "I'm sorry, I don't think that I've seen you here before. What's your name, sweetheart?" he asked her politely.

"Stacey," she replied, nervously looking over her shoulder to her coworker and then in the direction of the corridor, where he presumed Manny's office and the restrooms were. "I'll get you that beer now," she said, quickly scooting away and making her way to the end of the bar to give the drink order to the bartender, who was the only male working with them.

Fromer gave the place a quick look over and then saw Manny. He was walking down the corridor and across to the bar, checking things out. He looked almost surprised when he spotted the Detective—almost.

"Well, hello there stranger. Long time no see!" Manny exclaimed, putting on fake pleasantries as he walked toward Fromer and sat down next to him.

"Hey, man, how's it going?" the Detective asked, as Stacey practically slid his beer glass down the bar, giving her boss a nervous smile, and headed over to the other waitress, who was eyeing them carefully.

"Can't complain! Everything's great! And what brings you in this evening?" Manny asked, glancing over his shoulder to both his waitresses, who had already made themselves scarce.

"I just happened to be in the neighborhood and thought I'd pop in," Fromer replied, taking a long sip from his beer, eyeing Manny carefully.

"It's a good thing you're out there, Detective—keeping everyone in line, that is," Manny said, chuckling.

"Yeah, well, I'm trying to, although it's not always as easy as it seems. There's a lot of rats out there," Fromer said, his eyes never leaving Manny's.

Manny fidgeted in his chair and smiled nervously at the detective. He had to be careful. *This guy just pops in whenever he feels like it, at any time of the day*, he thought. He had to make sure to have his older girls working in the evening, like Stephanie, wherever the hell she was these days. Just thinking about her put him in a sour mood. "Well, you keep doing what you're doing, Detective, and I'm sure that the streets will be a better place," Manny said, clearing his throat.

Steven Fromer raised his beer to Manny and nodded as he took another long sip, finishing off his beer and loudly setting his glass down, catching the attention of the bartender.

"Can I get you another one, buddy?" Manny asked good-naturedly, giving a quick nod to his bartender, motioning him to pour another beer. Inwardly he hoped that the prick would just leave.

"No, thanks," Detective Fromer said, both to Manny for offering and to the bartender, who was just about to pour him another one. "I think I'll just head on home." He rose from his chair and reached for his wallet.

"Detective! This one's on me, buddy!" Manny said, thrilled to see him leave.

"Well, thank you, Manny," he said, putting his wallet back into his pocket. "I'll see you around." He gave Manny a quick wink, turned, and walked out, noticing that the waitresses hadn't yet emerged from wherever they were hiding. Something was not right. However, it was late, and he was anticipating a warm bed and a good night's sleep.

—

A week had passed since Stephanie had been to work, and the thought of seeing Manny again made her nauseous. She wasn't at all sure how he'd react to her absence of the last week, although she sensed that he'd be furious with her. The calls he had made had stopped after a couple of days, which caused her to be more edgy. Her nerves were getting to her, and she felt highly anxious, which disrupted her sleep. She really didn't want to work there anymore; but she didn't think that there was anything out there for her, especially since she lacked the education that she needed to get herself a decent job and make decent money. She'd made a few phone calls inquiring about waitressing positions, but she'd had no luck, and even though she'd gone to a couple of establishments in person, both had turned her down flat. It had been the same song and dance: employer's being forced to let some of their staff go because there simply wasn't enough business to go around; there was no chance of hiring someone new. Given her situation, her lack of education, and her need to make her rent as well as her other expenses, she had come to the unfortunate conclusion to return to The Blue Lagoon and work for Manny again. The thought didn't please her—not one bit—but she had to eat and pay her bills. She had no one, and it had been a week since she'd taken home any money at all. She had been eating pasta and canned soup every day for the past week, and her phone bill had just come in, not to mention her rent was soon coming up.

Stephanie felt extremely tired as she drove herself to work that early afternoon. She reluctantly walked in, feeling as though she were going to her execution. She spotted Laurie almost immediately, and she quickly walked past her, making her way to the back. She was instantly met by Manny, who was just coming out of his office. She froze in her tracks at the sight of him. He gave her a quick look over and a sly smile crept up, taking Stephanie completely by surprise.

"Well, hello there, Steffy. How very nice of you to honor us with your presence." He snickered, which only made her feel more awkward.

"Um, hi, Manny," she managed to say in a meek voice. "I'm sorry I didn't get back to you," she started rambling. "I was sick for a few days, and—"

"Oh, don't worry about it, Steph!" Manny interrupted, putting his arm around her shoulder and leading her to his office. "Everyone needs a break once in a while, isn't that right?" he bellowed, smiling from ear to ear.

Once they were in his office, Manny closed the door behind them, and before she knew what was happening, he had helped her remove the light sweater that she was wearing. "Here, let me help you with this, sweetheart," he said as he hung it up on the hook by the door. She just stood there, dumbfounded, obviously taken by surprise by his good-natured tone. She had been expecting to be grilled through the flames, and he knew that. He was two steps ahead of her, and he didn't want to scare her off.

"So," Manny said, as he walked up to her, putting his hands into his pockets. "Are we ready to begin working again?" he asked in a much more serious tone.

"Um, yeah I guess so. Manny, since we're alone now, I really needed to talk to you about something," she said stammering.

"Sure, go ahead," he said, already figuring out what she was going to say.

"Well," she continued, looking down at her shoes. "Um, well, I'd like to continue working for you, but, um, well, I don't want to do anything sexual ever again with you—or with anyone else," she concluded, alluding to the sex she was forced to have with Laurie. She slowly lifted her chin up to face his beady eyes that were penetrating right through her.

"Oh, is that right?" he said as he walked behind his desk and sat on his chair, putting his feet up. "Please, sit down." He motioned to her, and she slowly sat on the chair across from him.

"You know Stephanie, you've been my oldest and top waitress in this joint. You know that don't you?" Manny asked, leaning back and placing his hands behind his head. Stephanie nodded in agreement. "And as the senior waitress, you make a lot more dough than anyone else in here," he continued. "You with me so far?" She nodded once more. "I depend a lot on you, and because I'm able to pay you so well and provide for all your necessities and then some, I expect certain, shall we say, 'favors,' if you know what I mean?" he continued. His voice was low, yet so powerful she thought she was going to faint. "Now I know that some things I've asked of you seem, shall we say, degrading to you, but they're necessary for me, if you catch my drift." The realization of what he was saying to her penetrated to her soul, her eyes growing the size of saucers, her heart rate increasing to the point where she felt she would faint.

"You know, Laurie didn't have a real problem with the two of you, um, getting it on, and do you know why that is?" Manny asked. Stephanie shook her head in response. "Because she knows what happens to girls that don't obey, and actually, I think that a little 'sugar' wouldn't hurt while you're at it, you know. It helped Laurie to relax a little. If you give it a chance, then you'll come to see that I'm right, and you'll find it *much* easier to do the things you're supposed to do. You might even enjoy yourself in the process," he concluded, smiling at her. "Stephanie, you're a very attractive young woman, and a woman with your looks shouldn't waste them. I'm sure you understand my position here. You scratch my back so to speak, and I'll scratch yours," he said simply.

Stephanie was shocked at his request. It was more of a demand, and she knew it. She took a deep breath and crossed her hands in front of her. "Are you saying that I *have* to do it?" she asked incredulously. She wasn't prepared for any of this. Manny's so called "charm" was all an act.

"Well, let me put it to you this way so you understand me. If you want to live in this world with food, paid rent, and all your necessities— and more money than you'll know what to do with—you'll see that what I'm asking for in return is no big deal. To make things easier for you, you just need to snort some candy here," he said as he pulled out a little white bag from his desk. "Trust me on this, sweetheart, you'll be rolling in the dough. Not only that, but I also have a couple of buddies that need a little, shall we say, TLC, and if they think that you'll do it for them, then there's a couple of regulars for you. A lot of money in your pocket my dear. And if I need some tender loving care, then I think I deserve to get some since I'm the one who's going to be providing your candy and all. Now I think that's a very fair request, don't you think?" he asked as he put his feet down from the desk and leaned closer to her.

She couldn't believe what she was hearing. He was asking her to sell her body—to sell her soul! Her body started to tremble, and her hands were as cold as ice. "But I don't want to do that anymore," she said in a quiet voice.

Manny laughed as he rose from his chair and walked around his desk to where she was sitting. "Oh, Stephanie," he said with a chuckle, placing his hand on his belt, his other hand tracing her lips. "You really don't know me very well do you? Even after four beautiful years together, you really don't realize what you have here do you?" he said, towering over her as he unbuckled his belt and started unzipping his pants. Ever so gently, he took her face with his hand and guided her lips to his already erect penis. She closed her eyes and did as she was told as he gently moved himself in and out of her mouth. "Come on, baby, show me what you've got!" he said. She didn't have a choice but to pleasure him orally, right there and then.

24

*I*t was a very long and difficult night, and the nightmares prevented Ashley from getting any sleep; images of being thrown to the ground and the hardness of his body pressing against her, making it difficult for her to breathe, not able to make a sound because her mouth was covered with his hand. She relived the terror and paralyzing fear she'd felt, repeatedly, every night. The nightmares of the rape and the beating would suddenly make her sit up in bed at all hours of the night, her body covered in sweat; her breathing would be hard and labored as she'd fight to calm herself, her eyes wide open in fear. Then images of her childhood would enter her mind, of the sexual abuse she'd endured from her stepfather while her mother turned a blind eye, leaving her only daughter to fend for herself. Ashley had never felt like she mattered, never felt protected or loved.

Her father had run out on her and her mother when Ashley was very young, and it didn't take long for her mother to get involved and then marry Jerry, her present husband, Ashley's stepfather. At first, he had been kind to her, but then, as she got older, the abuse started. He'd enter her room late at night and talk to her. It didn't take long before he'd fondle her and masturbate in front of her, all the while reassuring her that it was his way of showing her that he loved her. Finally, he made his move and ordered Ashley to give him oral sex until he was ready, then had intercourse with her. When she approached her mother with everything that was happening at night while she was working late or sleeping, her mother just spat in her face and called her a lying whore.

For another few years she endured the sexual abuse. When she turned sixteen, she ran away from home. She lived on the streets for a while—shelters and the occasional friend's house, until she met Tom Greene. Almost immediately, Tom became her boyfriend, and he showered her with gifts. They also shared his bed. Ashley hadn't been aware of his addiction to alcohol, and when he'd come home in a drunken stupor, it always ended with him becoming physically abusive. She tried to get away on several occasions, but he'd always find her, and threaten that if she ever left him, he would kill her. Somehow, she stayed with him for a few years, mostly out of fear and because she had nowhere else to go. He owned her, as he told her so often, and, like a piece of property, he did as he pleased with her, however and whenever it suited him. Whatever Tom wanted; Tom got. If he wanted to have sex with her three or four times a day, she had to be submissive to him.

She had been under his watchful eye for so long that when she did finally leave, it took her over two months to finally start to feel free again. That was when she came across Manny, who hired her immediately. It didn't take long for him to request a blow job, and when she told him that she wouldn't, he got very angry with her and threatened to "fire her ass" as he had put it. She knew that there wasn't anywhere else she could go, so she did the only thing she could to survive.

As she thought about it now, it sickened her to know that she had been giving oral sex to men as early as ten years of age, starting from her stepfather, who was also responsible for taking her virginity at eleven. Now, here she was, at twenty-two, alone and in the hospital, unsure of what kind of future was in store for her. No one from work had even bothered to visit her, but she was aware of the detective's strict orders to the staff. She had been kept under watchful eyes, and she was grateful for the care she was receiving from everyone, particularly one nurse, Gayle Thorton. She was always there for her, including one night when she had woken up in a cold sweat, screaming and trembling. It was Gayle that had sat with her and comforted her the rest of the night. Gayle had stayed with her until she was finally able to fall asleep again, even long after her shift was up. It scared her to think that one day soon she'd be released from the hospital. She had nowhere to go and no one who cared, and it scared her.

—

Back at the Newman's, things were unusually quiet. After their "talk" night before, Nicole felt a little bit more than perplexed. It had felt good to get things out in the open, but her emotions were still raw. Listening to Jack open up about Jonathan's death was an enormous relief to her, since she hadn't been able to talk about him before without Jack getting upset. It felt like a ton of bricks had been lifted from her chest; but she felt the stab of betrayal when she thought about Jack's short but painful interaction with the young woman. Even though he had been honest with her, it still didn't change the fact that he had come so close to another woman—a woman he had just met. All Nicole had right now was his word, and if she was really being honest with herself, she had doubts about his whereabouts over the last year or so. She loved him, and she knew he loved her; last night proved that, even with all that was happening with them, they still shared a powerful chemistry together.

She thought about the young woman who was in the hospital and how she'd got there. Nicole knew Jack, and there was absolutely no way that he could've, or even would've, beaten and raped the girl. Not Jack! But then again, how did Nicole know that for sure? No! Her husband was not a beast. He had never in their entire marriage laid a hand on her, nor had he ever forced himself on her. Ever. This was all going to sort itself, and they would resume their lives again. She placed her hand on her stomach, noticing that there was now a physical bump there.

She was just over three months pregnant, and her clothes were fitting tighter on her.

"Nicole, you want some coffee?" Jack called from downstairs. He had woken before Nicole and was already in the middle of making breakfast.

"No, thanks," she called back from their bedroom. She was unsure of how to feel about him this morning. She dressed quickly and went downstairs. It was another beautiful sunny day, and the sun was shining through to the back of their house. Nicole had always loved mornings in their house; it was so cheerful and sunny. She only wished her mood matched the weather.

As she entered the kitchen, she smiled, noticing that the table was set for two. Jack had placed two coffee mugs, two juice glasses, and two plates holding bacon and eggs with toast. To top it all off, he had a small vase in the middle with a single red rose in it. She smiled once again at the obvious effort he had put into preparing a beautiful breakfast for two. "Wow! What's all this?" she asked, suddenly feeling famished.

"Well, I just thought we could have a nice breakfast," Jack answered as he pulled out a chair for her. "Besides, you didn't eat very much last night, Nick," he said as she sat down.

"I know," Nicole replied as he sat across from her. "It was a little unsettling to say the least." She placed a napkin on her lap.

Jack extended his hand from across the table, taking her hand into his own. "Nicole, you know that I love you, don't you?" he asked, his eyes fixed on her.

"Yes, I do. I love you too," she answered, gazing into his hazel eyes.

"Now, what do you say we eat breakfast and then head up north to Wasaga Beach. We could take our swimsuits and spend the day at the beach? What do you think?" he asked as he chewed on a piece of bacon.

"You know what? That sounds good to me! I think that a change in scenery will do us some good," she replied happily. "It's a beautiful day, that's for sure," she continued. "Jack, next week I'm scheduled to see the doctor about the baby and all. Would you like to come with me?" she asked, feeling hopeful.

"Sure, babe. I'll see what I can do with work. By the way, how are you feeling? Is the baby kicking yet?" Jack asked, taking a sip of coffee.

"No, not yet," Nicole answered, pulling up her shirt and giving him full view of her stomach. "But look, I'm actually showing! It feels so real now!" She beamed happily, stroking her stomach.

Jack got up from his chair, went to his wife, bent down, and kissed her tenderly on her growing belly. Then he got up and kissed her softly on her lips, tasting the lip gloss she had just applied moments ago. "We're going to be so happy, baby," he said, looking down into her crystal blue eyes. "All of this mess is going to blow over. I promise you that," he said with conviction. She nodded, wanting so desperately to believe him.

They finished up their breakfast, and they chatted easily about the baby they were expecting and all that was to come. Nicole almost felt complete, but the whole Ashley mess was looming over her like a dark cloud. She decided that, for the moment, all she could do was to be patient and enjoy the day with her husband. They cleaned up the kitchen after they ate, retrieved their swimsuits, towels, and a bottle of sunscreen, and headed up north to the beach. *It's all going to work out,* she thought to herself. Today they were going to enjoy the beautiful day that awaited them.

CHAPTER

25

Stephanie was back to square one, and she felt more humiliated than ever before. After she'd serviced Manny, he'd ordered her to get her "ass back to work." She didn't think that she had any choice, so she put on her apron and went out to the bar. Laurie approached Stephanie, wanting to talk to her, but the humiliation that Stephanie felt prevented her from looking Laurie in the eyes. Stephanie kept to herself for the rest of the day and served the patrons with little enthusiasm and minimal conversation. She couldn't believe what she'd gotten herself into. She wished she had never laid eyes on that low-life bastard of a boss, but she knew she had absolutely no choice in the matter. Stephanie just had to make sure that, from now on, she would protect herself with birth control. She most definitely didn't need another pregnancy, particularly with the scum she was working for. She needed to nail him somehow. She didn't know how, but somehow, she needed to get him for all his wrong doings. She was so lost in thought that she wasn't aware that Laurie had been talking to her.

"Steph, are you alright?" Laurie asked her at the bar.

"Yeah, I'm fine," she responded, lying to her. Who was she kidding? She wasn't fine at all. And yet, from what Stephanie observed, Laurie seemed to be more than OK. She assumed that Laurie would been just as distraught as she was, but that didn't seem to be the case. *Maybe he just laid off from her*, she thought to herself. "Laurie, excuse me please, but I've got to take an order," she said curtly, and before Laurie could respond, Stephanie was already at another table nearby taking a drink order. Laurie just shrugged and continued with her work.

Unbeknownst to Stephanie, Manny had already talked to Laurie about her future obligations to him and to whoever needed servicing. Manny was occasionally watching Stephanie's behavior at work, and he wasn't impressed by what he saw. She used to be an outgoing, flirtatious waitress that all the customers knew and loved, but today, she was cold and indifferent with the customers. He would talk to her at the end of her shift, but now, he had some dealings with Freddie that needed taking care of.

Freddie had been on his case for a while now, and Manny needed to come up with some money and fast. He sneered at the thought of putting his two top girls to work—there was no better time than the present. He would provide them each with a "customer," and he would arrange it for tonight. But first, he had to get another couple of girls to work the floor, since Stephanie and Laurie would be in the back room working. He had to make sure to hire a couple of age-appropriate girls to serve liquor since most of his current girls were underage. With the detective sniffing around so much, he didn't need any hassles.

Manny made a mental note to himself to hire a girl who was efficient with her job as a waitress. Now that he had Laurie and Stephanie taking care of other things, he didn't need to jeopardize himself with the other girls. He would be strictly professional, so to speak. With Laurie and Stephanie, all he had to do was make them snort some coke—shake things up a bit—and then they would be good to go.

Never in a million years had he ever thought he'd be in this kind of business, but if it all worked out the way that he planned, then he'd be sitting on a gold mine. It would be easy for him to get a few johns for the girls, and he'd benefit from it all, big time! They wouldn't need to waitress anymore, since they'd be busy enough with their other duties. He snickered as he walked to his office and proceeded to make a couple of phone calls.

—

It was late afternoon, and Steven Fromer had just finished helping his grown daughter move the last of her things into her new apartment. It had been a long day for him, and he plopped himself on his La-Z-Boy at home and cracked open a cold beer as he contemplated the whole Ashley case. There were still some holes in the case, but all the evidence so far pointed to Jack Newman. Jack's story seemed justifiable, he reasoned with himself, but there was no concrete evidence to prove that he didn't do it. After meeting with him a week ago, Fromer had sensed that he was a family man, but he also recalled the anger that he'd witnessed when confronting Jack. Detective Fromer decided that he had enough evidence to arrest him. He assumed that it wasn't going to go well, since he hadn't even communicated with Jack since the questioning.

He could picture the scenario that went down between Jack and Ashley: They are attracted to one another, and they go to the nearby park to "get to know each other better." Jack receives a phone call from his wife, and so Ashley changes her mind. Jack doesn't take well to rejection and tries to be forceful; Ashley gets angry and slaps him. His anger gets out of control, and he decides he's going to get what he wants, with or without her permission.

Fromer took a swig from his beer as he continued to play out the possible scenario that could have gone down between the two. Ashley probably put up a good fight, and that's when Jack lost it and beat the crap out of her in hopes of killing her, of course. But then again, why would he bother to put a mask on? Maybe he'd left her, like he said when he was questioned, but decided to go back to her, wearing a mask that he kept in his truck, and teach her a lesson that she'd never forget. Although, according to Jack, he put the brakes on after he received the phone call from his wife, Ashley got upset, they had words, and she slapped him. Then she ended up getting raped and beaten. Either way, Jack had been the only one at the park with Ashley, except for the cab driver who saw them arguing from a distance. The cabby witnessed her slapping him and left the two alone, not thinking anything serious was about to take place. Jack had no other alibi to support his story. He had told his wife that he was getting a couple of quotes, which was work related, but he was with Ashley at the park, taking inventory of his own. Fromer needed to deal with this, and he knew it wasn't going to be easy.

———

Back at the hospital, Ashley had just been given the news that she was going to be released the next day. Her body had almost fully recovered from the assault, and physically, she looked like any other girl off the street. She thought she'd be thrilled to receive the news, but surprisingly, she wasn't. In the hospital, she felt safe and taken care of, which was something she hadn't ever experienced in her life. It was always about surviving, taking it one day at a time, and now she'd been told by her doctor that she was free to leave. The problem was, where would she go? She had no family, and the room that she had been renting from a friend no longer existed. Ashley's roommate and so called "friend" had sent her a text message telling her that she could no longer stay there, and since Ashley was paying for her room on a monthly basis, there was no lease involved, therefore, her hands were tied. She just had to get over there and pick up her personal belongings, which were basically her clothes and makeup. She had nothing else. She looked solemn when her nurse came in to see her.

"Well! How is my favorite patient doing today?" asked Gayle Thorton, beaming.

"OK, I guess," Ashley responded with little enthusiasm. "And what about you?" she asked her nurse, who was really the only person on the face of the earth that gave a damn about her.

"I am thrilled! I've just been told of your release tomorrow!" she said with great spirit.

"Oh, so you've heard," Ashley replied, looking down at her hands. She really didn't want to leave the only place that offered her comfort. The truth was, she was terrified, knowing that she had nowhere to go.

"Of course I know!" Gayle smiled at her young patient. She went over to the other side of Ashley's bed and sat down beside her. "Ashley, honey, I'm so happy you're finally healthy enough to leave this place," she said with motherly tenderness. Ashley just kept her head down, staring at her hands. "I'm also aware that you don't have anywhere to go, am I right?" Gayle asked her, trying to get some eye contact with her.

"Yeah, I suppose you're right," Ashley said in a low voice, her eyes glued to her hands that were folded in front of her.

Gayle took Ashley's hands gently and held them in her own as she lowered her voice to her. "Ashley, honey, I've been thinking. I knew this day would come. And since the day you were brought in here and placed in my care, I've grown very fond of you," Gayle squeezed Ashley's hands and continued. "I'm going to share something with you, something very personal. I once had a little girl, my only child, and I loved her very much," she said quietly as Ashley lifted her head and gazed into Gayle's eyes with surprise.

"What happened to her? Your little girl I mean?" Ashley asked in wonder, her eyes as big as saucers.

Gayle cleared her throat as she continued, her eyes brimming with tears. "My daughter's name was Rebecca, and she was five years old when she was diagnosed with leukemia," she continued. Ashley raised her eyebrows in great surprise. "Anyway, to make a long story short, she was very sick for a long time, being in and out of the hospital, until finally, she passed away. Rebecca was only thirteen years old. I loved her very much, and I miss her a great deal," she continued as she wiped her eyes. "There isn't a day that goes by that I don't think about her. She was my universe. I had dreams of being there for her for high school graduation and, of course, her wedding day. I will obviously never get a chance to experience any of those things with her, and countless other things that a parent has the privilege of experiencing with her only daughter, which brings me to you Ashley," she said, clearing her throat, looking directly into Ashley's eyes.

"How long ago did she die?" Ashley asked sympathetically, forgetting for a moment about her own problems, her heart going out to the person who had nursed her back to health and held her late at night when she would waken from her nightmares.

"Rebecca died ten years ago. She would've been twenty-three years old right now," Gayle said, wiping her eyes as she thought of her. "Ashley, honey, I know that I'm not your mother. Heck, I'm not even related to you," she continued, giving a short laugh. "Anyway, I've come to care about you a lot, and I know that you're not a little girl, but I was just thinking that maybe, just maybe, you could come and live with me and my cat. His name is Simon." Ashley sat dumbfounded by what she was hearing. "I wouldn't mind having someone around, and I just thought that since you didn't have anywhere to go, well, maybe you'd come and live with me," Gayle said hopefully. "I wouldn't try to be your mom, although I honestly wouldn't mind having a daughter like you. And maybe, in time, you could think of me as your mom, if you wanted to that is," she said, looking intently at Ashley, wanting desperately for Ashley to agree to come and live with her. She had grown to love the young woman that she'd cared for over the past few weeks. "I don't expect you to answer me right now, but—"

"Yes," Ashley said simply, interrupting the amazing woman that sat before her. "I would love to come and live with you," she said, her voice breaking, her eyes brimming with tears.

"Really?" Gayle asked, taken by surprise. Ashley nodded in agreement. "Oh, Ashley, honey, I'm so happy! I promise you; you won't regret it!" she exclaimed happily. The two women embraced. There were tears in Gayle's eyes, and when they released their embrace, Gayle noticed that Ashley, too, was glassy-eyed.

"Thank you, Gayle! Thank you so much for your generosity," Ashley said as she wiped some fresh tears from her face. "You don't know how much this means to me."

"Honey, the way I see it, we're going to get along just fine. Now wipe those tears off your beautiful face, and give me a hug," Gayle said with excitement. Ashley got up from her bed and hugged Gayle, feeling the closest that she'd ever felt with anyone. She knew in her heart that this woman, the nurse that opened her heart and her home to her, would always have a special place in Ashley's heart. As the two women hugged for what seemed like an eternity, Ashley couldn't help but think of this experience with Gayle as unmistakably karma. She had always believed in karma. Everything happened for a reason; and the only thing that Ashley felt certain of at this very moment was that she felt safer and more loved than she had ever felt in her life.

26

The drive home from Wasaga Beach was only a couple of hours, and Nicole felt a quiet tranquility within her. Her and Jack had sunbathed in the hot sun and swum in the lake, splashing one another like two children, laughing and teasing each other. They'd had lunch on the boardwalk and then taken a long walk on the beach, hand in hand, like two people in love. It was a beautiful day, and the beach had been swamped with people, but they hadn't minded. It had been good for them to get out of the city and get the fresh north air that always seemed to give one's mind more clarity. As they drove home, Nicole couldn't help but feel lighthearted—the stress of the past week had started to wear her down. She glanced over to her husband, who was driving, and he glanced back at her, sporting his most handsome smile. He held her hand as they drove, one of their favorite songs playing in the background.

"I had a great day," Nicole said quietly, feeling sleepy.

"I did too. I love you," Jack replied, squeezing her hand as they drove down Airport Road.

"Love you more," she said, her eyelids feeling heavy as she started to drift off. She leaned her head to the side as Jack drove.

He continued to drive up and down the hilly road and smiled to himself as he glanced over to his sleeping wife, who looked so peaceful sleeping next to him. Jack turned his focus to the rest of the drive home, which, judging by the traffic that was starting to build up, was likely going to be at least a couple of hours, if not more.

—

Manny had been busy in his office that Sunday afternoon, planning for the evening. Business had been pretty good considering that it was summer, and he smiled slyly, as he anticipated a very productive evening for Stephanie. He had spoken to Freddie and invited him to come into his office for a drink. Freddie naturally assumed that he'd be receiving the money he was so anxiously waiting for, as his patience was starting to wear thin. Manny reassured him that it wouldn't be long before he got his money and had explained to him that he wanted to give him an incentive for his patience. Manny licked his lips as he thought about the plan he had in mind. He was certain that a blow job from Stephanie, perhaps a little more, would be just enough to get Freddie off his back, for a little while at least. What better way to "help" his "friend" in his time of need. In the meantime, Manny had a little stash of coke in his drawer. It would help Stephanie perk up a bit. Since their little talk, she had been more than a little uptight with him, and he needed her to be more cooperative. Tonight, he thought, would be the beginning of his new and improved business.

Stephanie had been busy from the moment she stepped foot in the bar, starting with the talk she'd had with her boss, which led to her giving him oral sex. It disgusted her to the core every time she thought about the new demand, he had placed on her, and it made her even more anxious, as she didn't know when or where he would come from, or what was expected of her. Manny had spent the better part of the day in his office, which worried her more than a little, and she and Laurie took care of the front, with Phil at the bar. She felt sick at the thought of her having to "service" anyone for money. What Manny was suggesting was prostitution, and it sickened her like nothing else. Stephanie was obviously nothing more than a whore, otherwise she wouldn't have been putting herself out there for him, or anyone. She couldn't believe that her life had come to this! One thing was for sure: she had to go on birth control, because the last thing she needed was another pregnancy from some guy who just used her for his own sexual interest.

As she wiped down the last table, she noticed a short, straggly man walk into the restaurant. After a moment, she approached him, all the while thinking that she couldn't wait to get the hell out of there.

"Hi, can I get you anything?" she asked him, pasting a fake smile.

"Yeah, sure, babe. Get me a beer," he responded, sneering at her. He wanted his drink before he met up with Manny. "Oh, by the way, toots, where's your boss?" he asked her directly.

"Umm, he's in his office. Is he expecting you?" she asked, wondering who he was and what connection he had with her boss.

"Oh yeah, he's expecting me alright. See if you could get him for me, will ya?" he asked, making Stephanie's skin crawl. She had never seen this man before, and she wondered what he could possibly want with Manny. Suddenly, an eerie feeling overcame her, making her want to vomit.

"Um, sure. I won't be long," she replied, trying to signal Laurie to get Manny from the office. Laurie, however, was busy talking to a gentleman that she was waiting on. With an air of annoyance, Stephanie reluctantly marched down the long corridor to Manny's office. She quietly knocked on the door, not wanting to disturb him, and when there was no answer, she slowly opened the door. To her surprise, there was Manny, just sitting at his desk as if expecting her and smiling. "Um, Manny, there's a man at the front asking for you," she said nervously.

"Is he a short, straggly little thing?" Manny asked her sarcastically. She nodded, surprised he'd used the exact description she had mentally made of the man.

Manny stood up from his chair and walked over to her. "Well, Steph, it looks like you're ready for a little treat." He snickered. "Come here, sweetheart, over by the couch." He smirked at her. "You've worked really hard today, haven't you?" he asked her as he led her to the couch, making her sit. He pulled out a little white pouch from his pocket, and when she shook her head to protest, he violently grabbed a fistful of her hair, making her body shake with terror. With his index finger, he put some of the white powder on the top of his hand. She was frozen in shock as he forcefully shoved her face to the white powder. She rejected it, spitting it out of her mouth toward Manny's face. He wiped his face with one sharp swipe and slapped her hard across her face. "You stupid bitch!" he yelled in her face. "Do you have any idea how much these costs?" He spat at her as she looked up at him in horror, her hand on her throbbing cheek where she had just been slapped. "Now, snort it slowly, and do it right, you hear?" Again, he forced her head down to the palm of his hand where a speckle of white powder awaited her, and this time, she did as she was told. Stephanie had never done cocaine before, and she was mortified as she incompetently snorted the substance against her will. Manny's other hand was on the back of her head, firmly holding her face down, making sure she snorted it all. She tried to resist, but he held her down roughly. She tried to breath but couldn't. When he was satisfied with her, he roughly tilted her head up for some fresh air and smiled slyly at the residue that lay on the top of her lip and around her nostrils. Tears stung her eyes, and she felt trapped, like an animal. She was aware of what he was doing to her but felt powerless against his strength.

"I want to go home!" she cried. "Please, let me go home!" she repeated over and over again as the tears escaped down her cheeks.

"Oh, sweetheart, you ain't going anywhere right now." Manny sneered. "Why, the fun is just beginning!" He laughed as he watched her. "Listen, you sit tight, and I'll be back in a jiffy." He felt a rush of anticipation at what was about to transpire. Her eyes were as wide as saucers, and the fear she displayed only increased his need for control.

Stephanie wanted to get up and bolt, but fear overtook her. She had never in her life taken drugs, and she felt frozen in fear. She didn't move for fear that he'd hurt her even more. She didn't know what to expect or what he had in mind to do with her. She sat on the couch as she awaited her fate, feeling extremely anxious. Her heart was racing, and her body started to tingle all over with euphoria. She wasn't sure if it was the drug, he'd just forced on her or if it was sheer panic that was surging within her.

It didn't take long for Manny to return with the man she'd served just minutes ago. They walked into the room, both smiling from ear to ear as Manny instructed her to remove her clothes. She tried to protest but found she couldn't. Somehow, Manny had claimed her soul.

"Come on, man! Is this a fucking joke?" the short, straggly man sneered with obvious annoyance.

"No! I told you, Freddie, she does as she's told." Manny replied angrily. "Stephanie, I said take off your clothes!" he ordered, his eyes narrowing toward her. "Now!"

Stephanie tried to remove her blouse, but her fingers were trembling, and she found she couldn't. Manny stepped in and roughly removed her shirt, exposing her top half, revealing her black lace bra. He pushed her back on the couch and pulled down her black pants, revealing her matching black panties. Freddie licked his lips hungrily at the sight of her, staring at the young woman's body like a dog in heat. He had been promised a good time, and a good time he was going to have! Stephanie's eyes grew wide as the realization of it all hit her like a ton of bricks. Manny was fully expecting her to have sex with this stranger, and she couldn't do anything about it.

"Go ahead, buddy. She's all yours." Manny sneered. "Do whatever you want with her, man. She can take it! She's been doing me for several years, haven't you, sweetheart?" He snickered.

Stephanie was mortified beyond belief, but knew Manny was right. She was his whore, and it didn't make a difference if she had sex at the street corner or right there in his office. A whore is what she must be, otherwise she wouldn't have been in this compromising position. Her body continued to tingle, and a surprising rush of excitement went through her like electricity, causing her to feel less anxious as Freddie approached her. His beady eyes were cemented on her as he removed his pants and underwear in one swift move. He walked right up to her and placed his dirty penis up and around her face as he sneered at her. He held his limp penis and circled it around her mouth for a few seconds before separating her lips and inserting it in her mouth, making her gasp. She finally did what was required of her as he went in and out of her with fury. Surprisingly, she sat up more comfortably, cupped his growing penis with one hand, and sucked him fiercely, feeling a sudden wave of superiority. She was going to give him the best blow job that he'd ever had, and she was feeling very stimulated by pleasuring him. Freddie grabbed her breasts, squeezing them hard while she continued to pleasure him orally, and it was at that point that Manny, satisfied by what he'd witnessed, decided to leave them alone and go out into the bar area.

Manny made himself a scotch, slurping it slowly, feeling like he was on top of the world. He couldn't believe how easy it was to get Stephanie to comply. He had big plans for her and keeping her was going to make him a shitload of money. He knew enough men to keep Stephanie busy every night; the coke was the key to getting what he wanted. He smiled as he lifted the glass to his lips and swallowed the last of the scotch. He visualized Stephanie blowing Freddie. She was a little vixen alright, and he was going to enjoy having her around. The little that he'd witnessed made him horny as hell, and he'd make sure that she gave him a little action before the night was over. After all, it was his idea in the first place!

CHAPTER

27

aurie was wiping down the last table. She turned around, only to see her boss at the bar with a smirk on his face as he raised his glass to her. She turned away quickly and continued with her side duties, not wanting any attention drawn to her. She wondered what had happened to Stephanie, since she had been in Manny's office for a while now. Stephanie had her own side duties to do before her shift ended, and Laurie was curious as to what was holding her up and if she was alright. She felt Manny's beady eyes on her, and it made her feel uneasy since she and her boss were the only two people left in the restaurant. Phil had left a little while ago, and Stephanie was down the hall in the office doing God knows what; but Laurie didn't want to stick around to find out.

Manny smiled at the prospect of Laurie being included in his newfound business. She would make him a killing—both girls were very attractive, and they had killer bodies. He glanced down at his watch and noticed that it had been about twenty minutes since he'd left Freddie with Stephanie. He decided he would go back, whether they were finished or not.

When he opened the door to his office, Stephanie was lying on the couch totally naked, and Freddie was standing in front of her pulling up his pants, sporting an ugly smile on his face, obviously satisfied with the sexual escapade he'd just experienced. He turned to see Manny, who looked equally pleased.

"Thanks, man! You weren't kidding about her," Freddie said as he zipped up his trousers. "Tell you what," he continued, "I'll keep you supplied as long as I get what I want when I want it." He glanced in Stephanie's direction.

"As long as you keep your end of the bargain and keep me fully stocked, we shouldn't have any problems. Stephanie here won't mind at all, isn't that right, sweetheart?" Manny said, turning to look at her. She just lay back on the couch, wide-eyed, her long shapely legs open, her belly and her face covered with semen. She was obviously in no shape to go home, so Manny decided he would take her to his place for the night. The thought of her staying with him and sharing his bed delighted him. He'd have to get her some decent clothes and feed her well, since he didn't want her dissolving to nothing but skin and bones! He needed her to look good if she was going to make him some money.

The two men exchanged their goodbyes, and Freddie exited from the back door. Manny ordered Stephanie, who hadn't moved since he'd entered the room, to clean herself up and change back into her clothes, which were sprawled across the floor.

He went out to the bar area and let Laurie go home for the night, making sure she'd be in the next evening. He called for Stephanie, who was still cleaning herself up, and told her that she'd be staying at his place for a while, and she nodded obediently.

Manny closed the bar and Stephanie followed him to his car. He unlocked it and shoved her roughly inside. He drove out of the parking lot and made his way to his condominium, which was less than a kilometer away. His condo was on the first floor, so he didn't have to worry about getting her in an elevator with a bunch of strangers. Attracting a lot of attention to himself and to her was most definitely not on his agenda, so living on the first level was ideal. Yeah, this was going to work out beautifully!

CHAPTER

28

rriving home, Jack pulled up in their driveway and glanced at his wife, who had been sleeping soundly beside him for the past half hour. It had been a long day, and he too was exhausted from the day on the beach. He reached over and gently stroked her hair, letting her know that they had arrived home. Nicole stirred and sleepily looked in his direction. She smiled at him, and he leaned over toward her, planting a kiss on her temple. "We're home, sleepyhead," he said warmly. "You go on inside, and I'll bring the stuff in." She nodded, got out of the car, and proceeded to walk up to their front door while Jack collected their beach bag from the trunk.

The sound of a car pulling up right behind him just as he locked the car prompted Jack to turn around. It was just after ten thirty, and Jack was puzzled as to who was visiting them at this hour of the night, since they weren't expecting anyone. As she was unlocking the front door, Nicole also turned to see who'd pulled up in their driveway. Curiosity got the better of her, and she walked back toward her husband. She figured it must be someone stopping to ask for directions. A man got out of the car and took two steps toward them, where the house pot lights shone on him, revealing Detective Fromer. Nicole suddenly felt like she was going to be sick.

"Good evening, Mr. and Mrs. Newman," Steven Fromer said politely.

"What's going on, Detective?" Jack asked, not appreciating the impromptu visit.

"I'm afraid I've got some bad news for you, Mr. Newman," he answered. Jack stood frozen in his tracks. "I have a warrant for your arrest—"

"What the fuck!" Jack interrupted just as a police cruiser pulled up behind the Detective's car.

"Oh my God!" Nicole cried, looking over to her husband and then back at the unwelcome intruder who was about to turn her life upside down.

"Like I said," Fromer continued. "You're under arrest for aggravated sexual assault. You have the right to remain silent. Anything you say or do can be used against you in a court of law. You have the right to an attorney. If you don't have one, one will be provided to you. Do you understand?" Steven Fromer said in a monotone, as if reading from a script, while Jack stood dumbfounded.

"Oh my God, Jack!" Nicole cried in shock.

"Are you insane?" Jack shouted, holding his head. "What the fuck are—"

"Jack, don't say anything!" Nicole cried as she ran to her husband while the Detective pulled out his handcuffs.

"No!" she cried out in desperation.

"Nicole! Calm down!" Jack shouted at her just as the detective put his hands behind his back and handcuffed him. The other officer took Jack and led him to the cruiser, which was parked right behind the detective. The officer opened the door to the back of the police car and, with his hand on the top of Jack's head, gently pushed him into the back seat. Jack felt powerless as the car door slammed shut beside him. From the inside of the cruiser, Jack looked out at his pregnant wife, completely shut out from her and unable to calm her as she clawed at the window that separated them. She was visibly upset and crying uncontrollably. It only took a moment before the officer got into the driver's seat and drove off to the station. Nicole looked on with tears streaming down her face.

Detective Fromer tried to console Nicole, who was sobbing, but she was inconsolable. It wasn't in his nature to just leave a young woman outside that late at night in the emotional state she was in, and when he tried to get her to enter her house, she told him where to go. She was angry and upset—understandably so—but he insisted she get in the house for her own safety, no matter what she thought of him. She finally surrendered and let herself in, slamming the door in his face. He understood her other half would be just as hostile, but that wasn't his problem. He'd had a job to do, and he'd done it.

29

*I*t was Monday morning, and Ashley was feeling lighthearted. Ever since her chat with her nurse, she'd felt more at ease. She didn't feel so alone anymore, and the prospect of living with Gayle had brightened her mood. She felt more alive and unusually calm this morning, and she couldn't wait to resume her life once again; this would be a new start, a new chapter. All her life she'd felt afraid and anxious, always looking over her shoulder, and now Gayle, the one person who cared for her and nursed her back to health, was opening her heart and home to her. It was nothing short of a miracle, and she couldn't be happier.

Ashley was supposed to be released some time midmorning, and although it was Gayle's day off from the hospital, she was going to pick Ashley up and take her to her home—a place where she would be safe. Ashley stood at the window and looked outside. It was July the first, Canada Day, and it was a beautiful day. The sun was already shining, promising another perfect day; the sky was baby blue, and from where she was standing, the grounds were well kept and beautifully manicured.

So far, the summer weather had been magnificent, with promising sunshine every day, but somehow, today felt different. It seemed even sunnier to her, and she put her hands on her hips and took a deep breath in, basking in the glory that she felt within her soul. It wasn't just Canada's birthday today—it was the first official day of her happiness. One thing she knew for sure was that living with Gayle would be everything she never knew existed. The two women had bonded, blood-related or not, and Ashley knew that she could never repay Gayle for all she had done for her and all she continued to do for her. Gayle had told her that she would be bringing Ashley a change of clothes before leaving the hospital since the clothes that she had worn the day of the attack were ripped to shreds. All Ashley had now was a hospital gown and a robe that Gayle had bought her.

"Good morning, sweetheart!" Gayle's bubbly voice interrupted her thoughts, prompting Ashley to turn around and face the woman who had already changed her life for the better. "And how are you this morning?" she asked as she approached Ashley, giving her a warm hug.

"I'm good … really good," she responded, smiling from ear to ear.

"Are you all ready to go, my dear?" Gayle asked her, stroking Ashley's hair.

"Ready as I'll ever be," she replied beaming.

"Here, I brought you a pair of shorts and a T-shirt that I think should fit you," Gayle said, beaming proudly as she removed some new clothes from an H&M bag with the tags still on them. "You're pretty small, so I hope these aren't too big," she said, laughing as she placed them on Ashley's body to check for size.

"No. I think they should be fine," Ashley replied, thankful to Gayle for being so thoughtful. The shorts were plain and black in color, and the T-shirt was a cotton blend, a V-neck in a shade of pale blue.

"Here, I also bought you a pair of flip-flops. I hope you like them; my niece helped me pick them," Gayle said as she pulled out a pair of black flip-flops that were perfect for this time of year. "She says that these are very popular with you young kids." She laughed.

"Jeez! Are you going to pull out a rabbit from there?" Ashley laughed good heartedly. "Gayle, thank you so much! Really, this was very nice of you. I don't know how I could ever repay you for your kindness," she said as her eyes started to brim with tears.

"Come on now. There's no need for tears today," Gayle responded, giving her a quick hug. "Your release papers are done, so we're good to go! Why don't you go on and change out of that gown, and we could go out and have some breakfast," she said enthusiastically. "Then, we can hit a mall and do a little shopping for you. Can't have you running around in nothing but these shorts and a T-shirt, can we?" she said giving her a friendly wink.

"Thanks, Gayle!" Ashley responded graciously, taking her new clothes from Gayle and happily heading for the bathroom. It was the first day of her new life. She had been miraculously given a second chance at happiness and a feeling of belonging.

CHAPTER

30

The night was exceptionally long for Nicole, but it was even longer for Jack. Once taken to the police station, he was fingerprinted, and his picture was taken. He was furious with them, but he had no choice but to cooperate. They put him in a cell on his own, about four by eight in size, and it was cold. All there was inside a sink and a toilet and a steel slab, which was his bed. There was no window, therefore no light, except for a small lightbulb hanging from the ceiling. He didn't sleep all night as he sat on the cold steel slab with his head between his legs. His mind and heart were racing; he wondered how the hell he'd gotten himself in this mess. Thoughts of Ashley raced through his mind as anger engulfed him. Retracing the events of that fateful night, regret hit him like a ton of bricks. If only he hadn't left the bar with her! He was angry with himself, and he was furious with her as he pondered her statement to the detective. She must've accused him, there was no other explanation for him spending the night in jail. He thought of Nicole and the emotional state that she had been in when he was taken away. He hoped to God that she was alright, especially since she was carrying his baby; but for the moment all he could do was wait, and his patience was wearing thin. He felt like he was in the middle of a nightmare, only he wasn't sleeping. This nightmare was real. He had been told that he had to wait until the next day at nine o'clock in the morning for his bail hearing, which gave him ample time to panic in fear and anxiety. He sat motionless till dawn, awaiting his fate.

If the night was—and it was painfully long—Jack survived his night in jail, and he was looking forward to being released. He had spent one night in jail, and even though he hadn't shut his eyes all night, he was wide awake and was already feeling nostalgic. He wanted desperately to see Nicole. He was sure that the night hadn't been a bed of roses for her either.

It didn't take very long in court. Fortunately for Jack, Nicole had come up with the bail money thanks to their savings and the help of her sister, Sara, and James. When Nicole had called them in hysterics the night before to tell them what had happened, they'd driven to her house immediately. Nicole had been completely beside herself, and it had taken both Sara and James to calm her down. They had reassured her that they were there for her and didn't believe that Jack was guilty. They'd reminded her how much Jack loved her, and that she should hang on to his love, and that everything would be alright. Sara had been particularly worried about her little sister since Nicole's life had been nothing short of a rollercoaster in the past two years. James had left after a couple of hours, but Sara had stayed with her all night. Sara had wanted to let their mother know what was going on with her youngest daughter but had decided against it. Noreen already had her hands full with taking care of their father, and she didn't need the extra stress in her life. Both James and Sara had promised to help Nicole out with the bail money, which was one hundred thousand dollars.

Jack was allowed to go back home, carry on with his life, and go to work, but he was to stay away from Ashley. He was not to be anywhere near her at any time until his court date, which was set for the following March. For the moment, he didn't care. He was just thrilled to go home to his wife.

They drove home in silence, both lost in their own thoughts. Nicole was quiet, and although she was relieved that Jack hadn't been kept in jail, she knew that the rest of her pregnancy would be a stressful one, with the court date looming over their heads. Life had not been easy for them lately, and she had to keep telling herself that she had a baby growing inside of her, which meant that she had to do everything in her power to take better care of herself. In her heart, she knew that Jack was innocent; but why was he the only suspect in this heinous crime? Life just didn't seem fair! But who said life was fair?

—

The rest of the summer flew by, and it was already into fall. The hot summer days and warm nights were replaced with crisp mornings and cool nights. Labor Day had come and gone, and the children were back at school. Fortunately for Nicole, she had her work at the salon to keep her mind occupied and get her through the days. She never mentioned anything to her coworkers about her situation, except for Diane. She trusted Diane to keep her secret, and it was nice to be able to confide in her. Diane's relationship with her live-in boyfriend was deteriorating, but Nicole always tried to encourage her, nonetheless. It helped her to focus on someone else rather than her own problems. By then, everyone at the salon knew about her pregnancy since she was just over five months pregnant. She went to her monthly doctor's appointments, and even with everything that was going on, her baby was thriving, and that was the only thing that mattered. Nicole worried about the future—the upcoming court date that was just a few months away. Would Jack be around for her and their baby, or would he be in jail serving time for a crime he didn't commit? Would she have to raise her baby all on her own? She wasn't prepared to do that, and every time she had these thoughts, she had to remind herself how much they loved each other.

In retrospect, Jack did everything in his power to remind his wife how much he loved her. Every day after work, he'd stop and pick her up some fresh flowers. He wasn't sure how long he had his freedom, and he wasn't about to waste any of it. He needed his wife to know how much she meant to him, and it was imperative that she carried their child to full term. He wouldn't be able to live with himself if anything happened to their baby, and for now, he just had to keep going. Jack continued to go to work and carry on as usual, and he would even start dinner on the odd days that he came home before her. Nicole was always grateful, but Jack felt that she was holding back. She seemed happy on the surface, but he was worried about her. He went with her to most of her doctor's appointments with her obstetrician, which wasn't always easy to do with his job; but his wife and baby were his top priority. He always looked forward to hearing their baby's heartbeat at each appointment, and it warmed his heart to the core when he thought about his new son or daughter coming into the world in just a few months. They even made love once or twice a week, but the passion they'd shared was replaced by fear—fear of the outcome of their future. At first, he thought it was just her pregnancy hormones, but he sensed there was more. They carried on like any normal married couple, and from the outside, their life seemed perfect. Only it wasn't, and he suspected it wouldn't be until he was cleared from this nightmare that plagued them.

31

$\mathcal{M}$anny smiled as he counted the dough. Once again, Stephanie had come through for him. He had the world by its balls, and nothing or no one was going to stop him. Stephanie was doing roughly two men every night, with his help of course. She had been living with him since the middle of June, which suited him just fine. She shared his bed and did what she was told. Stephanie no longer fought him on the guys he paraded into the bar every night. She would wait in the office, have a few lines of coke, and the party would begin. At first Manny thought he'd use Laurie to do the same, but she was needed more in the restaurant now that she was his top waitress. Between Phil and Laurie, the front was practically running itself. Freddie still supplied ample drugs to Manny, only now it wasn't just cocaine but crystal meth. Stephanie had grown quite dependent on it, which worried Manny somewhat—not because he cared for her well-being, but rather, he was concerned about her being strung out all the time.

There were the regulars, some from his drug dealings and others who were married but needed something extra on the side. Manny made it clear to the men that they needed to wear protection, and, as well, he had Stephanie on birth control. He didn't need her getting pregnant or getting some deadly disease. He needed to have her relatively healthy, apart from the drugs that she had grown so fond of.

He owned her and controlled her like a puppet, and she knew it. Stephanie wouldn't dare try to defy him, especially since he had almost beat her senselessly a couple of months before when she had threatened to report him to the police. She had been just coming down from a high, and she had been in the bathroom when she'd started screaming. Reality of what her life had become had suddenly hit her, and when Manny had entered the bathroom, she had been hunched over on the toilet seat with a razor in her hand, contemplating slitting her wrist. Manny had grabbed the razor from her hand and slapped her hard, sending her reeling across the floor. And when she'd stood up, she had been full of rage and remorse. Stephanie had continued to cry and scream at him over what he'd done to her, completely hysterical, all the while threatening to report him, and that was when he'd lost it. He'd slapped and punched her so hard that, by the time he'd been finished with her, she'd been unrecognizable—her face covered in blood and her lips and eyes doubled in size.

Manny had kept her at his place for the next few days, letting her recover, before he'd brought her back to work. He didn't need her in hysterics in the presence of his employees or her customers. He'd made sure she stayed in by taking her cell phone and locking her inside his apartment. Manny had brought her food every day, and when she'd begged him for a hit, he'd made her wait another couple of days before giving her the drug she so desperately craved. Stephanie had been like a deranged animal by the time he'd given her the cocaine. He hadn't been about to give in to her addiction that easy. As a matter of fact, she'd then apologized for her outburst, and even given him a blow job for her gratefulness. Oh yeah! It was too easy with her.

—

Ashley was thriving day by day. Living with Gayle proved to be everything she'd hoped for—and more. Gayle was able to pull some strings at the hospital, getting her some part-time work at the gift shop. When they were home, they would usually have dinner, pop some popcorn, and watch a movie together. A few times, they went out for supper—simple outings like burger places or Pizza Hut. They visited the CN Tower together, and another time, they spent the day at Niagara Falls, which was one place that Ashley had never visited. They also went to Canada's Wonderland, which turned out to be a wild day for both. They went on all the rides and enjoyed all the events that the park had to offer. It was a day filled with fun and laughter, which was something that Ashley had never experienced before. She had always lived in fear, and now all she felt was pure joy and stability.

The summer was just as wonderful for Gayle as it was for Ashley, since they spent practically all their free time together. They truly bonded, and even though Gayle was old enough to be Ashley's mother, the age difference fulfilled a need for both. Gayle desperately missed doting on a daughter, and Ashley desperately needed a mother figure to take care of her and love her. They fit together like a hand in glove, and they enjoyed each other's company. Ashley finally felt a sense of belonging, living with Gayle, and even though there was over two decades between them, Ashley never felt like she was missing out on anything with people her own age. Gayle tried on numerous occasions to persuade her to go out with a couple of other girls that worked with her at the gift shop, but Ashley had no interest. She never even bothered to go to The Blue Lagoon to see her coworkers. She had only been working there for a couple of months, and she never heard from any of them. Ashley's mission was to try to clear from her mind that fateful, horrible day. Her nightmares had subsided somewhat, but from time to time, she would still wake up in a cold sweat, only now her nightmares included the molestations from her stepfather and the abuse she'd endured from her boyfriend. Gayle reassured her that, over time, her nightmares would subside. She even talked to Ashley about seeking a therapist, a professional to talk to, but Ashley wasn't interested. Gayle was all that she needed. Trusting anyone else was going to take time. A lifetime perhaps.

Over the course of the summer, Ashley confided to Gayle about her ugly and painful past; Gayle was incredibly sympathetic and supportive, and most importantly, nonjudgmental. Ashley had always felt that somehow everything that had happened was her fault. Gayle continued to give Ashley the support that she so desperately needed, telling her all the while that she wasn't responsible for any of the abuse that she had endured. Gayle found it incomprehensible that a mother could turn her back on her own daughter. It was the love Gayle had had for her own daughter—and lost—that she was able to give wholeheartedly to Ashley.

32

Nicole was walking into work, admiring the decorations that were already displayed throughout the mall. It was nearing Christmas, and everyone was busy with the holiday bustle. Even Santa Claus had a place in the mall—the elves and parents lined up with their small children, dressed up in bright holiday colors, waiting to get their pictures taken with Santa. People were everywhere, and almost everyone had shopping bags in their hands. It had always been Nicole's favorite time of year, until her son passed away. Now she smiled as she thought of the baby that was soon to arrive, after the holidays. She had already made plans to stop working when the holidays were over, since that put her in the beginning of her ninth month. Her baby was due to be born sometime in the middle of January, and her pregnant belly had grown considerably for her tall but slim frame. The holiday music was playing throughout the mall, and as she entered the salon, she was smiling from ear to ear.

"Hey, look who's here! It's Mrs. Claus herself," Tony, her boss, said cheerfully while cashing out a client.

"Very funny!" Nicole responded playfully as she checked the appointment book at the front desk. He wasn't far from the truth though. She really did feel as big as a house, with her protruding eight-month belly.

"You sure you can still do hair, Nikki?" he asked, chuckling. "I mean, look at you, girl! You look like you're going to deliver any minute," he teased.

"Don't worry your curly head," she replied. The truth was, it was very difficult for her to do shampoos and haircuts since her belly came between her and her client, and it had become increasingly hard on her back. "Actually, I think this is going to be my final week, and then I'm going on maternity leave." She announced, holding her stomach with one hand, and her lower back with the other.

"Ya think?" he asked playfully, wondering how she'd even managed so far.

"What's this I hear? You're finishing the end of the week?" Armando asked. He was in the middle of a haircut and had tuned in to their conversation.

"Yeah, I know. I think I'm finally ready to turn in my scissors for a while," she admitted to them. "I find I'm tired all the time, and even sleep has become almost nonexistent," she said, lowering herself into a free hydraulic chair that no one used.

"I hope everything else isn't nonexistent!" Tony laughed, causing everyone else who was listening to giggle in unison.

"Leave it to Tony to say something like that!" Nicole laughed, thankful for the slow night that was awaiting her.

"Hey, Nikki," called Diane from her station. "Have you two thought of names for the baby?" she asked enthusiastically.

"Well, we've come up with a few, but nothing concrete yet. We don't even know what we're having," Nicole replied.

"Didn't you have an X-ray or something?" Claire, another older stylist, asked.

"It's not an X-ray, you bubblehead. It's an ultrasound," Tony corrected her.

"So, who gives a shit!" Claire replied, annoyed at his insult. "Whatever it's called, didn't you have it done on you?" she asked, turning her attention away from her boss to Nicole, who smiled sympathetically at the older stylist. Claire had never married and never had children.

"I did, Claire, but we didn't want to know the sex of the baby. We want it to be a surprise. Frankly, we just want a healthy baby," she replied, running a soothing hand over her unborn baby.

"Wow! You guys must be so excited!" Diane asked, feeling envious of her. Things between her and Fernando were starting to fizzle out, but she was truly happy for her friend.

"Yeah, of course we're excited. I just wish it would come sooner than later, if you know what I mean," Nicole said, sitting up in her chair and rubbing her back.

"Don't worry, Nikki! From the looks of you, it won't be too much longer," Diane said sympathetically. "I remember when I was pregnant with Martin, I couldn't wait for him to be born, and when he finally arrived, well, let's just say that I haven't had a good night's sleep since!" She laughed.

"I know. It was the same for me when Jonathan was born," Nicole said sadly.

"Just don't let the kid pop out here, alright? This ain't no hospital," Tony said, walking to the front desk. "Things like that freak me out."

"Well, in that case, I'm going to camp out over here until I go into labor!" Nicole laughed, visualizing him freaking out if that did happen.

"I don't think you have to try too hard, you know. You shouldn't even be here in your, let's say, delicate condition," he said, teasing her. He always loved teasing her.

Fortunately for Nicole, the rest of the day was slow; yet she found it difficult to go home. Jack was a sweetheart to her, making her breakfast, helping her around the house, even offering to put her shoes on for her, since she couldn't bend forward with her huge pregnant belly protruding as much as it did. But even with everything going smoothly at home, she couldn't help but feel a certain amount of anxiety. Her baby was due in a matter of a few weeks, and her husband was still considered to be the prime suspect in Ashley's attack. Every day she prayed that he would be cleared from the nightmare they had been living and everything would go back to normal, but the fact was, he was still under the microscope, and that concerned her a great deal. It stirred up more emotion than she felt she needed, which only confused her more. Nicole didn't know if it was her hormones acting up or the slight, taunting doubts about her own husband that were creeping into her thoughts. Sometimes she wondered if Jack's guilt was the real reason for his attentiveness toward her but thinking so badly about him only fueled her anxiety. She was hoping for a miracle at this point. In her heart of hearts, she knew that the man she knew and loved could never commit such a heinous crime, which only frustrated her more. They hadn't heard from the detective at all, and Nicole wondered if she should approach him. She needed some solid reassurance from him.

When she pulled up in their driveway, she was met with Jack, who had just arrived home at the same time as her. He got out of his truck and helped her out of her car, greeting her with a kiss.

"Hey, you! How are you?" he asked, helping her to the front door of the house. There was already a light dusting of snow, and with the cold air, Jack was concerned that it might freeze. He made a mental note to himself to throw some salt on the walkway and driveway.

"I'm still wobbling around as you can see," Nicole responded with a chuckle. "I can't wait to have this kid, let me tell you," she said after Jack opened the front door and led her inside.

"I know, babe. Just be patient now. We're almost there," he said, helping her remove her coat. "Honey, I hope you told your bosses that this was your last day. You're already long overdue you know—I mean, look at you," he said, bending down to her protruding belly and planting a kiss on it.

"Don't worry, I've told them that this was my last week," she reassured him.

"What, last week! Are you kidding me? Babe, I don't want you driving around unnecessarily, let alone working! Come on now, take it easy. The baby will be here soon, and you're going to need all the rest you can get now. By the way, I was just wondering … do you think that your mom would be able to come over for a couple of weeks when the baby arrives? I'll be working, and I don't want you here alone," he said as he led her into the family room. They sat downside by side on the oversized couch.

"Actually, I thought about the same thing, but my mom has her hands full with my dad, and I don't want to put her on the spot. But I'm sure that Sara will be popping over. And then there's Emily," Nicole said, noticing his frown. "Don't worry, baby, I'll be just fine," she said stroking his arm. "But it's sweet of you to think of me. You do remember, this isn't our first baby. I'm perfectly capable of taking care of things," she said defensively.

"Don't take it that way, Nikki. I know you are. I just thought it would be best if you had some extra help, that's all," Jack said gently, stroking the back of her hair. "I'm going to be working most of the time, and I'd feel more comfortable if you weren't alone, especially if …"

"If what?" Nicole interrupted, turning to look at him more closely, panic setting in.

"If nothing, OK? I just don't want you to be alone … if I'm not around for you," he replied quietly as he turned to meet her eyes with his own. "Babe, I don't mean to scare you or anything, but if the detective doesn't come up with anyone, I'm going to be heading toward the slammer, and—"

"Don't talk that way," Nicole said, her eyes welling up with tears.

"Nick, we have to face it," Jack said gently, turning his body toward her and taking her face in his hands. "There's a good chance that I might be found guilty," he continued, as tears started to roll down her cheeks. "Nikki, please be strong, and …"

"No!" she cried out. "I won't hear of it!" It pained her to think that there was a chance she'd have to raise their baby on her own.

"Nicole …"

"No!" she cried stubbornly. "You're going to be right here the whole time, and we're going to raise our baby together, you hear?" She wasn't sure if she were trying to convince him or herself.

He nodded silently and took her in his arms. He held her as she cried. His heart felt like it was torn in a million pieces. It was obvious to him that she couldn't handle the possibility that he wouldn't be around if he was sent to prison. He held her tightly, his chest wet from her tears.

"Jack, promise me you won't go anywhere! Promise me, Jack!" She cried into his sweater.

"I promise you" was all he could say, but in his heart, he wasn't so sure.

CHAPTER

33

Steven Fromer was just finishing off his dinner, and once more his wife was visiting their daughter at her new apartment. He contemplated watching some television, but instead, decided he would go out for a drink. He hadn't visited his "friend" at The Blue Lagoon for a while and decided he would pay him a surprise visit. Something about the guy hadn't sat well with him right from the beginning; plus, Fromer needed to unwind.

He hadn't been able to come up with any other suspects, other than Jack, in the Ashley case. Jack was the only one present at the time and place of the attack, and it was Ashley's word against his; even though she couldn't fill in all the details of the night of the attack, Jack was the only one who she remembered. And yet, in all the years he'd had on the police force, his gut told him that Jack just didn't fit the profile. It bothered Fromer that there were no other leads. He had called Ashley a couple of times, but both times, she and Gayle were out. He was curious as to how Ashley was doing, but on the flip side, he figured that no news was good news. Fromer put his jacket on and headed toward the bar. He needed a stiff drink just about now.

———

"Pleeease!" she begged. "I just need a little bit!" Stephanie was referring to some ecstasy, which was another drug that she had become very fond of.

"Cut it out, will ya! You're starting to get on my nerves," Manny yelled at her, taking her wrist and twisting it hard, causing her to cry out. "I told you once, and I'm going to tell you again, I don't got any. You got that? You've become a junkie, you know that?" he yelled in her face.

"I'm sorry," she apologized meekly. "I promise, I'll be good to you. Please," she begged in desperation. "How about some powder? I need something, please, Manny!"

"Alright! Stop whining!" he shouted, going into his secret compartment where he kept his stash of cocaine, retrieving a small packet, and slamming the drawer shut in anger. He was the one who'd introduced the shit to her, and now she couldn't function without it. She was completely out of control, but there was nothing he could do about it. The money she was making for him was ending up in her nostrils, and she was starting to piss him off. However, the men really liked her, as the coke made her more compliant, and often, she'd go off into her own little world and dance for them sexually, and that really turned them on. She was in high demand by many of the regular men, most married and some single. She'd really put on a show for them, and the guys would get off just by watching her touch herself in ways that would make them want her even more. Freddie kept an ample supply for Manny, since he visited Stephanie almost daily. She was doing roughly six men a night now, sometimes two at a time, and the best part of it all was that Manny got to watch some of it. The johns demanded privacy, but Manny had set up a button-sized video camera in the top corner of the room at an angle that gave him a good view of everything that went on in there. It turned him on immensely, having live porn right there in his own domain. It took real talent to do what he was doing and get laid daily. Stephanie was his whore to do what he wanted, and that's exactly what he did.

After she finished snorting the coke up her nose, Manny decided he would get some action before the others, so he grabbed her by her hair and roughly shoved his penis in her mouth. She immediately went into action and sucked him hard. He always enjoyed sex, but he thoroughly enjoyed getting it orally, and when he finally ejaculated in her mouth, he sighed and smiled. Now she was ready to bring in the cash.

—

As he entered the bar, Fromer was immediately approached by a young waitress, who greeted him with a smile. The place was packed with people, all the little booths were taken, and the bar was full. The noise level was almost deafening with what seemed to be the new music of this generation; the beat was alright, but the words were offensive. It was unmistakably busy tonight, and he wondered if there was anything else going on this evening; he knew that on some nights there was karaoke and comedy. He walked over to the bar and took a seat. He couldn't believe how busy it was. He scanned the place quickly and took notice of three girls working the floor and the bartender. The place was jumping, the atmosphere was nice, and he found he was nodding to the beat of the music.

"Hey, man, what can I get you?" asked the bartender, a tall man who Fromer recognized almost immediately.

"Hey, I'll have a beer, please. A draft—Stella," answered the detective. The place was happening, and he looked around the bar quickly to see if the big boss was around. There was a lot of hustle and bustle, but everything looked to be running smoothly.

"Here you go, man," the bartender said as he placed an ice-cold glass of beer in front of him. Before Fromer could thank him, the bartender was already taking another order at the end of the bar. The detective took a long swig of his beer, relishing the ice-cold liquid gold. He still hadn't spotted the owner yet and wondered where he could be, with the bar being as busy as it was tonight. Fromer wondered if Manny was in his office. It seemed like every time he popped into this joint, Manny was hiding out in his office. He finished off the rest of his beer and glanced at the bartender with a nod.

"Would you like another beer?" asked the bartender, looking directly at him.

"Yeah, I'll have one more, man," replied the detective. "It's busy tonight," Fromer said, wanting to start up a conversation. Another ice-cold glass of beer was placed in front of him. He hadn't seen the bartender in a few months.

"Not bad," replied the bartender as he wiped the counter and turned to take another drink order.

"Hey, can you pass the peanuts, buddy," asked another guy sitting at the bar. The bartender grabbed the small bowl of peanuts and slid it in front of him.

"So, where's the big man?" asked the detective, helping himself to a handful of nuts.

"Who, Manny?" asked the bartender, taking a drink of water.

"Yeah, Manny," said the detective, taking a swig of his beer.

"Yeah, well, he's usually here. Spends a lot of time in his office," the bartender replied, leaning back and crossing his arms in front of him.

"How long have you worked here," asked the detective, taking another handful of nuts; they were spicy and sweet at the same time.

"I'd say about a year or so," he answered. "I work here most evenings and on the weekends." The bartender took another drink of water, making eye contact with the other patrons to see if anyone needed anything.

"And how do you like working for him?" Fromer asked, chewing on the nuts. He wondered how he'd never tasted anything quite so good before.

"He's alright," the bartender stated bluntly, wondering what the detective was getting at. "I mean, he's fair. He gave me a job when I needed work. I do my work, I get paid, end of story," he said, making it known that the questions about his boss ended there.

"So, what can you tell me about the girls that work here? Are they happy working here?" Fromer knew he was probing him, but he was curious. He hadn't liked Manny from the first time he'd met him, although he wasn't sure why. Having over thirty years' experience under his belt taught him to trust his gut, and his gut told him that there was a lot more to Manny—he was sure of that.

"I can't speak for the girls, but they seem happy enough. To be honest with you, the girls and I don't really interact much," the bartender responded. "You'd have to ask them." And at that moment, one of the waitresses approached the bar, placing a drink order. "Excuse me," he said quickly to the detective, exiting their chat.

"Of course," nodded the detective, watching the bartender prepare the drink order. He looked around again, hoping he'd see Manny, but he was nowhere in sight. Fromer looked back at the bartender as he finished off his beer. He caught his eye and nodded, signaling him for the bill, which the bartender brought him immediately.

"One more thing," Fromer continued as he reached into his wallet to pay for the beers. "What can you tell me about Ashley?" He paid the bartender what he owed him and waited for him to cash him out.

"What about her?" the bartender asked, looking slightly annoyed with all the questions that were being thrown at him. He gave Fromer his change. "What exactly are you asking me?" he said, narrowing his eyes at him.

The detective put the change in his wallet and looked directly at him. "It's Phil, right?" he asked, to which Phil nodded. "It's no secret what happened to her. I'm sure you've heard," Fromer said, eyeing him carefully.

"Yeah, I heard," Phil answered, taking another drink of water, giving a quick nod to a guy at the end of the bar with a drink order. He turned to prepare the drink and started talking to the customer. After a minute or so, he looked over his shoulder very casually to see if the detective was still there just as the detective turned his back and started walking out of the bar.

Fromer noted that their conversation had come to a halt, prompting him to leave, for now. He drove home in deep thought, questioning who was responsible for beating and raping this young girl.

CHAPTER

34

*G*ayle and Ashley were sitting at the kitchen table sipping their morning coffee after eating a breakfast that Gayle had cooked up. They had developed a nice routine in the months that they had been living together. Ashley was happy and thriving in her work at the hospital as well in her home life with Gayle. She was truly content with her life and living with Gayle made Ashley feel felt like she truly belonged and was wanted; in the short months of living with her, Ashley felt like Gayle truly was her mom. She knew how lucky she was to have met this wonderful woman who had opened her heart and her home to her. It was sheer luck to have had Gayle as her nurse after the attack. Many nights, Ashley would lie in her bed and think about what Gayle brought to her life. The emptiness she'd felt after the attack, the loneliness and the fear she'd felt once she was conscious, made her wish she had died. She had questioned the purpose of her life on numerous occasions, questioned why she had survived the brutal attack. It still chilled her to the bone when the memory of it flooded her brain when she least expected it. Many nights, particularly in the beginning, she'd be jolted awake, covered in a cold sweat, trembling in fear as the image of the savage beating played in her mind like a record, repeatedly, causing her to gasp for breath.

But Gayle was always immediately by her side, holding her and stroking her hair and telling her that everything was going to be alright. But would the nightmares ever stop? She still had no memory of who had attacked her, and that worried her. There was still no word from the detective; she had his business card tucked away in her nightstand. Ashley tried to remember all the details of the attack, but other than what she'd told the detective, nothing new surfaced. She often wondered if she couldn't remember because her mind was protecting her, shielding her from more pain and anxiety. Why couldn't she remember the details of the rape and the beating, at least up to the point where she'd lost consciousness? Maybe her mind was instantly throwing the whole incident under the carpet, helping her to go on, until the nights set in at least.

Her job at the hospital was what most people would define as boring, but Ashley found it refreshing. It was the first time in her life that she felt safe—that was something new to her. Her life had been anything but "safe."

Ashley was raised by a single mother who, over the years, had brought many different men into their tiny one-bedroom apartment. Her mother was in and out of relationships with all kinds of men, mostly abusive men, and when she finally settled with one man, she endured even more abuse from him—only this time, the abuse trickled down to Ashley. It started with a slap. At first, her mother tried to physically defend her, coming between Ashley and her boyfriend; but that would anger him even more, and he'd end up beating both. Her mother had been young herself when she'd had Ashley and hadn't had the most loving upbringing. How could she give love to her daughter when she'd never received it herself? How could she give something that she'd never had? And because it was a small one-bedroom apartment, Ashley had nowhere to go. School was her only escape, but unfortunately Ashley wasn't the best student. She couldn't concentrate on her studies and completing her homework was almost impossible. She didn't have any siblings or family that she could turn to, and she'd never met her biological father. Anytime she inquired about her father, her mother would get angry with her and order her to go and do her homework. Ashley slept in the living room on a pullout couch—sleep was almost impossible with such limited living quarters.

Things got bad for Ashley when her mother got a job working nights at an all-night gas station. Ashley spent many uncomfortable evenings alone with her stepdad. She was just hitting puberty when he started making advances toward her. It was subtle at first, touching her behind when she walked past him; then he'd want to watch a movie with her, only his choice of movie was not an appropriate family movie that normal families watched together. He had his own movie that he liked to watch, and he called it their "special" movie. He would make her sit very close to him while he watched his "special" movie of various people having sex among each other. When she tried to get up from the couch to go to the bathroom, he grabbed her arm and told her to be a good little girl and make Daddy "happy."

Making Daddy "happy" meant fondling his manhood, and he had shown her how to do it. Although she was very young, she knew that it was wrong, and when she finally gathered the courage to tell her mother what Eddie had made her do to him, her mother didn't hold her and comfort her and tell her that everything was going to be OK. Instead, she got very hostile with Ashley and started shouting obscenities at her, calling her a lying little whore. And when Ashley cried and tried to convince her mother that she was, in fact, telling the truth, her mother slapped her hard in the face, causing her to fall to the ground. Ashley still remembered the sting of the slap because it was the first time her mother had laid a hand on her. She had received a couple of slaps from her stepdad beforehand but never from her mother. The slap she received from her mother left her feeling shocked, alone, and confused—confused as to why her own mother didn't believe what she was telling her. In many ways, the hard slap she received from her mother was far worse than what Eddie did to her, because she'd naturally assumed that her own mother would protect her. But she didn't. Ashley was left feeling completely and totally alone.

Over the next couple of years, the sexual abuse escalated with Eddie. He was having sex with her a couple of times a week while her mother worked. And even on the nights that her mother had a day off, he would occasionally wander into the living room in the middle of the night and expect her to have intercourse with him. She never understood how her mother could be in such denial about her husband and carry on like nothing was happening. Did she not notice that her daughter's schoolwork was suffering or that she had become withdrawn? How could her mother be so oblivious to the sexual abuse that was happening right under her nose? However, Ashley's relationship with her mother had changed dramatically. Her mother treated her like a stranger—only talked to her when necessary. Her mother had become very cold and indifferent toward her daughter, and Ashley decided then and there that she needed to leave and never return. But where would she go?

She was only fifteen years old when she finally got the courage to leave for good. She left in the morning with her backpack and the clothes on her back as though she were going to school, only she didn't go to school. She hit the streets, wandering around downtown Toronto. She wondered if her mom would care enough to look for her when she discovered that her daughter wasn't coming home, but Ashley knew deep down in her heart that her absence would probably be a blessing to her mother; Ashley had never felt wanted from as young as she could remember.

After hours of walking in and out of stores on the streets, she ended up sleeping on the platform at the train station. She had already eaten her peanut butter and jelly sandwich that she had packed and drunk her juice box, but she was still hungry. She had also packed a granola bar, but she was saving it for the morning.

Ashley ended up staying at a shelter. And soon she met a man who she thought was the love of her life, a man she thought would take care of her—they would live happily ever after; but he ended up abusing her, just like all the different men that her mother had brought home over the years. She ended up fleeing from him, leaving him bleeding on the ground after stabbing him during yet another abusive episode.

Sitting in Gayle's kitchen, Ashley closed her eyes and shuddered at the memory: Ashley had prepared a nice dinner for the two of them and had the table nicely set; but he came home drunk and belligerent, looking for a fight. She nervously tried to reason with him in hopes of having a nice dinner, but he wouldn't have it. He started accusing her of sleeping around, calling her all kinds of names, and when she turned to go into the kitchen, he grabbed her by the hair and yanked her back to him, demanding to know who she'd been sleeping with. Again, she tried to reassure him that none of what he was saying was true, that she loved him very much. That was when he slammed his fist on the table, sending everything flying to the ground. He slapped her so hard that she went down, with all the food and broken dishes clattering around her. Before she knew what was happening, he was on top of her, choking her, calling her a lying whore. It was at that moment that she managed, barely, to reach beside her where one of the steak knives was lying; she tried very hard to keep it together while he had both his hands around her throat, trying to choke her. She managed to grab the knife and stab him in the chest.

Fresh tears rolled down Ashley's cheeks at the memory of that fateful day: the look of shock on his face, as well her own disbelief that she could commit such a heinous act to another human being. She had managed to squirm herself out from under him, gasping for air, and left him on the ground with a steak knife in his back. She had flown out of the apartment crying, knowing that she had probably killed him.

Suddenly, Ashley was sobbing uncontrollably and gasping for air. Gayle was immediately by her side, holding Ashley's crumbled body to her chest, stroking her head and quietly soothing her.

"It's OK, sweetheart, let it all out," she said gently. It pained her to see Ashley go through so much heartache. Gayle had noticed how quiet Ashley had become as they sat together. The enormous pain that this young woman was experiencing and the torment she had endured had become very clear to Gayle.

Ashley continued to sob on Gayle's chest, soaking her blouse with tears that continued to fall. "Shhhh ... it's alright. Everything's going to be alright, love," Gayle's soft voice soothed, her heart breaking into a million pieces for Ashley as tears stung her eyes.

CHAPTER

35

Nicole found it extremely difficult to move around, and she wondered if she was going to get to full term with her pregnancy. Her pregnant belly was bigger than she could ever have imagined. She wobbled her way to the kitchen and was making herself a mint tea when Jack came up behind her and wrapped his arms around her, planting a soft kiss on the side of her neck.

"Good morning my very pregnant wife," he said lovingly. "And how are you feeling this morning?"

Nicole turned herself around to face him, smiling at him with love in her eyes. "Ginormous! Like a house is how I feel. Look at me, babe! I've never looked and felt so huge in my entire life." She laughed, rubbing her big belly. "You'd think I'm carrying triplets by the look of me!"

"You look wonderfully radiant, baby," Jack replied, leaning in front of her and planting soft kisses on her belly. "It looks like our baby might be coming sooner than we think, eh?" He stood up and took Nicole's hands into his.

"God, I hope not," she answered. "We still have another month to go." She looked a little worried. She was at the point now where she couldn't sleep, and her frequent trips to the washroom during the night didn't help. The truth was, Nicole was anxious a lot of the time, not only because of the anticipation of giving birth, but also because of the dark cloud that loomed over her head with the whole Ashley situation. She worried that her husband was going to be taken away from her and their baby. They tried to make the best of their situation, and in the last months, Jack had become so incredibly sweet toward her and attentive to her needs. His work had slowed down considerably, which was not unusual for the time of year—Christmas was only two days away—but that worked in her favor since he was home a lot more. He had taken on the cleaning of the house and some of the cooking. Jack wasn't the best cook, and he knew it, but Nicole loved him for trying. He had even taken on the laundry, which was a first for him. He had gotten quite good at it, making sure to separate the clothes like she had shown him two months prior. He was fully aware of his wife's perfectionism, and he tried his best to keep up to her standards.

"Come sit down, sweetheart," he said to her, taking her gently by the hand and leading her to the sofa, helping her sit comfortably, bringing the ottoman closer to her. "Here, put your feet up." Jack helped her lift her legs and sat beside her. "Can you believe that Christmas is in just a couple more days?" He took her hand in his and turned to face her.

"I know, I can't believe how time flies!" Nicole exclaimed with excitement. "It seems like just yesterday we found out we were going to have a baby, and look at us now," she said, looking at him, smiling. "Christmas has always been my favorite holiday." She leaned toward him and kissed him lightly on the lips.

"Mine too," Jack replied. "You know, we haven't discussed any names for our baby," he said as he squeezed her hand. "You're just about ready to pop that kid out any day."

"Well, I hope not! I'm not due for another few weeks, give or take," she exclaimed, rubbing her belly. "You hear that, baby?" She nervously looked down at her pregnant belly. Truth be told, Nicole was getting quite anxious about the delivery as well as the whole situation with her husband. She hoped that the stress of it all didn't hasten the birth of their baby. "To be honest with you, I haven't even thought about names."

"Well, how about we pick some out—a girl's name as well as a boy's name," he said, smiling at her. "I was thinking that if it's a boy, we could name him Leo. What do you think?" He was eyeing her for reaction. "And if we have a girl, we could name her Grace. It's sweet and simple, and it's one syllable," he said, causing her to smile lovingly at her husband, who had obviously given some thought to choosing names for their unborn child. It warmed her heart as she thought about how close they were to seeing their baby. Their unplanned baby had become the link that bonded them again as husband and wife.

Nicole leaned into her husband and kissed him lightly on the lips. "I'm impressed, Mr. Newman," she said to him. "You're going to be an amazing daddy to our little one, no matter what we have." She took his hand and placed it on her stomach, placing her hand on top of his. "I love the names you've chosen, Jack," she said softly. She'd had an ultra-sound a few months ago, and everything, so far, was normal with the baby. When the technician asked them if they wanted to know the sex of the baby, they both declined, wanting it to be a surprise. They just wanted a healthy baby, and it didn't matter to either of them what they were having. They had been given a second chance at their marriage with this baby, and they were both fully on board and looking forward to their little bundle of love.

"Nikki, I have an idea," Jack said, with a twinkle in his eye. "Let's go and get our picture taken with Santa at the mall," he said enthusiastically, almost childlike.

"Shouldn't we wait till next Christmas to have it done with our baby?" she asked, confused.

"We're going to go again next year with our baby, but I want a picture with my beautiful pregnant wife and Santa. We could get ready and go right now. Then we could pick something up for dinner and come home and relax right here by the Christmas tree and watch a movie. How does that sound to you?" Jack felt like he had when they'd first started dating. He was aware of how anxious she had been in the past few months, and he wanted to do something to ease her anxiety. "Come on, it'll be fun!" he exclaimed eagerly.

"OK, sounds like fun!" She was smiling from ear to ear. It was so spontaneous, and she loved it.

"That's great, let's go." He helped her off the couch, and they went upstairs to change for the mall. It was two days before Christmas, and they were as happy as two peas in a pod. They couldn't wait to hit the mall and let the child in them come out as they posed with Santa Claus.

CHAPTER

36

*P*hil had cleaned up the bar area, had the glasses washing, and was wiping the counter surface when Manny strolled through. The two waitresses had left for the night after they did their side duties. Manny looked over at Phil and gave the restaurant a quick look over, noticing that everything was clean, and the floor was vacuumed, which left him to do the cash.

"How was business tonight?" Manny asked Phil as he helped himself to a scotch at the bar. A sly smile crept over his face as he thought about his other business that was going on in the back of the restaurant. He had three regular johns for Stephanie, who came in almost every day. Manny had trained her well, making sure that she got her "candy" just before one of her clients would arrive. By now, Stephanie was addicted, not only to cocaine and ecstasy but heroine as well. He had introduced it to her just a short while ago, and she loved it. One night, for example, she had serviced three men at once, and had been only too happy to do it. The money that he'd received that night was over the top, and as a bonus, Manny got hold of some heroine, which he shot up her arm after she serviced him too. The greatest part was that he got to watch every-thing that went on in that room. That button-sized camera that he had installed months before really came in handy.

"It was good, actually," Phil answered. He finished cleaning up and watched Manny as he drank his scotch while doing the cash. "Umm, Manny, I have a favor I need to ask you," Phil said, approaching him.

"Yeah, what's up?" Manny replied without looking up at Phil.

"I need some money," he said matter-of-factly, "and lots of it."

Manny looked up from what he was doing, glaring at Phil. He didn't like the tone in his voice. "What kind of money are we talking about?"

"Fifty thousand dollars is what I want," Phil said, staring him down. He was very aware of what had been going on for the past two years in the bar, particularly in the last few months. Manny thought he was being smart in having the men enter the restaurant from the back door, but Phil had run into a few men in the parking lot when he'd gone to get more supplies or thrown out the trash. He had also noticed that Stephanie had changed enormously in the past few months. She barely waitressed anymore, and yet he'd see her all the time going in the office with a dazed look on her face. Men were coming and going all the time, and Phil kept quiet about it until now.

Manny let out a snort and laughed. "Are you kidding me? What the fuck do you need fifty thousand dollars for? And what the fuck gave you the idea that I would just give it to you?" he said angrily, wondering where this was coming from.

"Well, let's just say that you *will* give me what I want, especially if you don't want any trouble. You have a very busy establishment here, and I'd think you'd want it to continue that way." Phil's eyes never left Manny's.

Manny stood up slowly, his eyes darkening. "Are you threatening me?" He took a step closer to Phil, not believing what he was hearing.

"Just asking for a favor, boss!" Phil laughed, lightening his tone. "You're making a ton of money in this joint right here, as well as in the back of the restaurant. Am I right?" he asked with a sly smile, letting Manny know that he was onto him.

"What the fuck do you need fifty thousand dollars for? You make a lot of money in here. So, what the fuck do you think you know?" Manny was getting angry, and from the tone in his voice, Phil knew that he knew what was going on.

"Let's just say that I know a lot more than you think I know. I know that you're using Stephanie to make you extra cash by making her fuck a lot of men. I've also noticed that you're rarely in the bar area because you're always in your office, taking care of your business. You're running a dirty business back there, and I know you're making a ton of money. I don't think that I'm asking a lot." Phil watched Manny twitch and take on a different look, his eyes darkening.

"So, you think you can threaten me? You don't know who you're messing with, buddy!" Manny shouted at him, taking a step toward him.

"I'd watch what you say to me boss," Phil said politely. "The detective was in here not too long-ago asking questions, and I covered your slimy ass. So, if you want me to keep quiet, you'll give me the money," he stated calmly. "Simple." Phil was enjoying watching his boss squirm.

"Oh yeah? What kind of questions was the detective asking?" Manny was more and more curious. It had been a while since the detective had come around, but then again, Manny didn't spend a lot of time in the bar area.

"He asked about Ashley, and what had happened to her. He was curious as to why you're never around."

"So, what about Ashley? What did he want to know? I thought I'd already dealt with him months ago," Manny said, lowering his tone, not liking where this conversation was going.

"About her getting attacked. I could've blown you to bits, but I didn't," Phil continued.

"What the fuck are you talking about, huh? What are you implying exactly?" Manny was in Phil's face now, and he was angry.

"I overheard you and Ashley hashing it out one day in your office. I was coming to talk to you about something, and I overheard Ashley telling you that if you wanted her to continue to work here, you'd have to stop making sexual advances and threats toward her, or she'd report you to the police. And you told her that if she ever breathed a word to anyone, she would live to regret it. Does any of this refresh your memory boss? We both know that she left from here and ended up getting attacked. Are you getting me?" Phil spoke to him in an even tone, looking directly into Manny's eyes, their noses practically touching. "So, you see, boss, I don't really see that you have a choice here. You either pay up, or I contact our little detective friend and fill him in on what's been happening around here. I really don't think he's going to be so happy with you." Phil was in the driver's seat, and it felt great. He watched the goings on in the restaurant with some of the girls carefully, and he was going to use this information to his advantage.

Manny stared at Phil as if meeting him for the first time, observing that they were the same height and built. He backed away from Phil and seated himself at the cash where he'd stood earlier. He took a long swig of the scotch he had poured himself. He hesitated and then took another mouthful, finishing his drink. "You think I had something to do with Ashley's attack?" He turned to look at Phil, waiting for a reply.

"As a matter of fact, I do. You had motive, and you'd threatened her. I heard you with my own ears," Phil responded. "So, if I were you, I'd just pay up, and you'll never hear another word from me."

"You think you're so smart, eh? Give me till after Christmas, and I'll give you five thousand dollars," he answered. Manny had to shut him up for now. There was too much at stake, and he didn't need any complications. He wasn't exactly a shiny penny, and he was involved in some very shady businesses, so he had to provide Phil with something to keep him quiet.

"No, I want five thousand now, and after Christmas, I want the rest," Phil stated in an even tone. "I'm serious, Manny. I'll go straight to the police if you don't give me what I want." His tone told Manny that he was serious about his threat. "And I want it in cash," Phil added.

"Fine," Manny answered. He went into his cash register, as well as his wallet, and counted out five thousand dollars. He'd give it to him now to shut him up and figure out what to do about the rest. He wasn't going to allow this punk to get away with extortion. "Here," he said gruffly, as he slammed five thousand dollars on the counter for Phil to take, his eyes dark with fury. "It's all there." He didn't like the predicament he was in, nor did he appreciate his opponent holding all the cards.

Phil smugly picked up the cash that Manny had just given him, putting forth a smile for Manny's benefit. "It's been a pleasure doing business with you, boss!" His sarcasm just angered Manny more, making his blood boil. "Merry Christmas to you!" And with that, Phil turned and walked out on Manny, leaving him stunned and angry as hell.

Phil's next step was to get the rest of the money he'd asked for and leave the province. He figured he'd go to the States. Fifty thousand dollars was sure to help him make a life there.

As he was leaving the restaurant, Phil ran into Stephanie, who was just entering from the front door. She looked like she had just woken up: her hair was a mess, and she looked ragged. She bumped into Phil as she made her way inside, acting skittish.

"Hey, Steph! What are you doing here?" She was obviously startled to see him.

Stephanie started to speak but had a hard time forming a sentence. "I, I'm just looking for Manny," she said nervously. "I need him. I need to see him badly," she rambled, her eyes darting everywhere. "Is he here?"

At that exact moment, Manny appeared from the back, and when he saw Stephanie, his dark mood only worsened. He caught her off guard as he grabbed her arm from behind and yanked her toward him. "What the hell are you doing here, and how the hell did you get out?" he shouted. He was not having a great night and seeing her show up in a heap of mess angered him to the core.

Stephanie started to whimper and cry. "I'm sorry, Manny. I need you sooo bad. Please don't be angry with me!" she pleaded as he pulled her roughly toward him, forcing her out the door. Manny was holding her by the arm with one hand and locking the door with the other. He noticed that Phil had made a quick exit, and he was relieved. He didn't need this right now.

"You stupid bitch! Shut the hell up!" Manny struggled with getting her into his car while she repeatedly kicked and screamed, pleading that she needed a hit. She was fighting with him as he shoved her in his car, and he struggled to get her seat belt on. He slapped her hard across the face and yelled at her. "Wait till I get you home!" He was furious with her, although he knew that she was desperate for her usual drugs. Manny drove off angrily and headed toward his condo, which wasn't too far from his bar, while Stephanie whimpered beside him. He thought about Phil and how he was going to deal with him. But right now, he had a pathetic whore that he needed to take care of.

CHAPTER

37

*F*eeling like the world had lifted from her chest after crying it out, Ashley felt like she was reborn, and for the first time in her life, felt a sense of peace within her. Gayle had become her colorful and bright rainbow after a dark and insufferable storm that she'd endured in her life. She felt love and acceptance in the purest form, and that was something foreign to her. Ashley had started to see a light at the end of a dark tunnel, and she was so grateful for this amazing woman, who had come into her life in her darkest hour. Gayle had become her friend, her confident, and her rock. It had become so clear to Ashley that their paths crossing was no coincidence. They both desperately needed each other, and it saddened her to know that Gayle had lost her one and only daughter. Ashley longed for a mother figure, someone to love and protect her; and Gayle had so much love to give and yearned for someone to love and care for like a daughter—it was fate that had brought them together.

Ashley was exhausted after the flood of emotions that had come out of her hours before, and she decided to turn in for the night. She found

Gayle in the living room, half asleep on the sofa with the television on. Ashley smiled warmly at the woman who selflessly gave so much to her. Gayle had worked a twelve-hour shift at the hospital and was obviously exhausted. It was evident to Ashley why Gayle has chosen nursing to be her profession—she clearly was a nurturer by nature. She walked up to Gayle and quietly placed her hand on her shoulder, being careful not to startle her.

Gayle slowly opened her eyes and looked up to see Ashley standing before her, smiling. "Hello, sweetheart," she said sleepily. "Is everything OK?"

"Everything's fine," Ashley said quietly. "I was just coming in to say good night to you. I'm sorry I woke you," she replied, desperately wanting to hug her. "How was work today?"

Gayle sat up in her seat and yawned. "Looong!" She laughed. "But it's all good. I was watching a movie, but I guess I fell asleep. These twelve-hour shifts are starting to get long for me," she added jokingly.

Without even thinking, Ashley spontaneously leaned toward Gayle and wrapped her arms around her. "I love you!" She spoke. Gayle was instantly caught off guard by her sudden display of affection, and she hugged her back lovingly.

"I love *you*, sweetheart," she replied quietly, wiping a single tear that escaped her eye. "My life, once again, has meaning."

—

Christmas Eve had arrived, and Gayle and Ashley filled the day with Christmas shopping. Both ladies had some time off for the holidays, and Ashley had managed to save up some money from working at the gift shop. She wanted to buy Gayle something unique, something special to let her know how much Gayle meant to her. They agreed to separate for an hour or so at the mall so they would each have a chance to shop for the other.

Listening to the Christmas music that played throughout the mall and seeing children dressed in holiday colors standing in line with their parents for Santa pictures brought a smile to Ashley's face. She visited a few different stores, looking at handbags, perfume, and a variety of trinkets. She finally settled on a porcelain figurine, the Virgin Mary and baby Jesus. Instantly, she knew that it was the perfect gift for Gayle. Ashley paid for it, smiling from ear to ear, and when asked if she wanted it wrapped, she nodded. When it was wrapped, Ashley thanked the merchant for the beautiful job she'd done. She contacted Gayle on her cell phone, and the ladies met up a few minutes later at Starbucks, where they enjoyed a cup of coffee and chatted easily, laughing and enjoying each other's company.

"What do you say we go home and order in a pizza, maybe watch a movie? How does that sound to you?" Gayle asked, looking forward to going home and putting her feet up. She, too, was feeling giddy after buying Ashley's Christmas present, looking forward to the next morning, where they'd wake up and open their gifts. She couldn't wait till Ashley saw what she'd bought for her.

"That sounds good. My feet are killing me!" Ashley laughed, feeling exhausted herself, but incredibly happy. They picked up the rest of their parcels and went home.

38

Christmas had come and gone, and Nicole's anxiety had risen to a whole new level. Anticipating the birth of their baby caused her to have a whirlwind of emotions. She found herself constantly reflecting on the time when she had been expecting her firstborn, the child she'd lost, the son she'd adored, Jonathan, her baby boy. Tears stung her eyes at the memories of the fateful day her little boy had died. Oh, how she'd loved him! He'd been the light of her life, her little sunshine, as she would so often refer to him. Losing him was the hardest, most painful thing that she had ever gone through; and now, here she was just weeks away from delivering another child. She was very excited about this new little human that she and Jack had created, but she also felt an enormous amount of guilt. Guilt for not being able to protect her child from harm, for not checking up on him sooner, because if she had, he'd still be with them today and not buried six feet under. Her head knew and accepted the fact that it was, indeed, an accident, but her heart felt different, and as happy and excited she was to be expecting another baby, there was always the feeling of "replacing Jonathan" that plagued her thoughts. She was certain that Jack had sensed that something wasn't right with her, but she was too afraid to open to him. The emotions flooded her mind, and she feared that if she expressed them to her husband, unresolved feelings about the death of their son would surface. She felt that they were finally in a good place, and she didn't want to revisit the enormous loss that almost cost them their marriage.

She was sitting on the love seat when her thoughts were interrupted by the doorbell. She slowly got up and wobbled her way to the front door, wondering who it was, because she wasn't expecting anyone. She peered through the side window before opening the door, and when she saw her sister, Sara, standing there, she was suddenly overcome with joy.

"Well, hello, stranger!" Sara exclaimed excitedly, leaning forward and hugging her younger sister. The two sisters hadn't seen one another during the holidays, since both of Sara's kids had gotten the chickenpox, so contact with them had been out of the question with Nicole being pregnant.

"Oh, Sara! It's so nice to see you! I've missed you so much!" Nicole answered, hugging Sara back and leading her inside, away from the cold and snow. Can I get you a coffee?"

"Oh, I'd love a cup of coffee," she answered as she removed her boots and jacket. "Oh, your house looks so festive, sis!" Sara commented, observing the well-lit Christmas tree that was so beautifully decorated with silver and white ornaments throughout, and a beautiful white and silver angel nestled at the top of the tree. The two sisters made their way to the family room, where Sara plopped herself on the couch. "Well, look at you!" Sara exclaimed excitedly, referring to Nicole's enormous baby bump. She was so happy for her sister and her brother-in-law.

"Yeah, look at me. I'm as big as a house!" Nicole laughed, stroking her baby belly. "New Years is in just a few days, and I haven't had a chance to get over to your house to drop off the kids' Christmas presents!" She felt bad that she hadn't made it a priority. "I did, however, wrap them, and they're right here under the tree." Nicole wobbled her way to the Christmas tree and tried to reach down to grab them.

"Nikki don't strain yourself, hon, I got it," Sara responded, getting

up quickly and reaching down to collect the boxes that were so beautifully wrapped. "You always were the better wrapper," she said, compli-
menting her younger sister as she placed the gifts carefully on the couch.
"You sure you got enough for them?" Sara laughed. The number of gifts
wasn't a surprise since her sister was always so generous with her niece
and nephew.

"Listen up, big sister, nothing is too much for my little munchkins.
How are they feeling?" Nicole asked, concerned about them having
chicken pox.

"They're a handful, I'll tell ya! But the worst is over at least. I didn't
want to take any chances on exposing you to anything, especially with
the baby and all."

"As much as I miss them, I understand." She wrapped her arm
around Sara, leading her into the kitchen. "Let's make some coffee and
sit and catch up," Nicole said.

"That sounds so good. I sooo needed a break from the kids. Once
James got home, I told him to hold the fort for a couple of hours because
I was just about ready to lose it with them!" She laughed, feeling over-
whelmed. "And so here I am! So, tell me, how are you?"

Nicole smiled as she prepared the coffee, not knowing where to begin but thankful for the timing of her sister's visit. Jack had gone to his
office to check on a few things, and it was a perfect time to visit with her
one and only sister. They both led busy lives, but when they talked on
the phone or got together, they never ran out of things to say.

ack at the condo, Stephanie was overwrought. Manny had once again left her home alone after she'd serviced two men for him at the bar. The condo had become a prison to her now, and she felt like a caged wild animal. She had just had sex with two men that Manny had produced for her, and she couldn't understand his displeasure in her with the most recent escapade. She hadn't put up a fight, and she'd done what she was told with them, but Manny was angry with her after the two men left the bar from the back door.

Stephanie was shaking like a leaf, and her body was covered in bruises from Manny's beating. He seemed so angry with her all the time, and she couldn't understand why. He had screamed and yelled at her, calling her the most degrading names, telling her that she'd better get with the program because he was losing johns over her behavior. She had begged him for a hit, and he'd refused her, saying that she had become a junkie, and that she was costing him more money than he was making. Stephanie had been begging him, all the while crying, asking for "just a little bit," referring to the heroine that she had grown to love and depend on. But he wouldn't give her any. He'd kicked her hard and shoved her on the bed, calling her a "stupid bitch."

Stephanie was curled up on her side in a fetal position, Manny having left her once again, storming out of the apartment. She didn't know how long it would be before he would return this time; this had become a common occurrence. She lay curled up for a while with her eyes open, feeling completely empty. The need for heroine overcame logic, and she immediately sat up in bed and looked around. She had seen where Manny stashed the drugs—he kept them locked in a safe in the closet. She thought of trying to break it open, but the last time she'd tried to do that, he'd caught her red-handed, and she'd paid for it dearly.

She stood up and walked toward the large closet that held her most prized possession, and as she did, a full-length mirror faced her. Stephanie froze on the spot, staring at the vision in front of her. Blinking back tears, she refocused as she examined the person in the mirror. She was appalled at the horrifying specimen that stared right back at her. She took a step closer to the offensive creature, shocked at what she was seeing. The reflection that stood before her was not the same person she once was. The once beautiful girl with the blonde hair, soft curves, and creamy complexion was now replaced by an alarmingly gaunt, skin-and-bones figure with transparent skin and straggly hair. She leaned forward toward the mirror and touched her face as she gazed at the empty eyes that stared back at her.

Stephanie looked at the clothes that hung on her bony and flimsy body. Her eyes were hollow and drawn and displayed emptiness and sadness. A single tear escaped one eye, soon followed by a flood of tears as she turned away from her own ugliness. She went back to the bed, lying on her side in a fetal position once again. The tears flowed easily, and she was overcome with shame and disgust. Stephanie was shocked at the hideous and ugly person she had become. At that point, she knew that she had no one in the world, no one who cared if she were dead or alive.

—

Gayle had a few minutes before she began her shift at the hospital, and she decided to run into the gift shop and say a quick hello to Ashley. She walked in and saw that Ashley was tending to a customer, giving her advice as to what to buy for the loved one she was visiting, so Gayle walked around the gift shop, careful not to intrude on her work. Ashley spotted Gayle right away and smiled in her direction, then turned her attention once again to her customer. After some idle conversation, Ashley cashed her out and wished her a good day. It brought a smile to Gayle's face, noting that the customer was satisfied with her purchase.

"Hello, sweetheart!" Gayle greeted her. "I missed you this morning, and since I had a few minutes before my shift began, thought I'd pop in and say hello," she said warmly, giving her a quick hug.

"I'm so glad you did," Ashley said as they broke their embrace. "By the way, I wanted to thank you again for this beautiful necklace!" She placed her hand on the delicate pearl pendant that hung on a 14-karat white-gold chain. "I absolutely love it!" She had received it from Gayle for Christmas, and it meant a lot to her. "I've already received so many compliments on it. Thank you."

"You've thanked me enough. You wear it in good health, sweetheart," Gayle responded cheerily. "Well, I better get going. It's a long shift, so I'll probably see you tomorrow," she said, giving Ashley a quick wink. "Don't work too hard!"

"Well, I've got a few hours to go, but I'll see you at breakfast tomorrow." Ashley knew that Gayle would be working a twelve-hour shift today, which meant that she'd be alone in the evening. They embraced again, and Gayle left the gift shop ready to face her long shift.

CHAPTER

40

After a long night of tossing and turning, Nicole decided to get out of bed and make herself a coffee. She was in the end of her pregnancy and had become increasingly uncomfortable. Sleep had become a thing of the past, for it didn't matter how she positioned herself, it was almost impossible to get any sleep, not to mention that she had to pee all the time. The baby had transitioned into birthing position, and her appointment with her doctor had gone as well as expected. The baby was thriving, and the heartbeat was strong. Jack had been with her to all her appointments, which made it more bearable for Nicole, since her anxiety hadn't changed.

Jack still hadn't been cleared from the whole mess with Ashley's attack, and that made Nicole nervous, but she never voiced her concerns to him for fear of upsetting him. She was thankful for her sister and her closest friend, who both checked up on her daily by telephone, even making surprise visits to her, bringing her food and treats, "for the baby." Her mother called her every single day, making sure that her youngest daughter was holding up OK. Nicole felt sorry for her—she had her hands full with her father, which didn't allow Noreen time to visit Nicole. His dementia had worsened, and he couldn't be left alone. Nicole sensed her mom's guilt every time they spoke on the telephone, but Nicole always reassured her that she was fine and that she had Sara and Emily checking up on her. It was just a matter of time until her unborn baby would make his or her appearance, and Nicole was elated. As usual, January had brought in freezing-cold weather and a massive amount of snow, so she was pretty much housebound. Fortunately for Nicole, Jack's workload was lighter in the winter, which allowed him to spend most days at home with his wife.

—

Phil waited patiently for the night to come to an end, cleaning and wiping down the bar, washing and drying the glasses, and putting up the chairs. He said good night to Laurie, who was just leaving work for the night, and made his way to the back of the restaurant toward Manny's office. Since the altercation with his boss, they hadn't said a single word about what had transpired between them: not about the five thousand dollars that Manny had given him on the spot, nor the implications that Phil had made regarding the sex trafficking that Manny was running on the side. Did Manny think that all was forgotten? That he didn't need to pay him the rest of the money that he'd demanded? He wondered what Manny was planning.

Phil drew in a deep breath and stepped into the office. Manny had his back to him and didn't notice that Phil was in the room. He looked like he was counting money, and when Phil cleared his throat to get his attention, Manny turned around instantly, obviously caught off guard.

At the same time, Laurie was walking toward her car in the parking lot. She reached into her purse to retrieve her keys, but then panic set in, as she realized they weren't there. She dug in further, hoping that they would miraculously appear, but they didn't seem to be there. She feverishly took apart her purse, going through every nook and cranny, but her keys were nowhere to be found. She had no choice but to go back inside the restaurant and look in the staff changeroom. She hoped and prayed they'd be there.

In the office, Manny glared at Phil. "What do you want?" Manny barked in obvious displeasure. "I thought you'd left already."

"Nope," Phil responded smugly, taking a step toward him. "It seems you still owe me quite a bit of money, boss."

"I don't owe you nothin'!" Manny growled, going back to what he was doing before Phil interrupted him.

"Um, yeah you do." Phil stood directly in front of Manny with his chest out, arms crossed in front of him.

Manny took a deep breath, put the money he was counting back in his pocket, and took a step toward Phil. "Listen, asshole!" he said in an even and threatening tone. "I've had just about enough of you, you hear?"

Without warning, Phil grabbed Manny by his shirt and shoved him back into his desk, taking Manny by complete surprise. Phil spoke to him in an equally threatening tone, his face right into his opponent's face. "I don't take well to being ignored or threatened, you understand? I've given you a few weeks to pay me the rest of the money, and you've been dodging me, and I don't like that. So quit the bullshit and pay up." Phil released his grip.

Manny cleared his throat, not liking where this conversation was going. He had been certain that he had pacified Phil with the five thousand he'd given him. "And what makes you think that I have that kind of money?" He asked Phil. "I think you should take the five thousand I've already given you and leave this joint. Forget you ever knew me. You don't know who you're messing with, buddy," Manny said evenly, straightening himself out. "Now get out of here and don't ever come back!" His eyes narrowed darkly.

"Oh, I ain't going anywhere, old man, not until you pay up," Phil answered. I've been here long enough to know what's been going on, and if you want to keep your nose clean, you'll do as I say." Phil was enjoying making Manny squirm.

"You don't know what you're talking about," Manny said, making his way to the other side of his desk. He sat in his chair, placed both his hands on the desk, and looked Phil right in the eyes.

"You know, Manny, I thought you were a little smarter than that. I know more than you think, and if you knew anything about me, you'd know I *always* get what I want." Phil wasn't about to let him off the hook.

"Well, I don't have that kind of money, so take a hike," Manny answered, unmoved by Phil's threat. He shuffled some papers on his desk, indicating that the conversation was over.

Phil took a step forward and smiled slyly. "This isn't over Manny—not by a long shot. I expect the rest of the money by the end of the week. And you better have it, or I'm likely to turn nasty, and you don't want to see that side of me, you understand?" Phil turned to leave, glancing back at Manny one more time, who ignored him by looking over some paperwork in front of him. Phil turned around angrily and walked out of the office, straight down the corridor, and out the front door.

41

*L*aurie put her hand to her mouth, stunned by the conversation she had just overheard between her boss and Phil. She had come back into the bar and gone straight to the staff room to look for her keys. She fumbled in her cubby, pulling out odds and ends in hopes of finding her keys. It was a mess in there, and she retrieved a couple of scarves, baseball caps, a couple of cardigans, and a pile of shoes, mostly high heels. There was an array of garments, and when she stooped down to move things out of the way, a light jingle caught her attention. She bent down further to see if it was her lost keys, and to her surprise as well as relief, her keychain was caught on a knit garment. When she lifted it up, she realized it was a black mask. She pulled it closer to her, releasing the hold the keys had on one of the eyeholes. Then she overheard Manny's voice from his office, which was adjacent to the staff room, and from the sound of his voice, he didn't seem very happy.

She stood still, not wanting to make any noise for fear of being heard. Laurie had just worked a long day, and her legs and back ached.

The last thing she needed was for Manny to call her in for sexual favors. She had wondered who her boss was yelling at, and after just a couple of minutes, she realized it was Phil. She turned off the light in the staff room, wanting to make herself scarce, but she was stuck, as she was frightfully aware that she was listening to something she wasn't supposed to hear. It had become very clear to her what had transpired between them. Phil was blackmailing Manny and was demanding money from him. How much money? She didn't know. But she did know, from what she overheard, that Manny had already given him five thousand dollars. Was Phil referring to the sex that was going on in the back of the bar? But how would Phil know about that? She stood very still as she listened to the two men, each threatening one another. What was going on? And come to think of it, where was Stephanie? Laurie hadn't seen her for a few weeks now, and when she had asked Manny where Stephanie was, he had just ordered her to get back to work.

Suddenly a thought occurred to her: Ashley had disappeared just like that, and now Stephanie was nowhere to be seen. She covered her mouth, willing herself to be extra quiet in fear of being heard by the two men. Her blood ran cold, and she was terrified as she stood there holding her breath. "I *always* get what I want" was what Phil told Manny. Laurie turned away, recalling a conversation she'd had months ago with Ashley while walking to their cars after a long night of work. Ashley had confided that Phil had made several advances toward her, insisting she give him a chance and go out with him. She'd told Laurie that Phil gave her the creeps, and she'd rejected him several times, and that the last time she'd rejected him he'd told her that, in the end, he *always* got what he wanted. A cold chill went through Laurie's body as she recalled their conversation. Could Manny or Phil be responsible for Ashley's attack? And what about Stephanie? Where was she? Manny had used Stephanie more than ever in the past few months, only she hadn't seen her for weeks now. Where was she?

Laurie was scared, not only for her own life, but for Stephanie's life. She had thought about Ashley more than once since her attack last summer. Laurie remembered Manny ordering her and Stephanie to stay away from the hospital against their better judgment. She wanted to go and visit Ashley, but she did as she was told and stayed away. Laurie wouldn't even know where or how to begin to try to find Ashley—her cell phone had been smashed during her attack. She recalled the detective who had questioned her regarding Ashley. He'd even given her his business card, asking that if she had any information to reach out to him. "Oh my God," she whispered in the dark as her whole body started to shake.

Laurie stood frozen in the dark staff room for what seemed like an eternity—though it was only a few minutes—wondering how she was going to get out of there safely and quietly without being heard or noticed. She didn't dare move a muscle when she heard someone with a heavy foot walk past her door, the footsteps loud and deliberate. She stood motionless as the steps got fainter until the sound of the front door to the bar slammed shut. She could hear Manny in his office, talking on the telephone with someone, telling whoever was on the other end of the conversation about the "problem" that he had to take care of. Manny mentioned that Phil was demanding forty-five thousand dollars, and angrily told the person he was talking to that he'd give him the money when hell froze over. So, Phil was blackmailing Manny for fifty thousand dollars! What the hell was going on? And what had she walked into?

42

*I*t had been an exceptionally long day, and Nicole felt drained. "You know what, babe?" she said as she plopped herself on the couch. "This baby doesn't seem to want to come out." She held her pregnant belly, talking more to the baby than to her husband.

"Well, you've had quite a day, Nikki," Jack answered, pulling her legs toward him on the couch and proceeding to massage her feet. "Whatever possessed you to clean the house today? I told you that I was going to clean the house tomorrow, didn't I?" he scolded her.

"Well, I didn't want to have the baby and leave a dirty house," Nicole replied. "You know very well how busy it's going to get once the baby comes, and the last thing that I wanted to worry about was cleaning," she said testily. "My sister offered to come and help me, but she's got enough to do with her own family, and I didn't want to impose." She let out a sigh of relief while Jack massaged her feet. "God, that feels good! I don't know what hurts more, my legs or my back," she said, stretching her upper body.

"Nikki, your OCD is relentless!" Jack laughed, getting his wife to turn and sit facing away from him so he could massage her back. "Our baby is not going to notice a bit of dust when he, or she, arrives." He knew how spotless Nicole kept their house, and he smiled as he leaned toward her, kissing her lightly on the back of her neck. "You know what I miss?" he said in a devilish tone.

"Oh, I know what you miss!" She smiled as he continued to plant soft kisses on the back of her neck. She had missed the intimacy with him in the past little while, but sex was the last thing on her mind these days. "Oh God, I have to pee again!" Nicole said in annoyance, trying to get off the couch. Jack got up immediately and took her hands in his own to help her up. She stood up and smiled at him, putting her arms around his neck. "Thanks for the massage," she said warmly.

"Anytime, sweetheart," he responded, leaning toward her with his arms around her waist. He bent his head to hers and kissed her long and hard. Just then, he felt a trickle of fluid hit the top of his feet, and when he looked down, he noticed there was a small puddle of clear fluid on the floor right under Nicole's feet, causing them both to look down. "Oh, wow! Did you just pee yourself, Nick?" He chuckled.

"No, I don't think so," she said, staring down in bewilderment as the clear liquid continued to trickle down her legs, onto the hardwood floor. Realizing what was happening, Nicole looked up at her husband in surprise. "Jack! I think my water just broke!" she exclaimed in shock. Her heart was beating wildly; she'd been taken completely by surprise. Suddenly, she felt a surge of emotions—panic as well as excitement.

Jack looked into her blue eyes and kissed her on the top of her head, holding her head with both hands. The realization that his wife was going to go into labor left him dumbstruck.

"Oh, Jack, I'm so scared!" Nicole wailed, looking down again at the clear liquid, confirming the fact that she was going to be having her baby, and soon.

"Don't be scared, baby," he reassured her, kissing her on the lips. "I'll get the overnight bag for the hospital, and you call the doctor. He's going to want us to go to the hospital immediately." He needed to stay calm during this process, for Nicole's sake.

Jack quickly sprinted upstairs to their bedroom, where Nicole kept the bag packed and ready to go. He admired her efficiency and detailed planning, and he hated to admit it, but as calm as he seemed, he was a nervous wreck. He ran downstairs quickly with the overnight bag in his hand while she was finishing up her brief conversation with her doctor, confirming that she was, in fact, in labor, and needed to get to the hospital immediately. Jack helped Nicole with her coat and boots, for it was a bitterly cold night, and it had snowed all day. He was relieved that her car was in the garage, ready to go; there was no way he'd be able to get her into his truck, which was too large for their garage.

Jack helped Nicole into the car, noticing she had become quiet. "Babe are you OK?" he asked. He threw the bag in the back seat while she clamped her seatbelt on.

"Yes, I'm fine," she replied in a shaky voice, her eyes widening in anticipation. Jack closed her door and quickly went around to the driver's seat. Nicole flinched beside him, and when he turned to look at her, there was no doubt in his mind that she was in labor. Luckily, the hospital was only ten minutes away from their house, and it was close to midnight, so the roads would be empty. Jack held her hand momentarily and gave it a reassuring squeeze.

"I love you," he told her simply. He put his seatbelt on and turned on the ignition. He put the gearshift in reverse and backed out of the garage. He glanced over to his wife once again, who flinched as she held her stomach. "I love you," Jack said to her with deep conviction.

"I love you too," Nicole answered shakily. Another contraction came, causing her to howl in pain. Jack put the car in drive and headed to the hospital.

CHAPTER

43

Manny was still on the telephone in his office, and Laurie decided that if she was going to leave without him knowing, it was now or never. She knew that if she didn't get out of there immediately, she'd be in trouble. She didn't know what she'd stumbled upon, but she knew one thing for sure: she didn't want to find out. From the sound of his conversation, Manny was going to be hanging up soon. Laurie needed to make an exit, and fast. She peered out into the narrow corridor and quietly tiptoed out of the changeroom holding her breath—she had to pass Manny's office to make her escape.

If Laurie was caught, how would she explain her being there? Manny would undoubtedly be angry with her, and from the sound of his voice and the mood that he was in, she didn't want to be around for that. She took a couple of steps toward his office, making sure to hold her breath, and when she reached the doorway to his office, she stood still, listening to him talking on the phone. Peering through the doorway, she saw that he was standing up with his back to her, looking down at a file. Hastily,

Laurie took two big quiet strides past the doorway, then walked down the rest of the corridor, making her way to the front door of the restaurant. She quickly and quietly let herself out, holding the door behind her, making sure it didn't slam shut.

Laurie quickened her steps as she walked toward her car, reclaimed her keys, unlocked her door, and got into the driver's seat. She was about to close the car door when, out of nowhere, a man appeared beside her, standing between her and the door to her car. Before Laurie knew what was happening, he'd grabbed her by the back of her hair and forced her out of her car. Sheer terror engulfed her, and when she tried to get a glimpse of him, he pulled her hair back roughly, causing her to stumble. Laurie tried to scream for help, but he covered her mouth with his hand and roughly dragged her to the back of her car. Her heart was beating wildly, and she panicked, unsure of what he was going to do with her.

"You scream and I swear I'll kill you!" he said as he leaned close to Laurie's ear. "Do you understand me?" She nodded, petrified for her life. He snatched her keys from out of her clenched hand and unlocked the trunk of her car. "Get in the trunk! Now!" he commanded, glancing back toward the restaurant, making sure that no one was around.

"No! Please don't do this," Laurie pleaded, noticing that the man's face was covered with a black mask with an opening only for the eyes and mouth. "I promise, I won't say an—"

"Shut up and get in the trunk! Now!" he yelled as he shoved her inside the trunk of her car.

Laurie sobbed uncontrollably. He bent down toward her, speaking low in her ear. "Did you think that you were going to get away just like that?" She shook her head in total panic just before he slammed the trunk shut. She started to kick and scream from the inside of the trunk, but he surprised her again by opening it up and grabbing her roughly by her face. "Shut the fuck up, or I'll kill you right here, right now!" He pulled a gun from his pocket and pointed it straight to her mouth. Laurie's eyes widened in bewilderment and fear. Seeing that she wouldn't dare move, he shoved her head back inside and slammed the trunk shut. He placed his gun back into his pocket and waited for Manny to come out of the restaurant. A few minutes later, he looked over to see Manny locking up, and he waited to make his move.

Manny was in a foul mood after the confrontation he'd had with Phil. "I'll take care of him," he mumbled out loud. He needed to get Phil off his back once and for all. He'd go home, make himself a stiff drink, and deal with another problem he had back at his condo. Manny frowned as he thought of Stephanie, whom he had left alone hours before. He didn't know what he was going to do with her, because she had become useless to him now. The few johns he'd set her up with weren't interested in her anymore. She had become unresponsive and increasingly dependent on cocaine as well as heroine. Her physical appearance had deteriorated drastically, and the men didn't find her attractive anymore. She had literally become skin and bones, and the johns complained that they felt like they were screwing a corpse. He knew that it was his fault that she had become a junkie—he was the one that introduced the drugs to her—but he didn't think that she'd become so dependent on them, and so quickly, and that angered him. Even the food he brought home to her didn't interest her. She'd nibble here and there, but food didn't interest her anymore. She had literally melted to nothing right before his eyes, and even he was turned off from her. He locked up and started walking toward his car, when unexpectedly, he felt something hard and pointy against his back.

"I told you that in the end, I *always* get what I want, didn't I?" A male voice sneered at him from behind.

"You son of a bitch," Manny muttered angrily, pissed off with himself that he hadn't foreseen this coming, feeling the hardness of the gun piercing into his back.

"Keep walking over there by the blue car," Phil commanded, referring to Laurie's car, the only other car in the parking lot. "Don't try anything, or you're a dead man, you hear?" Phil warned. "You're going to drive to your place, and you're going to pay up."

"And what makes you think that I've got that kind of cash?" Manny replied angrily, regretting not getting rid of Phil sooner.

"Oh, I'm convinced you have a ton of money at your place," Phil answered. "Now move it!" He pressed his gun to Manny's back even harder, causing Manny to flinch.

Phil led Manny to Laurie's blue Chevy with the gun to his back, checking the parking lot, making sure that no one was around. With his free hand, he opened the driver's door and shoved Manny inside, pointing the gun to his face. "Put your belt on," he ordered him. Manny grunted but did as he was told. What other choice did he have? Once Manny's belt was on, Phil swiftly went to the other side of the car, continuing to point his gun at Manny. He opened the passenger door and slid in beside him, his gun pressing hard to Manny's side, and his free hand inserting the car key into the ignition.

"You fuck!" Manny shouted, rage building within him, feeling weak and small.

Phil dug his gun into his side even harder, causing Manny to cry out in pain. "Shut the fuck up, you douche bag! You don't feel too powerful now, eh?" Phil taunted. "Drive to your place *now*, and you don't get hurt, understand? And don't even think about driving anywhere else, because I know where you live. Got it?"

Manny let out a sigh. The gun pressed hard into his side, which made it difficult for him to breath, and as cold as it was, he was perspiring profusely. "Can you ease up on the gun?" Manny said with great difficulty. "I can't breathe." Phil eased up on the pressure but kept the gun to Manny's side, letting him know that he was in charge and that he meant business.

"Now *go*!" Phil ordered. Manny put the car in drive and proceeded to drive out of the parking lot toward his condo.

CHAPTER

44

ack in the trunk of the car, Laurie squirmed and whimpered in desperation. She was claustrophobic and lying there in the dark caused her adrenaline to skyrocket. She told herself that she needed to calm down, but the thought of what he was planning to do with her terrified her. Was he going to take her to the woods, where he would no doubt rape and kill her and then dispose of her body? Suddenly, Ashley entered her thoughts, and Laurie wondered if she'd experienced the same thing with her attacker. Her heart was beating wildly, and when she realized the car was moving, she knew she had to act fast. She fumbled in the dark, feeling her surroundings, when she remembered that she still had her cell phone in her back pocket. In the very limited space she had, she squirmed and shimmied her body and was able to retrieve her cell phone from her back pocket. She was starting to hyperventilate as panic took over. Holding her cell phone in front of her, she tapped on it and watched as her iPhone lit up. "Oh God! Please help me!" she cried. She slid her figure along the screen in an upward motion, and then she had to key in her code to unlock her phone. With shaking fingers, she quickly tapped her four-digit code, but it wouldn't unlock; she had tapped it too quickly, so she had to start again. She took a deep breath and, slowly and deliberately, tapped in her four-digit code again; this time, it unlocked. She dialed 911 and held her breath as she waited for an operator to pick up.

"911. What is your emergency?" said the operator—a female's voice. Her heart was beating so fast, and she took another deep breath in relief that she'd gotten through.

"Help me! Please help me!" Laurie cried into the phone in desperation.

"What is your emergency, ma'am?" repeated the operator.

"I'm in the trunk of my car, and I don't know where I'm going!" she rambled quickly, trying not to hyperventilate.

"What is your name, please?" asked the operator in a standard monotone voice. "Take a deep breath and try to calm down," she continued, showing some empathy toward Laurie.

"Laurie. Laurie Jefferson," she answered her quickly, taking deep breaths. "Please help me!" Laurie pleaded to the operator, the one person that could possibly save her from this madman.

"OK, calm down … have you been kidnapped?" the operator asked.

"Yes. No. I don't know!" she responded in total panic, wondering why this operator wasn't getting her any help already.

"Laurie, can you tell me what the make of the car is you're in? The color? Year?" The operator asked in a calm voice.

"Yeah, it's my car! It's a—oh my God, it's a blue Chevrolet Cruze!" Laurie replied breathlessly.

"What's the year of your car, Laurie?" the operator asked her.

"Um … oh God! I bought it used about two years ago," she said frantically, trying to remember the year of the car. "Oh, I think it's a 2015!" she answered back quickly, not sure how much time she had left until the car stopped, and then it would be too late. She imagined him taking her into the dark woods where he would savagely rape her and strangle her to death.

"OK, Laurie, you're doing good. Now tell me what happened? How did you get in the trunk?" the operator asked.

Breathlessly, Laurie responded, "I was leaving work, The Blue Lagoon restaurant, and this psycho got me in the parking lot, and he had a gun, and he forced me into the trunk!" Her heart was beating a million miles a minute.

"Do you know this man, Laurie?" she asked.

"No, I don't. He threatened he was going to kill me! Please help me, please!" Laurie cried.

"Did he say where he was taking you, Laurie?" asked the operator in a calm voice.

"No! He just shoved me in my trunk and told me that if I tried anything, he'd kill me! I think he was the one who attacked Ashley. Last summer. I don't know for sure, but this guy is sick. Please get me out of here!" she begged. "Oh! I remember a detective came into the restaurant asking for information about her. She was in the hospital, but I didn't know anything. Oh my God! What was his name?" Laurie said in frustration. "She was found raped and beaten and left for dead, only she didn't die. Oh my God! He's going to do the same to me! Please help me!" she cried hysterically, not sure herself if she was making any sense at all.

"Laurie, I'm tracing your call, OK? Stay with me, alright?" the operator told her, her cool-as-a-cucumber voice giving Laurie a small shred of hope. "We're going to find you, OK?" Laurie nodded, pressing the cell phone into her ear, her heart beating so fast and so loud that she was certain it could be heard from outside.

"Please hurry! I'm so scared. He's going to kill me. I know he is," she sobbed uncontrollably. Suddenly, she remembered the name of the detective that had questioned her at her work so many months before. The only reason she remembered his name was because she had just recently changed purses, and she had come across the business card that he'd given her. She'd been just starting her shift, so she'd just thrown it in. "Fromer! The detective's name was Steven Fromer!" Laurie said, feeling thankful for her memory as well for changing purses. She remembered vividly cleaning out her purse and discovering the card.

"OK, Laurie, so the detective's name was Steven Fromer, correct?" the operator asked.

"Yes! Please find him. He would remember me. Please hurry!" suddenly, the car came to a halt. Her heart felt like it was going to jump out of her chest. "Oh my God! The car stopped!" Laurie said in a low voice, a new wave of panic setting in.

"OK, Laurie, you listen to me, OK? Try very hard not to hang up on me, OK?" the operator advised calmly. "I need you to stay calm. Can you do that? Can you place your phone somewhere on you where he won't notice it?" Laurie nodded her head quickly, afraid to speak. "Just keep your phone on, OK? I'm going to get you help as fast as I can, alright?" the operator spoke in an even and clear tone.

45

"Oh my God, it hurts!" Nicole wailed in agony. "This one's a bad one! Aaaaaagh!" She doubled over in obvious pain. Despite the heavy snow, Jack had driven his wife to the hospital in no time. It was late in the night, so the roads were clear, but by the time they arrived, Nicole was already in active labor. He checked her in immediately, and she was wheeled away by a nurse. He wanted to be with his wife, but the nurse at the desk needed the standard information, reassuring him that she was in good hands and that he'd be with her shortly. In the meantime, Nicole was disrobed and put on a gurney. She was in excruciating pain as one contraction flowed into another with no break in between. She wrestled in her bed, wincing with each contraction, as they wouldn't let up, all the while looking around frantically for her husband as well as her doctor, who hadn't yet arrived. She had forgotten how incredibly painful labor was, even though it had been just a few years ago since she'd given birth to Jonathan.

The nurse that was tending to her was efficient and exceptionally calm, speaking to Nicole in a soothing voice. "You're doing great,

Nicole!" she said as she assessed her labor. The nurse took her blood pressure, her pulse, and checked the baby's position and heartbeat. She had Nicole hooked up to the machine that monitored the length and strength of the contractions, making note that they were frequent and strong, and from the looks of her patient, it was apparent that this baby was not going to wait for the doctor. "Nicole, honey, I'm going to do a vaginal exam to check the status of your cervix." By the look on Nicole's face, the nurse wasn't sure that she had even processed what she'd told her. She quickly spread Nicole's legs, checking her cervix as Nicole screamed in agony.

"Where's my husband? Ohhhh, God! It hurts *so* bad!" Nicole cried. "Where's my husband?" she cried in frustration, wondering why her husband wasn't with her during the most significant moment of their lives.

"I'm sure he'll be here in no time, honey," the nurse answered her, focused on her examination. "Oh my!" she smiled warmly at Nicole. "Your baby will be coming out in no time. You're at 9 my dear," she commented as Nicole wailed and moved around incessantly. "Nicole, I want you to breath, OK? Is this your first baby?" the nurse asked, making a feeble effort to distract her.

"Noooo!" Nicole hollered, rolling around in the hospital bed like a deranged animal. Just then, Jack came racing in the room and beelined straight to Nicole's side, looking just as frantic as his wife. The nurse smiled warmly at the young couple.

"So, Mr. Newman, your wife tells me this isn't your first rodeo?" she asked with a smile. She glanced at her watch and wondered where the doctor was.

Jack was by his wife's side, supporting her head with one hand, his other hand in hers, which she gripped and squeezed so forcefully that he wasn't sure it would be in one piece by the time it was all over. "Umm, no," he answered the nurse vaguely, feeling a tug in his heart as he glanced at his wife, who was in obvious excruciating pain.

Another nurse entered the room motioning the nurse in charge to step outside so she could have a word with her. Nicole and Jack looked at one another in panic as the two nurses stepped out of the room.

"Why did she leave? What's wrong? Is it our baby?" Nicole asked him in sheer panic, twisting and turning in obvious pain, leaving Jack to soothe and comfort his wife, all the while asking himself the same questions.

Their attending nurse entered their room quickly, and both Nicole and Jack's eyes fixated on her, pleading for answers. She cleared her throat and proceeded to care for her patient. Nicole let out another scream as she situated herself in a birthing position, breathing rapidly and heavily as her husband supported her head and her back.

"Where's our doctor? Shouldn't he have been here by now?" Jack asked the nurse quietly as he leaned in toward her, away from Nicole's earshot. He didn't want to alarm her in the middle of her labor.

"Mr. Newman, your doctor won't be here in time for the birth," she answered him in a low tone. "His car broke down halfway here, but another doctor will be here shortly, OK?" she continued, making sure that her patient stayed as calm as possible. "Nicole I'm going to check your cervix once more, alright?" Nicole nodded obediently.

The nurse examined her, and satisfied with the status of her examination, gave Jack a nod, indicating that it was time. Jack stayed by Nicole's side, coaching her to breathe and following the nurse's instructions, occasionally wiping Nicole's damp forehead with a towel. At that point, a doctor stepped into the birthing room and stood with his arms crossed in front of his chest, observing the nurse expertly coach Nicole and her husband during the delivery.

"Come on, Nicole, push! You can do this!" the nurse encouraged from across her, aiding her, as the baby was already crowning. Jack was right by his wife's side, supporting her and telling her how great she was doing, and how much he loved her. Nicole continued to push, and she squeezed Jack's hand, causing him to wince in pain as Nicole begged the nurse to take the baby out of her. The nurse smiled in return, recalling how many expectant mothers begged her to do the same, as if she was pulling out a turkey from the oven.

"OK, honey, one more push will do it! Come on, Nicole! You can do it!" she exclaimed, cheering Nicole on while the doctor observed from behind, noting how experienced, as well as compassionate, the nurse was during the whole birthing process.

"I can't!" Nicole cried, and she flopped back onto her bed in exhaustion. "I'm so tired!"

"Come on, baby! You can do it! Just one more push!" Jack said encouragingly, kissing her on the top of her head and helping her up in birthing position again.

"You've got this, Nicole! Come on, girl! Just one more push!" the nurse exclaimed, giving her a nod that told her this would be it.

Nicole took a deep breath and, with all her emotions and determination from her months of agony, pushed with all the power she could muster. "Aaaaaaagh!" Nicole roared out so powerfully that her voice was unrecognizable. She filled the room with all the intensity that was deep within her soul as their baby made its way into the world.

Smiling from ear to ear and filled with emotion, the nurse cleaned up the infant as the doctor looked on, thankful for the successful delivery. The doctor nodded at the nurse in approval. Nicole lay back in her bed in relief and exhaustion, her eyes fixated on the tiny human that had just come out of her. She looked up at Jack, who had tears in his eyes, and he leaned into her and gently kissed her on the lips. The nurse asked if Jack wanted to cut the umbilical cord, which he did diligently, and then she gently placed their newborn on Nicole's chest, making skin-on-skin contact between mother and child.

"Congratulations, you two! You have a daughter!" the nurse told them both with tears of joy in her eyes. It wasn't very often that she delivered babies, but when she did, it always had a profound effect on her.

Nicole burst into tears of joy and relief as she held her baby girl. She was in disbelief as she caressed her tiny but beautiful face. She leaned into the infant and kissed the top of her head. Jack was equally moved, as he'd just witnessed the birth of their baby, relieved that everything had gone without a hitch, except for their own doctor not being present for the delivery. He looked down at his wife and child with love and adoration as fresh tears poured down his face.

"Oh, Jack, she's beautiful!" Nicole exclaimed as she held the baby's hand in her own. She looked up at Jack, who was equally fascinated by the tiny miracle that lay on her chest.

"Just like her mama," he replied quietly. He leaned down and kissed the top of the infant's head and then gently kissed his wife on the lips. "I love you, baby," he said, feeling overwhelmed with love for the woman who had just made him the daddy of a perfect little girl.

"I love you too," Nicole replied, feeling tired but incredibly overjoyed and grateful for the little miracle that had already transformed their lives.

CHAPTER

46

The trunk flew open, and the assailant was standing right over Laurie with a gun pointing at her. Before she could scream for help, he grabbed her roughly by her hair and put the gun against her face. "Don't even think of doing anything stupid, you hear?" He spoke gruffly. "You make any noise, and I'll kill you instantly. Do you understand?" he warned, speaking into her face. Laurie nodded, her eyes wide open in terror. She got a glimpse of his eyes through the holes of his black mask. She had managed to place her cell phone inside her jacket pocket, and as far as she knew, the cell phone was still on. She was trembling so much that she thought she was going to pass out; the horror of this unpredictable situation was getting more and more intense.

Inwardly, Laurie prayed that help would get to her before he could kill her. What reason would he have to spare her? It was just a matter of time before he'd take her to the woods and, ultimately, kill her.

"Now, get out and walk with me as though we're together, you hear?" he ordered. To prove his point, he placed his gun right to the side of her head. Laurie gasped, her heart beating a million miles per second.

She nodded again, afraid for her life, as he roughly pulled her out of the trunk, causing her to stumble and fall because her right leg had fallen asleep. He grabbed her by the arm and jerked her up, leading her to the front of her car, which was when she spotted Manny, who was sitting in the driver's seat of her car.

"Look who I've got with me, sweetheart!" he said slyly as he removed his mask, leaving Laurie shocked.

"Phil!" she whispered out loud. She stared at him, stunned by what was transpiring before her eyes and suddenly more afraid than ever.

Phil held her arm firmly with one hand. With the other, he held a gun that pointed in Manny's direction. Phil motioned him to get out of the car. Manny and Laurie stared at one another in confusion. For the whole drive, Phil had ordered Manny to stay in the car until told otherwise, shoving his gun into Manny's side or the side of Manny's head, threatening that he would blow his head off if he moved. Manny did what he was told, inwardly planning how he was going to escape.

"You're both going to walk in the building with me like there's nothing going on, you hear?" Phil warned both, looking around the empty parking lot. "If you say one word, just one word from either of you, you both die." Laurie and Manny looked at one another and started to walk toward the high rise. Phil walked behind them, pointing the gun, which he had covered with his scarf, at their backs.

Manny let them inside the building with a quick swipe from his fob. Unfortunately for Laurie and Manny, the lobby was empty. Phil made sure to keep his gun covered for fear of getting caught by any cameras the lobby might have. Manny grunted and led them down the hall, past the elevators, and to his apartment. He was on the main floor, which was fortunate for Phil. Manny stood outside his apartment and looked at his opponent.

"Open the door, boss," Phil commanded Manny. Laurie's body shook in fear. She wondered what this deranged bartender had in mind for the two of them. She silently wondered if her cell was still on and if the 911 call was still active.

Manny unlocked the door, and as soon as it opened, Phil shoved him roughly inside. Quickly and effortlessly, he pushed Laurie inside the apartment and then let himself in, shutting the door and locking it behind him. Phil ordered them both to remove their shoes and jackets, leaving Laurie standing there in sheer panic. She had removed her boots, but she didn't want to remove her jacket, since her cell phone was in her pocket.

"Do it!" Phil shouted, startling her. "Take your jacket off!" He pointed the gun in her direction.

"Can I leave it on?" she replied meekly. "I'm so cold," she added, bunching herself together to show him how cold she was, which wasn't exactly a lie—she was shivering in fear.

"No! Take it off and get over there in the living room. *Now!*" Phil commanded. Manny had already removed his jacket and shoes and was in his living room, watching the altercation between Laurie and Phil. He didn't understand what Laurie had to do with him and Phil. Manny had just remembered that he had Stephanie inside his bedroom and wondered if she was asleep. He didn't want Phil knowing she was there. He just wanted to get his gun, which he kept in the safe, and shoot the prick in the balls.

Reluctantly, Laurie slowly removed her jacket and held it over her arm as she walked toward the two men, eyeing Phil and exchanging looks with Manny. She had feared Manny in the few years that she'd worked for him, but the fear she felt for Phil at this moment far surpassed anything she'd ever felt before. Laurie knew that she'd been at the wrong place at the wrong time. She feared that Phil was going to kill them both, and soon if help didn't find them.

Phil ordered Laurie to sit on the couch, not quite sure what he was going to do with her. She wasn't part of his plan tonight, but he couldn't let her go after he'd discovered that she'd been in the restaurant and heard everything that he and Manny had discussed. He wanted all his fifty thousand dollars so he could get the hell out of the province and head to the US. He had come from Montreal, and no one here knew of his shady past. He was a sex offender and had done some jail time, and as soon as he'd completed his seven-year sentence, he'd headed to Ontario to start fresh. It hadn't been too long after that he'd started working at The Blue Lagoon. He had set his sights on Ashley from the beginning of her employment, but she'd never paid any attention to him. He'd asked her out on a few occasions, but she'd turned him down every time, which angered him to the core.

"So, what now?" Manny asked as he stared his lunatic bartender in the eye.

"What now? Are you serious?" Phil sneered back at him. Laurie looked from Manny to Phil. She placed her jacket slowly on the arm of the couch, making sure that the pocket that held her cell phone was on top. She slowly sat on the couch and prayed to God that the cops were on their way.

"You're going to get me the money that we talked about, that's what you're going to do!" Phil said, walking toward Manny with the gun still in his hand.

"And if I don't?" Manny asked, challenging him. He knew that he was playing with fire, but he was going to stall Phil until he figured out a plan.

Phil let out a laugh, and he walked right up to Manny's face, their noses almost touching. "You will give me the rest of the money, or you and your little friend here can kiss your lives goodbye!" he said smugly.

"I've already given you five thousand dollars," Manny answered testily, his eyes fixed on Phil, standing his ground.

"Well, you still owe me forty-five thousand dollars, and I'm not leaving here until you pay me," Phil replied, looking Manny straight in the eye. "I call the shots here," he added, taking a step back.

Suddenly, there was a sound. It was coming from the end of the long hallway, shifting everyone's attention. *Shit!* Manny thought instantly, flinching in nervousness. Stephanie, no doubt, had been awakened by the commotion and was trying to open the bedroom door.

"Who's here?" Phil asked Manny gruffly, taking a step toward him and grabbing Manny by the front of his shirt.

"No one in particular," Manny muttered, trying to think of what to do.

"Let me outta here!" A female voice screamed from the bedroom down the hall. Laurie stood up, as she recognized the voice instantly. "Hello! Is anybody there? Help me!" the voice cried out.

Laurie knew right off the bat that the woman that was pleading for help was her coworker, Stephanie. She hadn't been around the restaurant in a while, and she had wondered what had happened to her.

"Get in there and let her out! Now!" Phil commanded, shoving Manny down the hall to the bedroom where he kept Stephanie. There was a lock on the outside of the door, and reluctantly, Manny unlocked it as Stephanie continued to call for help. Phil and Manny both went inside, coming face-to-face with Stephanie, who looked like a frightened animal. She looked from Manny to Phil and back to Manny, wondering why the bartender was with Manny. Was he going to make her have sex with Phil now? Was that his plan? Or were they supposed to have a three-some? She panicked and felt sick to her stomach at the thought of that.

Phil noticed immediately that Stephanie looked a mess. She was painfully thin, her arms were bruised, and her hair was dry and matted. Manny stood there for a moment, trying to think of a way to get to his safe, where he kept his gun. Laurie stood out in the hallway, catching a glimpse of Stephanie, shocked at what was left of her. Manny grabbed Stephanie and shoved her on the bed, ordering her to keep her mouth shut. Phil looked back at Manny in surprise. He hadn't seen Stephanie since the night she'd shown up at the restaurant looking for Manny. She looked even thinner than when he'd last seen her, and when Phil took a better look at her, he realized that Manny not only used her for prostitution but also had her hooked-on drugs.

"You devil, you!" Phil sneered at Manny. I knew you were doing her regularly as well as renting her out, but I didn't know you made her into a junkie." He laughed. "And you get to keep the prize to yourself." Manny stood there, feeling his anger rise.

Laurie, who was standing at the doorway, rushed into the bedroom to Stephanie's side, holding her close to her. Stephanie started to cry as she buried her head in Laurie's chest.

"Well, isn't this sweet." Phil scoffed. "This is going to be easier than I thought." He pointed the gun down by his side. "It's too bad you couldn't save your other coworker." He laughed, looking directly at Laurie. She looked up at him in disbelief. "Yeah! The bitch thought she could lead me on, repeatedly, and treat me like I was a leper!" Phil shouted as Manny and Laurie stared at him. "She thought she was too good for me. And then to watch her flirt with that asshole at the bar right in front of me. Well, I fixed her alright! I'm only sorry that the slut didn't die! But she might as well have. She was attacked and that asshole is taking the heat for it!" he yelled triumphantly. It was obvious to Manny and Laurie that he was talking about Ashley.

Manny lunged toward Phil and tried to grab the gun from his hand but missed, causing Phil to fall backward. Manny lunged at him again and wrestled him to the ground, throwing punches to his face; but Phil fought back and kicked him in the groin, causing Manny to yell out in pain. The two young women looked on in terror, not knowing what to do. Laurie quickly released her hold on Stephanie and helped her off the bed, indicating the door, hoping to escape while the two men continued to fight. Phil and Manny were on the ground, punching and kicking one another, both men equally strong considering that Manny was quite a few years older than Phil. The girls ran toward the open doorway, Stephanie just a couple of feet behind Laurie, when Stephanie noticed Phil's gun on the ground, just a few feet away from the fighting duo.

Laurie was already out in the hallway, and when she turned around and noticed that Stephanie wasn't with her, she ran back toward the bedroom, only to see Stephanie kneeling and reaching for the gun. "Stephanie, *no!*" she shouted at her in panic. Both Manny and Phil stopped fighting and looked over to see that Stephanie had the gun in her hand. Manny jumped up and out of Phil's hold and lunged in Stephanie's direction to get the gun from her, but it was too late. She stood facing them with the gun pointing at them, her hands shaking uncontrollably.

"Stephanie, *no!* Don't do it!" Laurie cried out. Suddenly, the door to the apartment flew open, and three policemen charged into the bedroom, only to see Stephanie pointing a gun in Phil and Manny's direction, threatening to pull the trigger.

"Put the gun down!" a policeman ordered Stephanie. "Now! You don't want to do this, miss." The officer approached her slowly while the other two officers moved behind Manny and Phil, who both had their hands up in surrender.

Stephanie stood frozen with both her arms straight out in front of her, the gun pointing in Manny's direction, looking straight into his eyes. "You used me," she said evenly, her eyes filling with tears.

"Miss, put the gun down!" the officer said sternly. "Now!"

"Stephanie, please put the gun down," Laurie pleaded, but Stephanie stood there frozen.

"You used me in the worst possible way, and I'll never be whole again because of you," Stephanie said to Manny directly, causing him to squirm with fear as he stared at the gun that was pointing at him. In the next instant, one of the officers lunged toward her, causing her to pull the trigger, firing two shots into Manny's chest before the gun flew out of her hand. Everyone watched in horror as Manny went down, blood splattering everywhere. Just as quick, the other officer shoved Phil to the ground face first, taking both his arms behind him and handcuffing him. Laurie was immediately by Stephanie's side, holding her tight and stroking her hair while Stephanie sobbed uncontrollably.

47

The sound of her baby cooing prompted Nicole to go to the nursery to check on her baby, but she found that Jack was already there, holding their baby girl in his arms and rocking her back and forth. He hadn't noticed that his wife was standing in the doorway observing them, and she smiled tenderly at the sight of her loving husband and their daughter together.

She couldn't believe how much their life had changed in the past few years. They had loved and lost their firstborn to a horrible accident, one that almost destroyed their marriage. Nicole missed her little boy terribly and suspected she always would, no matter how many years went by. Until her dying day, Jonathan would always hold a special place in her heart, and she was certain that, one day, they would be together again. It pained her that her little boy wasn't with them anymore. She was sure that if he were still alive, he would've been the most loving and protective big brother to his little sister. It made her sad to think of this vision because they would've been the perfect little family, but as she watched Jack slowly and gently place their three-month-old baby back in the crib, she knew she had another chance of being the best mother she could possibly be.

She entered the nursery and put her arms around her husband from behind. They both looked down at their sleeping angel. After some deliberation, they'd decided that they would name their beautiful baby Hope because it seemed like it was the most suitable name for the child that had brought her parents back together. They had both been in a bad place emotionally since the death of their firstborn, and they had both suffered silently in an immeasurable amount of pain. The crippling and paralyzing pain that they'd endured prevented them from leaning on each other or reaching out to a support group of other parents who'd lost a child. However, now that Hope was born, they mutually decided that they still needed to seek out a support group to finally help them deal with their loss. It was already arranged: Nicole's sister would babysit baby Hope for them once a week so that they could go to the meetings that they so desperately needed. At least Jack had been cleared of all charges, and they were able to live freely once again without the dark cloud that had been looming over them for months. Their future looked bright and sunny, their baby was thriving, and nothing—no one—was going to get in their way of a happy life.

As for Stephanie, charges were never laid in the shooting of Manny, but she was ordered to undergo psychiatric treatment as well as drug rehab. She had a very long way to go, but she was on the road to recovery, thanking God every day for another chance of living the best life she could live. She stayed in a well-known rehabilitation center, taking it one day at a time, trying her very best to stay clean.

Laurie had quit her job as a waitress and was working as a salesgirl in a big department store. It was very different from waitressing, and she welcomed her new career choice.

Phil was charged with aggravated assault in the rape and beating of Ashley, as well as kidnapping and assault and battery. He was awaiting trial. Detective Fromer was going to make sure that he went to jail for a very long time.

Ashley continued to live with Gayle, and their relationship flourished to a level that she'd never imagined. She had made the decision to go back to school in the fall and work toward becoming a nurse. She loved working at the hospital because it reminded her of the care she'd received from Gayle while she was in the hospital. Ashley would be forever grateful for everything that Gayle had done for her, and for the first time in her life, she felt love from a woman, a stranger who had opened up her heart as well as her home to her. Gayle shared the day-to-day experiences that she had with her patients at the hospital with Ashley, and recently, she had shared the birth of a baby girl that she'd delivered herself with a doctor's supervision. From what Gayle had told her, this young couple's doctor didn't end up making it to the hospital in time to deliver their baby because his car had broken down on his way, and she had been the attending nurse. Gayle told Ashley that it was one of the most amazing feelings she had ever experienced in all her years of nursing. It was then that Ashley decided that she wanted to become a nurse.

Life, as we know it, is a journey that's very different for everyone. It has ups, and it has downs, and at times, when we feel like giving up because it becomes too difficult to manage, we're somehow given the strength to go on the best way we know how, using the tools that we've been given. God has a plan for each one of us, and it's up to us to discover how to survive this world of wonder; a world that is full of adventure, love, and ugliness. Some people seem to have it easier than others— "the grass is greener on the other side." What seems perfect to one can be far from perfect. The strength within us and the will to live a better life are what bring us closer together, and when the stormy clouds fill the sky and darkness overshadows, in the end, the clouds dissipate, and the sun rises once again.

CPSIA information can be obtained
at www.ICGtesting.com
Printed in the USA
LVHW100143310123
738243LV00008B/320/J

9 781665 736015